Can the CIA go on television tonight and tell the American public that the Democratic party has just nominated a KGB agent as its candidate for the presidency?

Who says so? Well, Kim Philby says so, folks. We know he's a traitor and all, but we've checked what he has to say and it makes sense to us.

Impossible, no one would believe it.

What *is* the CIA to do?

For that matter, what is the KGB to do?

The answers are the key to one of the best thrillers you will read this year!

TROTSKY'S RUN
Richard Hoyt

A TOM DOHERTY ASSOCIATES BOOK

Copyright © 1982 by Richard Hoyt

A Tor Book

Published by Tom Doherty Associates, 8-10 W. 36th St., New York City, NY 10018

First printing, August 1983

Reprinted by arrangement with William Morrow and Co., Inc.

ISBN: 0-523-48079-2

Printed in the United States of America

Distributed by Pinnacle Books, 1430 Broadway, New York, NY 10018

For John E. Brown

PROLOGUE

In the face of a deteriorating British economy and the rise of the Nazis on the European continent, Marxism became fashionable among undergraduates at Cambridge and Oxford universities between 1930 and 1936. The Soviet Union was fascinated by the potential of so many impressionable young minds. In due time, agents of the KGB arrived on the British campuses to recruit "sleepers" or "moles" to burrow into the British establishment. As we know it now, their take included:

Donald Maclean, a graduate of Cambridge, a British diplomat and KGB agent who in 1947 had an unrestricted, nonescort pass to the Atomic Energy Commission facilities at Los Alamos, New Mexico. Maclean used this pass—given as a courtesy to the British—after hours, several times a week, over a period of months. Not even the head of the American atomic program had such a pass.

Maclean defected to the Soviet Union in 1951.

Guy Burgess, also a Cambridge man and a friend of Maclean's, worked first for MI 5, British counterintelligence, and later the British foreign service. He was a Soviet spy all the while. Burgess defected to the Soviet Union with Maclean in 1951.

Kim Philby, a Cambridge man and KGB agent, rose high in the ranks of MI 6, the British secret service. Philby was in charge of putting British spy nets into place in Eastern Europe at the end of World War II, and was later a member of a select committee established to share British secrets with the CIA. Philby defected to the Soviet Union in 1963.

Sir Anthony Blunt spied for the Kremlin as an MI-5 operative. Blunt was a friend of Burgess. He rose to become art advisor to Queen Elizabeth II. Blunt was also a Cambridge man.

Charles Howard "Dick" Ellis, Britian's number-three intelligence officer at the end of World War II, spied for both Nazi Germany and the Soviet Union. Ellis, a career intelligence officer who died in 1975 at the age of eighty, made a confession in 1965 that was never made public.

Tom Driberg, a left-wing member of Commons for thirty-two years and the Labor party chairman in 1957-58, was a double agent working for MI 5 and the KGB. Driberg died in 1976.

Sir Roger Hollis, former head of MI 5, is alleged to have been a KGB agent. Former Prime Minister Sir Harold Wilson, in office during a 1970s investigation of Hollis, told the House of Commons he set up a Hollis inquiry because there were "reasons for anxiety" about Hollis's prewar connections. The probe concluded Hollis was not a double agent, although there was not 100 percent proof of innocence. Hollis died in 1973.

The man who assassinated Leon Trotsky was born Jaime Ramon Mercader del Rio, in Barcelona, on February 7, 1913. For most of his life, however, he called himself Jacson-Mornard Vandendreschd. He was born in Tehran in 1904, he said, the son of a Belgian diplomat and writer. More often, he simply called himself Jacques Mornard.

On the day of the ice pick, he carried a passport that originally belonged to a Yugoslav-Canadian named Tony Babich. Babich surrendered it in Spain when he went to fight Franco and the Fascists. When Babich was killed in battle, his passport was added to the collection used by Joseph Stalin's agents all over the world. Soviet forgers put a simple Frank Jacson on Babich's passport. What the forger didn't know was that there was no Jacsons in the English-speaking world.

Or so it is claimed. No matter.

What does matter is that Jacson or Mornard was, in 1940, a handsome, well-traveled man; women admired him. In the course of his adventures he met and charmed a rather plain young woman named Sylvia Agelof.

Miss Agelof was a secretarial assistant to Leon Trotsky, born Lev Davidovich Bronstein, on November 7, 1879.

What matters in the chronicles of history is that in May 1940 Trotsky was in exile in Mexico City, having fled there to avoid Stalin's vengeance. The latter was bent on erasing from memory the name of Trotsky who, along with a man named V.I. Ulyanov—also known as Lenin—had brought off the Bolshevik Revolution.

In May 1940, agents of Stalin's secret police, the GPU, had tried unsuccessfully to machine-gun Trotsky at the residence of the revolutionary artist Diego Rivera. Rivera lived in what was called his blue house at 127 Avenida de Londres in a part of Mexico City called Coyoacán. After the attempt on his life, Trotsky moved to his own quarters—a fortresslike compound in another area of the Coyoacán district.

It was there that Jacques Mornard, a.k.a. Frank Jacson, delivered Sylvia Agelof for work in the morning and picked her up again in the evening.

The day of the ice pick came in August 1940.

Trotsky woke with energy that morning. He fed the chickens and rabbits on his patio and turned his attention to an article about the military conscription in America. Trotsky thought young American draftees should be encouraged to revolt and shoot their officers. He had lived his life according to political fantasies and mad prophecies. At least one of them had come true. Despite exile, despite the awful purges, despite Joseph Stalin, the indomitable Leon Trotsky never gave up. He would not give up. He could not give up. That's the way he was.

He worked alone in his whitewashed study. It

was a comfortable place. Trotsky liked it. There was a map of Mexico on the wall. Trotsky sat on a cane-bottomed chair at a long table piled neatly with manuscripts and books. There was a glue pot, pens and pencils in a jar, a pair of scissors, an ivory paper cutter, a long-stemmed black lamp.

Under the table was a switch that activated an alarm system. There was a Colt .38 automatic in a drawer, and on the table itself a .25 automatic served as a paperweight. Both were oiled and loaded. It was a practical room, utilitarian and plain. There were no paintings or photographs on the wall: there were only pen and pencil for Trotsky to write with and two pistols with which to defend himself.

Nothing more.

At five that afternoon Trotsky and his wife, Natalie, took tea as they did at that time every day. A half hour later, his tea finished, Trotsky fed his rabbits in the company of Mornard. Mornard was there to show Trotsky an article he had written. Although it was a sunny day, he wore a hat and carried an overcoat draped over his arm.

Trotsky's wife asked Mornard why he carried an overcoat on a hot day.

"The sun won't last long," he said. "It might rain." The truth was Mornard had a revolver, a dagger, and an ice pick concealed under the overcoat.

Natalie asked how Sylvia was doing.

"Sylvia? Sylvia?" Mornard paused as though he hadn't heard the name before. "She is always well."

Mornard followed Trotsky into the study where Trotsky sat to read the typewritten article. Mornard threw his overcoat on the table to block access to the alarm switch.

About thirty seconds later, Mornard brought the flattened end of the ice pick down on the thinning white hair of Trotsky's bare head. The needle-sharp pointed end would have entered five or six inches into Trotsky's brain and remained there. Trotsky would have died instantly without making any sound.

Instead, the slightly curved, two-inch-wide blade penetrated the side of Trotsky's skull, sinking about two and a half inches deep.

Trotsky rose from his chair and struggled with Mornard, a stronger, taller man. Trotsky's glasses were smashed and he could hardly see, but he struggled, screaming a wild, unearthly scream.

He was felled at about 5:35 P.M. Mornard was captured by Trotsky's bodyguards and the ambulance was called fifteen minutes later. Paralysis was setting in on the left side of Trotsky's body by the time the ambulance arrived from the Green Cross Emergency Hospital in Mexico City. The ambulance sped through the city streets at high speeds, but Trotsky was in a coma by the time he reached the hospital.

The doctors examined his skull and concluded that an operation was necessary.

The first report was fairly straightforward, all things considered:

"The following lesions were discovered: fracture of the right parietal bone with bone

splinters projecting into the brain substance;
damaging of the meninges and destruction of the
brain substance, and hernia of same. The prog-
nosis is very grave, although the immediate results of the operation are satisfactory."

Trotsky died at 7:25 P.M. the following evening.
It was reported that within a few minutes of
death, Trotsky's breathing became very rapid.
Those near him said it was as though he was
racing to complete the journey—a romantic
notion befitting a man of Trotsky's passion and
place in history.

Others suggested the rapid breathing was sheer,
murderous rage. For Trotsky's followers, the
manner of his dying was clear: somehow, someday, somewhere, he would have his revenge.

Kim Philby was apparently recruited by the
Soviets at Cambridge University in 1931. After
Cambridge, Philby traveled on the European con-
tinent, where he witnessed the rise of fascism. In
1934, he married an Austrian Communist, Litzi
Friedman, in Vienna. On his return to Great
Britain, however, he joined the pro-Nazi Anglo-
German Fellowship. He separated from Litzi, and
in 1935 went to Spain as a correspondent for the
Times of London. He was considered a pro-Franco
journalist.

Philby went to France in 1940 to report for the
Times, and was evacuated to Britain in 1941.
Through old Cambridge connections he was recruited into the British intelligence service. Philby
was put to work training agents for undercover

work and soon was planning espionage operations. Philby was a stutterer and drank too much,
but he was trusted and efficient—perfectly placed
to give the Soviet Union full details of British
agents in Nazi-occupied Eastern Europe.

In 1949, the British assigned Philby to Washington, where he helped organize an Anglo-American
plan to place agents in Communist Albania. Hundreds of these agents were caught and executed.
Philby was also the ranking British member of an
Anglo-American committee designed to pool intelligence data.

The Americans grew suspicious of Philby, however. And in 1951, Philby learned that Burgess and
Maclean—the latter had helped steal secrets of the
American hydrogen bomb for the Soviets—were
under suspicion. Philby warned both men and
they flew safely to Moscow. Philby was recalled to
London, questioned, and fired. The British refused
to concede he was a Soviet agent, however. Philby
had a list of prominent supporters, including
Prime Minister Harold Macmillan.

In 1956, British intelligence set up Philby as a
journalist in the Middle East. In 1962, a senior
KGB man, Anatoli Dolnytsin, defected to London.
Dolnytsin alleged that the Soviets had had an
agent active in the Secret Intelligence Service
until 1951, although he didn't know the spy's
name.

The suspicions surrounding Philby refused to go
away. Philby himself stayed put in Lebanon.

There is some confusion as to exactly how Philby left Beirut. The American Central Intelligence

Agency and British SIS have their theories, of course, but they remain unconfirmed. Philby himself has never discussed how he escaped. He did tell one of his children that he arrived in Moscow with his feet bruised from a long and difficult walk. One of the better theories, it is said, has it that Philby—possessing forged papers identifying him as a Turkish diplomatic courier—was driven to the Syrian border in a Turkish truck. He crossed Syria into Turkey, then crossed the Turkish border into Soviet Armenia using contacts he had with the Armenian community in Cyprus.

No matter. The secret life of Harold Adrian Russell Philby was over. Philby, nicknamed Kim by his father, Harry St. John Philby, had been a Soviet spy in the British Secret Intelligence Service for thirty years.

The end had come, finally, when the British trapped George Blake, an SIS agent who had worked for the Soviets for nearly ten years. The British learned of Blake from Colonel Michal Goleniewski, chief of Polish intelligence. Goleniewski was in a position to betray Philby as well.

The British had a problem. They had already acquitted Philby in a secret trial. The Prime Minister had defended him in Parliament. Philby was a Cambridge man. He was a helluva guy. He was a hard drinker but held his booze well. He was bright and apparently lacked guile; men liked him. Despite his stutter, he had a certain shaggy charm; women liked him as well.

The British, being a civilized people, decided

they should have a chat with Philby. The man they
sent, a close friend of Philby's, had once been area
head of the SIS in Beirut. There followed the usual
battle of wits at which Philby was by then something of an expert. The SIS interrogator did his
best, but Philby repeated his oft-told explanations
of his past. The SIS man finally laid it on the line:
Her Majesty's Government now knew for a fact he
was a Soviet spy and had been one for years. Philby shrugged, admitted it, and told the SIS man,
"Knowing what I did, I could not have done anything else."

The SIS man returned to London. Philby returned to the hotel bars in Beirut, where he spent his
time getting pissed on Scotch whiskey.

The British were faced with four choices. They
could kill him in Lebanon, but that was messy and
dangerous. They could remove him forcibly to
London. They could try to persuade him to return
on his own and face charges. Or they could break
him in a way that would be impossible in London
and force him into exile.

The latter was the most attractive option. It
would be good for SIS morale, and the first allegations were emerging of what was to become the
Profumo Affair. A spy trial the British did not
need.

A second SIS man visited Philby in December
1962. The second man was less amiable than the
first and more determined.

On the night of January 23, 1963, Philby was to
attend a dinner party at the home of Glen Balfour
Paul, first secretary at the British embassy. On the

way he stopped his taxi and got out "to send a cable from the post office." Philby never made the party.

So that was the end. Philby emerged in Moscow six months later. On July 3, 1963, *Izvestia* announced that by unanimous vote of the Presidium, H.A.R. Philby had been made a citizen of the Soviet Union.

MOSCOW

Philby's Story

1

He emerged each night at midnight from the flat he shared with his Russian wife. He walked for two hours almost to the minute, bundled against the weather and puffing one cigarette after another. His routine never varied. He opened the door, looked up at a streetlight, down at his solid, serviceable shoes, grinned an odd grin, and lit an English cigarette. His KGB tails reported, accurately, that he met no one, talked to no one; he merely walked, his breath coming in quick, soft puffs in the coldness of the Russian night.

The Russians, being a suspicious people, were immediately alarmed. What was this all about? Why was he walking? Routine inquiries were made; it was discovered that he had some weeks earlier reported a severe case of insomnia to his physician. The physician, a woman who had treated him almost from the moment of his arrival

from Beirut years earlier, told him to cut down on
his drinking. She prescribed sleeping pills. He had
always been a drinker, a legacy of his past. His
liver worried her as much as his insomnia. He returned a week later to complain the pills didn't
work. The physician prescribed a different,
stronger drug. That too was ineffective, he reported. The KGB returned with more questions
for the physician. She told them again her patient
couldn't sleep. That sometimes happened to a man
his age, she said. Given his history, she said, his
lack of sleep was understandable. That answer
annoyed her interrogators.

He was apparently able to do with less sleep because each morning he arose in time to catch the
Moscow subway to Dzerzhinsky Square, where he
worked for the KGB. He had reached his seven-
tieth birthday and was beyond retirement age, but
was considered valuable, nevertheless, for his
knowledge of "sleepers" or "moles," depending on
whether you are a traditionalist or a reader of
John le Carré spy novels.

He began walking in late March and the weeks
passed. When June came he was still walking, a
ruddy-complexioned man with strawberry-blond
hair, wrinkled bags under blue eyes, and large-
lobed ears. His face had a slightly bloated look
from years of drinking, but there was energy in his
step yet. When June turned to July and the summer nights were warm, he walked with extra zest.
The KGB, ever suspicious, watched each night. He
was watched during August. He was watched
when a chill returned in September. He was

watched when the frost came in October. When the winter returned in November, he emerged each night, bundled in ever thicker layers of overcoats as the weeks went by. Only in December and January, when the temperatures plunged well below zero, did he stop his walks.

When he stopped walking, his KGB watchers reported, a light remained on in his flat until 2:00 A.M. He could be seen pacing, cigarette or drink in hand, or sitting, book in his lap. By January, interest in his behavior began to decline at Moscow Center, KGB headquarters. The men detailed to watch him became bored; they had other people to watch. There is never a lack of surveillance details in Moscow. Their man was an insomniac; he could not sleep. They knew of Kim Philby's past, of course, but still could not understand Ivan Konsomov's passionate interest in his behavior. Men were needed elsewhere. Still, the KGB was Konsomov's responsibility. Comrade Konsomov was ambitious; he took no chances.

When the weather began to thaw in March, Kim Philby put down his books and booze—well, some of the booze—and returned to the sidewalks. He picked up where he had left off in November. He looked up at the streetlight, then down at his shoes. He grinned. He lit an English cigarette. The routine was the same.

When he started walking again, Konsomov's interest was stirred once more. Men were again detailed to follow him. But nothing unusual happened. It was just as before. The KGB's interest began to decline. He was boring; that's all there was to it.

There came a suggestion that Philby return to his books and booze to put himself to sleep; Philby said that just didn't work. That was true, apparently; as it turned out he had visited his physician repeatedly in the winter, complaining that without his walks he could hardly endure. He cursed the Russian winters. In recognition of his years of service to Mother Russia, Philby was allowed to continue his walking.

So each night a slightly inebriated Kim Philby, carrying with him the knowledge that he had betrayed his colleagues, his class, and his country, that he was the single, most outrageous traitor of the twentieth century, this Kim Philby walked.

Comrade Konsomov watched.

Comrade Philby walked.

2

The public normally regards a change of Presidents as anxiously as it does a squall. Lives and fortunes are at the mercy of the cold waters of history, buffeted hard by winds that never cease. People wonder if the buoys by which they reckon their lives will somehow shift in the wind. Ask a sailor when he's drunk or wrapped in the softness of a woman and he'll tell you about the buoys:

"Red right coming in. Red left going out. Remember that, mate, and you'll be fine."

Derek Townes untied his Gucci oxfords, steadied himself with a hand on a roughly hewn, eight-foot wooden statue of Chingachgook, the last of the Mohicans, and put his feet on the varnished birch of the window sill. The wind ruffled the surface of Massabesic Lake, causing feathery whitecaps on the tops of swells.

Townes took a sip of New Hampshire branch and Mr. Daniel's best; he smiled at the sight of a

catamaran tacking into the wind. The cat was
hiked up on one pontoon; its skipper, a teenager in
a red nylon Windbreaker, was gutting it out, his
slender back arched with effort to get farther out
on the airborne runner. Townes had once sailed
but no longer had time, just as he no longer had
time to watch a ball game on the tube or have sex
with his wife. Tacking into the wind was an ex-
hilarating experience. It took nerve to go flat out
like that. The kid on the boat had nerve; if he cut it
too fine, a gust would take him over. It was a
lovely sight. Politics and the accumulation of
power were much the same, Townes reflected.
You had to take a chance. You had to go for it.

Townes had requested that the lake side of the
Iroquois Lodge be roped off from the public. New
Hampshire authorities had been obliging. The
Secret Service was grateful: crowds made them
nervous. Derek Townes would be President, a
natural lure for nuts and screwballs. So the public
milled about in the Grand Ballroom, drinks in hand,
laughing, talking about what Townes would likely
do about the high cost of medical care and the necessity, for the time being, of giving up on all the
sanctimonious anti-nuke talk. There was a country
to run. They were there waiting to catch a glimpse of
Derek Townes at his hour. The networks, waiting
to record it all on videotape, crowded the parking
lots with their trucks.

It had been perfectly normal, given the history
of American political life, for President James
Burack to name his successor. Burack was dying

of emphysema in his first term. The tobacco
people and the Republican party cursed the gods.
Burack's disease was doing to the tobacco industry what the Food and Drug Administration,
the National Institutes of Health, and the Department of Health had failed to do: cause smoking to
become unfashionable. And the Republicans, what
could they do? Burack was dying.

Everything Townes said and did from now on
had to be said and done with an eye on how it
would come across on the ubiquitous eye of television. It was ridiculous to any marginally educated and aware voter. No matter. It didn't
make any difference that Burack hadn't been an
especially effective President; the media hoorah
over his illness took the spotlight. Wholly un-
founded comparisons were made between Burack
and Jefferson, Burack and Lincoln, Burack and
the Roosevelts, Burack and Harry Truman. The
coverage was intended to be a touching tribute to
a man both well intentioned and earnest if not
especially dynamic; he had sort of held the economy together and the country was not at war.
For that at least the public was grateful. Any television reporter worth his pancake makeup dreamed of putting on videotape the Burack equivalent
of Lou Gehrig's farewell address at Yankee
Stadium. In an effort to boost their Nielsens, the
networks spared no expense on the Burack story;
the result was that he was ever present on television and on the covers of magazines. Television
reporters, in search of poignancy, struggled in a

tar pit of the maudlin. It was awful. Few people could understand how an intelligent adult could put up with it, but Burack did.

The result was that when President Burack said he thought the voters of New Hampshire should cast their mark for Townes, they voted for Townes. There was no doubt that Townes would crush his three opponents in the New Hampshire primary. And there seemed no reason to suppose that the sentiment would ease in any of the primaries coming up. Money that might have gone to his opponents was coming to him; he was a winner. The unions were already lining up their political action committees. Industry was there too, money in hand. Everybody wanted to make sure Derck Townes was acquainted with the fundamentals of proper thinking.

To celebrate, Townes gave himself the luxury of an hour alone in the bar. His aides and assistants were in their rooms making phone calls, changing clothes, and getting ready for the triumphant evening ahead. The men on his staff would be taking showers and there, lathered with soap, would dream of eight years of media attention, of being recognized on the street, of having their cocks sucked by beautiful women in Marriott hotels. The women, in bathtubs so as not to mess their hair, would dream of meeting and marrying one of the powerful, attractive men who surround an American President, or of using their contacts to move into a career on television.

Townes helped himself to some more whiskey. It was over, weeks of giving speeches and shaking hands in supermarket parking lots in small towns with names like Ossipee, Exeter, Nashua, Marlboro, Weare, and Northwood Narrows. You call a citizen of Boston a Bostonian. What about a resident of Ossipee? What do you do? It turned out the residents of Ossipee didn't care if they were called Occipeans, Ossipepoids, or Ossipissers as long as they got their quadrennial turn in the national limelight. Theirs was the starting gate for the presidential horse race; you had to win New Hampshire to prove you were a winner.

The attention lavished on them made the Hampshiremen cantankerous and demanding; Townes's chief aide, Irv Cohn, had gotten in the habit of flipping the locals the finger when their backs were turned, until Townes made him stop.

It was Cohn, a large, slouching, gruff-voiced man, who interrupted Townes's privacy. He closed the carved wooden door to the Redman's Bar.

Townes stood up and looked at Chingachgook's wooden beak and the two holes that were the pupils of his eyes "How's Susan?"

Cohn cleared his throat. "She's fine, Derek."

"We don't need her numb from vodka when the television people show up."

"She's sober, Derek. She said no more Sacramentos, no more Denvers." Cohn stared at his feet.

"What do you think?"

"I think she'll keep her word. She doesn't want to be pictured like Teddy's wife. She knows what Betty Ford went through. She said she understands the importance of coming off well tonight. I think she's ready. The problem, I think, is going to be me."

Townes glared at his friend. "We've been through that before."

"We have to face facts, Derek. Remember what happened to Tom Eagleton. This is something the public just cannot take."

"I disagree."

Cohn stood and left the room without looking back.

Townes took another drink. Irv Cohn had been his good friend since the protests on the steps in front of Sproul Hall with Mario Savio. He closed his eyes and remembered Berkeley. That was a long time ago. He had come a long way.

If he was going to be President, he wanted Irv to be with him.

3

Susan Townes was lying naked on a double bed in her room on the Iroquois's second floor. She had tired of reading *Cosmo* and sailed the magazine across the room. There was a Paul Newman movie on the television, *Sweet Bird of Youth*, but the sound was turned down; Susan, who was a few years shy of forty, was not interested.

She sat up on the bed and turned, looking at her profile in the mirror above the dresser. Her breasts were on the smallish side, so the accumulated effect of gravity and thirty-eight years was not much. They looked good, she thought. She twisted on the bed and looked at her other profile. Just as good. The more provocative part of her breasts was the nipples, the tips of which stood straight out, roughly the size of her thumb from tip to joint. Derek used to love them. He used to work on them with his tongue or he would take a nipple in his teeth and pull, applying enough pressure to make Susan arch her back and twist, sucking air in between clenched teeth. It had been lovely. Susan retrieved her glass from the floor and took another sip of bourbon.

She was sixteen years old, an early admit at Cal-Berkeley when Derek Townes first discovered those nipples. She remembered clearly how Derek had casually slid his hand down her blouse, how he had inhaled involuntarily when her nipples pushed against his palms. Derek thought she was eighteen.

They slept together that night and the night following. Derek was twenty-five, staying on at Berkeley to earn a second degree—in economics—at the urging of his friend, Dr. Nicholas Ostrov. "You need economics to go with your political science," Ostrov told him. "Then do graduate work." Ostrov believed economics to be at the heart of all human behavior.

Susan got off the bed, put her drink on the dresser, and, using a hand mirror to complement the mirror on the dresser, took a look at her butt. Ostrov could have his economics. Susan was an erotic woman; she wanted nothing more than to be totally, completely in love. Love was what mattered. She always had a good figure. Her ass looked fine; there were no dimples of fat. Her thighs were solid.

Derek had once been a good lover. He liked her butt as much as he did her nipples. One of their favorites had been for her to lean naked against a wall—butt out—while he worked her by hand from behind. She knew he liked to see her ass move and she obliged. She moved her rump in sensuous circles, tightening and loosening her cheeks, occasionally arching her spine to give him a better look at the moistness between her legs. She remembered the shuddering loveliness of the orgasms that washed across her body until at last he slid into her with a stinging slap on the ass, sign that it was time for her to put it into high gear. That she was pleased to do.

The year they met was 1964, the year of Mario Savio's free speech movement on the steps of Sproul Hall at Berkeley. It was a lovely time, sitting with Derek as he talked economics with Ostrov far into the night, marching in protest against the "Do not fold, spindle or mutilate" mentality of a university grown too large. She remembered the first time they had been gassed. A university administrator with a bullhorn had promised he would call the police, but nobody believed him, not really. They went right ahead with their speeches and name calling. When the police arrived with flashing lights on the tops of their squad cars, the students had been shocked. Police were for crooks. Susan thought reason would prevail and the cops would leave. But no, they donned masks, formed a line, and began marching shoulder to shoulder straight at the students.

Susan realized she was on her own; she was an adult. Her eyes had burned like fire when the tear gas came, but when it was over they felt like heroes. They had been tear-gassed! They were students, there at Berkeley to learn, and pigs in masks had gassed them! The feeling of solidarity and togetherness of those gassed was something Susan would never forget. And the pigs were proof of their assertion that an ugly, latent streak of fascism was surfacing in the United States. The television networks put it on videotape for all the world to see. Newcomers to the movement, those drawn to Berkeley by the media coverage but who hadn't had an opportunity to be gassed, were envious. It was great, when you were stoned on good Colombian, to describe the gas floating across the campus and give initiates advice on what to do when their time came.

The next year, in 1965, Susan transferred to Columbia to be with Derek. She was from Escondido, near San Diego. Her parents weren't anxious for her to move to New York but thought Derek Townes could do no wrong. His father, John, a Wall Street lawyer, had in some fashion served every Democratic President since Franklin Roosevelt. Derek had a future. At Columbia it was Mark Rudd and barricades at Morningside Heights. Derek's father and his mother, Hanna, a pretty woman who collected antiques, were patient with his radical phase. They believed it was something that would go away, like pimples. They thought Susan was wonderful.

In 1968, when the anti-war movement was at its peak, Derek, by then having earned his master's degree, suddenly tired of protest. He married Susan and the two of them moved to Albany, where Derek took a job as legislative assistant to a Democratic assemblyman. It was the beginning of his rise in politics, a rise almost without setback.

Susan took another sip of bourbon and slid back onto the bed. She explored the depression in the tip of one nipple with the edge of a slender fingernail. They really had been man and wife in those days. They did things married people do. It was different now. They had not had sex in four months. She was on the road; he was on the road. When their paths did cross it was for dinner in a motel, dinner shared with Derek's aide and advisors. When they met they fought. She was exhausted or he was exhausted. There was no warmth, no passion, no touching.

Susan plucked an ice cube out of her drink to see what it would do to her nipple. She stiffened at the touch. She had threatened to walk out on him in a motel in Des Moines, where they lived while he kissed the asses of Iowa Democrats who could give him caucus votes. He must have kissed sweetly because he won them all.

"Later," he told her in Des Moines. "Things will settle down and fall into place later, after November. We'll have a routine in the White House; we won't be on the road all the time. We can go up to Camp David for the weekends. We can have a baby then if you'd like. The honeymoon from the press lasts less than a year. We'll need a little pick-me-up the following fall. A baby would be nice."

Remembering that conversation, Susan Townes poured herself another drink. She was getting too old to be a mother. She couldn't divorce him. That was impossible. She tried to console herself that it would be fun, what with the travel, the power, the attention, the stories about her in the women's magazines. Just now, however, she was horny; women got that way too.

Men just didn't seem to understand.

Susan remembered that John Kennedy was said to have had young women smuggled into the White House all the time. She wondered if, while her husband worried about inflation, competition with Japanese steel, and the rest, if she might not do the same thing. After all, women were claiming more and more prerogatives formerly reserved for men. Why not? She could get relief from a young stud, a gigolo, someone with energy and a real wad between his legs. She could do her revolving butt routine for someone who hadn't seen it before. There was life there yet.

She poured herself another drink. She knew perfectly well she couldn't get away with that. She was certain she would be an alcoholic one day, the subject of pathetic articles in the press.

Susan Townes took her nipple between thumb and forefinger. She wished she could go back. She remembered Savio's speeches. She remembered the cops with their hard faces and batons. She remembered smoking pot and drinking jug wine in Derek's loft. She remembered Derek telling her to do her breasts while she lay back, eyes closed, spine arched, legs spread wide. He did her by hand, down below, as Susan did now, telling her how beautiful she was.

That was all gone now. Past. They would be President and Mrs. Derek Townes. She would be the First Lady.

4

The Soviets were always at a loss as to what to do with visitors from the West. When faced with a group of left-wing history professors, as they were now, there were problems. Should the Soviets provide the professors with spartan food and accommodations so as to impress them with the sacrifices made on behalf of the people, to assure them they were being treated no differently than ordinary Russians? Or should they flatter the professors, seeing to it that they had all the vodka they could drink and could tell their friends back home they were served Russian caviar, the rarest and most expensive in the world? There were arguments on both sides. Those urging austerity for visitors held that it was important that the Soviets appear to go about business as usual; there was no reason to curry the favors of Westerners, thank you. Others argued that was idealistic

nonsense—an American is an American. No matter what the professed ideology of an American
professor, he or she will in the end be most
impressed by extra attention.

The latter group argued that if American professors were paid sufficiently well, they would all
be capitalists. Having been excluded from material reward, the argument ran, the professors had
nothing better to do than attack the system that
valued plumbers higher. If the Soviets worked it
right, the Americans might conclude the Soviets
valued intelligence and inquiring minds, and they
also might overlook the obvious shortage of con-
sumer goods for the average Russian.

It was for that reason that the Soviets dug deep
into their treasury to build an impressive Olympic
stadium and athletic complex only to have that
fucking Jimmy Carter screw them out of being
telecast daily on NBC to a gullible American
public.

It was decided the historians would get the
caviar and vodka treatment. They were, after all,
in charge of educating impressionable young
minds. Trusting not in God but the certainties of
economic determinism, the Soviets nevertheless
knew that as they sowed, so should they reap.

A Soviet trade union was chosen as the proper
host for the professors. They were given the usual
tours of factories and a communal farm just outside Moscow that was subsidized by the State as a
showpiece for visitors. After the tours, there was a
reception at a lush and ornate hotel built in the
nineteenth century. The hotel, originally named

after Czar Nicholas, was now called the Hotel
Ulanov, after a Soviet general. The Hotel Ulanov
featured an impressive banquet room with a long
table upon which the trade union—again subsidized by a special State fund for just that purpose—heaped Polish ham, Hungarian cheese,
Czech pilsner beer in tubs of ice, caviar, plates of
smoked sturgeon, smoked reindeer, and other
delicacies intended to impress the visitor with the
diversity of the Communist world.

There had been one request—by a professor
from Temple University in Philadelphia—that had
caused some concern. The professor, whose radical credentials were impressive, was writing a
book on the cold war and wished to chat with Kim
Philby. The initial Soviet reaction was to turn him
down until a check was run. It was discovered that
the professor had once been cited for contempt of
Congress and had written a book about the
American intelligence establishment in which he
listed the names of more than a dozen CIA agents
in Europe. He had the book published in Great
Britain so as to avoid being censored by Langley,
the CIA's administrative headquarters, but the
damage was done. The administration at Temple
was chagrined, but nothing could be done. The
professor was tenured. Viewing all this, the
Soviets agreed to his request to chat with Philby.
What was the harm? The KGB would have a man
at Philby's side, of course. Just in case.

Just in case of what, nobody was certain.

The Soviets did know that the American embassy would assign one of its intelligence

operatives to accompany the professors. The
names of those assigned to the embassy by Langley were well known. The man chosen to babysit
the professors was an eccentric named James Burlane, a Russian linguist long an employee of the
Central Intelligence Agency.

Burlane was surprised to learn that Kim Philby
would be allowed to mingle with the professors.
With the exception of writers working on articles
and books about Philby that were obvious propa-
ganda, the Soviets saw to it that Philby was
isolated from possibly infectious contact with
Westerners. In the first years, Philby himself had
been understandably alarmed that the British or
the Americans might try to waste him out of
revenge. That fear had passed, however, and
Philby had earned the Soviets' trust.

Or rather, earned their trust so far as any Soviet
citizen is ever trusted. In Philby's case that meant
a KGB man at his elbow whenever there was any
doubt.

The buffet was an early-evening affair and
Philby, spotting the booze with the accuracy of a
surface-to-air missile, established his base at the
center of the table—between the Czech pilsner and
Russian vodka. After a couple of straight shots
with a beer chaser, he was charming and witty in
that worldly British sort of way that annoyed
many of his colleagues in the KGB. The professors
regarded him with much the same enthusiasm as
teenagers in the presence of a rock star or television personality. Being professors and all, they
didn't want to appear anxious and therefore
provincial. Philby was a hero in their eyes; it was

due to his efforts that the Communists were able to execute dozens of spies parachuting onto Albanian soil. Gawking was boorish. So one at a time they slipped casually up to him, had a drink, offered a secretly rehearsed spontaneous remark or joke, then moved on, rehearsing—and already embellishing—a marvelous anecdote about ''accidentally'' bumping into Kim Philby at a gathering sponsored by a Soviet trade union.

James Burlane, a tall, casual, cynical man, himself a bit drunk from the free vodka, made his way toward Philby too. He didn't expect to learn anything, but he liked anecdotes as well. Besides, there was the fun of torturing the KGB, which knew damn well he was with the CIA.

''Ahh, Mr. Philby. I'm pleased to meet you. I've heard a lot about you,'' Burlane grinned. The KGB man at Philby's elbow looked stern-faced.

''Mister?'' Philby asked. He poured himself another shot of vodka.

''Burlane.''

''And you are w-with?''

''The American embassy here. I'm acting as a host of sorts, I guess, to ensure that our people have a good time.'' He looked at the KGB man and smirked.

Philby took a package of cigarettes from his jacket pocket and removed the seal from the package. ''Oh, I thought you were another p-professor. I shouldn't be surprised, I guess.'' Philby shook his head and smiled. ''At least I don't have to ask you know you like M-Moscow. You already know.''

''It isn't bad duty, I suppose. This is a nice

spread." Burlane retrieved a cold bottle of beer from a tub of ice.

"Would you like a cigarette? They're English, I'm afraid. I've never gotten out of the habit. English cigarettes and the *Times*." He gave the package a slight flip, keeping one finger partly over one cigarette. Burlane took the one remaining. It was a casual offering, quickly done.

"Thank you," said Burlane.

"If you smoke them too far down they get a bit strong, though; that's the only drawback."

Burlane lit the cigarette and inhaled deeply. With his tongue he felt a small nipple in the butt of the cigarette. "Pleased to have met you, Mr. Philby. My colleagues will be envious."

Philby grinned and turned his attention to a slender professor of economics from SUNY, Stony Brook.

Burlane helped himself to some more vodka, smoked the cigarette halfway down, and went to the toilet, beer in hand. He was followed, as he knew he would be, by one of Philby's colleagues from Moscow Center. The urinal was old-fashioned, rising all the way from the floor. Spreading cracks in the enamel were filled with aged, yellow urine crystals. Burlane put his bottle of Czech beer on a ledge on top of the urinal. As he unzipped his pants, he removed the plastic capsule from the butt of the cigarette with his teeth and swallowed it. He twisted the butt of the cigarette with his fingers and flipped it disdainfully into the bottom of the urinal. His bladder was bursting. He laced it to the butt, tightening his stomach with effort and spreading brown flecks of tobacco across the bottom of the urinal; he managed to push the sodden mess from one side to the other. Not bad. It was white, booze piss.

The man who had followed him into the toilet had taken the urinal next to his.

"Have a good one," Burlane said cheerfully. He shook it more vigorously than he had to and zipped his pants.

"Asshole," the man muttered in English.

Burlane pretended not to hear. "Man, I really had to go." He flushed the urinal, leaving the remains of the butt clinging to the strainer at the drain. The Communists were humorless, conniving fuckers. Burlane had the idea that it somehow tormented the Soviets more to be screwed by someone who laughed at them at the same time. He drank too much, it was true, and he had his problems, but when he put it to the Soviets, he did it in a grand, flamboyant manner.

"You wanna suck on the butt, Ivan?" he said to the man at the next urinal.

The Russian glared at him with hatred.

"You people are such pricks, do you know that?" Burlane bunched up his face, tightened his stomach, and let go a big fart.

5

The shad began their annual run on the Potomac a month after the Hampshiremen blessed Derek Townes and Kim Philby began to walk again in Moscow. Every spring when the shad begin to move, men and their sons gather on the Potomac to cast lures into the water. This is all reported in the *Washington Post*. After the first newspaper article, it's hard to get to the water. The shad are something you can know and count on in Washington, like summer sweat and the leaves turning gold the third week of October.

On the day James Burlane arrived at Langley with Philby's microfilm, Ara Schott parked his car on the District side of the Key Bridge and hiked down to the shore. The better part of the run was over, but for Schott watching the fishermen was one of the pleasures of living in Washington. Schott knew how to steam the shad so their bones dissolve. He liked rockfish, too, and crabs steamed with lots of Chesapeake Bay spice. Schott sat atop a flat rock and picked at his fingernails with a pocket knife. He was late for work but he didn't care. The people at Langley understood: the shad were running.

Ara Schott was a contemplative, thoughtful man. For him the annual migration of fish was a sweet and poignant ritual in a violent world. Schott knew about violence. Better than the fishermen with their lures, he knew deception and treachery. He was director of counterintelligence for the Central Intelligence Agency.

Schott himself rarely got an opportunity to fish. He didn't have time. He did fish when he got a chance; he knew quite a lot about it, mostly from texts. He had a first edition of Isaac Walton. He knew about catfish in Arkansas, carp in Nebraska, pike in Minnesota. He knew about nymphs, bucktails, and the paraphernalia of fly-fishing. It was the idea of the bait or lure that fascinated him. Schott subscribed to *Field and Stream* magazine. In the evenings, relaxed with a cold bottle of National Bohemian, he read about fishing for tarpon off the Florida Keys, trout in Idaho, and salmon in Oregon.

What fascinated Schott was the fact that in order to be successful, a fisherman had to know the ways of fish. He had to *know* fish. That seemed obvious to Schott. It wasn't simple though; it was complex in the extreme.

Schott knew that bass spawn in the sand. They feed on the surface early in the morning and late in the afternoon. In the heat of the day they retreat to the deep water where it's cool; they lie there, sluggish, surly, unmoving. Schott knew that steelhead in the Northwest will mouth a lure then spit it out like a child approaching chicken liver for the first time. Fishermen drift salmon eggs on the bottom, pencil weights going bump, bump, bump until there is a pause or hesitation in the line.

Then they set the hook. Only then. Schott was convinced that in some ways men are not a whole lot different from fish. It's not that he put too fine a point on it. There were similarities, that's all.

Schott believed that odd facts and arcane bits of information will trail a double agent in much the same way that sea gulls follow the annual run of smelt up the Columbia River. He lived by details, much to the annoyance of his colleagues in operations, who did not like to deep-six a good scheme because Ara Schott couldn't account for a mustache trimmed incorrectly or a shoe of an outdated style. A man in counterintelligence must attend to facts, of course; it's part of his job. But with Schott it went beyond that; they said it was because he was German.

Schott was a rather tall man with a strong jaw, intelligent blue eyes, and a cleft in his chin. He was of German ancestry; that was true. His grandfather had emigrated to the United States from Hamburg. His father was a foreman in a York, Pennsylvania, textile mill. Ara attended Pennsylvania State University on a national merit scholarship and discovered he had an aptitude for languages. He was recruited out of Penn State by

the CIA and put to work first as an analyst, then as
a translator of Slavic languages in counterintelligence. In a way, he was out of place at Langley.
His colleagues had mostly attended prep schools,
Yale and Harvard. They were clever, gleeful cold
warriors, convinced they would prevail in the end.
But Ara Schott flourished in the bureaucratic
anonymity. He was polite and patient. He was
thorough. He was careful. The agency, recognizing
his quick mind, moved him into an executive
position. It was one of those rare occasions when
the right man was promoted.

By the time he was thirty-five, Ara Schott was in
charge of counterintelligence, not to be confused
with the DCI, director of Central Intelligence.
Schott was respected by his counterparts in Moscow Center. He was an effective brake on his more
energetic colleagues who seemed bent on forever
launching elaborate and unworkable ploys against
the demon Communists.

Schott was said to be even more cautious than
James Angleton. It was Angleton, whose tenure as
chief of counterintelligence was something of a
myth at Langley, who turned down an offer of information by a Soviet named Oleg Pentkovskiy in
1960. Angleton said he didn't trust Pentkovskiy's
bona fides. Pentkovskiy was in the Kremlin, Angleton's colleagues pleaded. "For God's sake, listen.
Let's find out," they said. Angleton said no. Well,
dammit, the Brits picked him up. The Americans
helped run him, much to the dismay of Angleton,
who continued to insist he was a double and ought
not to be trusted. Pentkovskiy gave the agency five

thousand frames of microfilmed documents, two pages to the frame. Still Angleton said no. Pentkovskiy gave the Americans the training manual for the Russian missiles in Cuba in 1962. Angleton said no; he wasn't satisfied. Pentkovskiy had to be a double. He had to be. "Believe him," Angleton said, "and you'll believe anything."

He was the same way with Yuri Nosenko, who fled the Soviet Union in late 1963, claiming to know for a fact that Lee Harvey Oswald was not working for the KGB. There was no way Nosenko could please Angleton. The result was that the director of the CIA at the time, Richard Helms, was forced to tell Chief Justice Earl Warren that the CIA just couldn't guarantee Nosenko's bona fides. Nosenko spent four years under round-the-clock guard in a padded cell. Angleton wouldn't be satisfied. Something didn't fit.

There were others after James Angleton, but eventually the burden fell on Ara Schott.

Schott walked slowly back up to his Toyota, looked back at the fishermen, and sighed. He had a ten-year-old son from a marriage that had been finished for five years. He felt a sadness for himself and for his son that was awful; somehow it was even worse now with the shad beginning to move. He would ask for his son on the weekend; perhaps the shad would still be there. Schott had remained single mostly because he found the routine of chasing women uncomfortable. He didn't like the bars where men and women gathered to meet one another. He felt self-conscious, if not a bit silly, trying to engage in the glib banter that was part of meeting someone. He was maybe lazy, too, and a bit cheap. It took effort to leave his condominium, and where would he go? He had few friends because he didn't try to befriend people. It was not that he was disliked or considered a drag. Schott merely stayed home, content to read, watch sports on television, and drink French table wines he bought at Pearson's on Wisconsin Avenue. After a year of isolation, Schott developed an understandable habit, which he reported to the DCI with an odd grin. Every once in a while, bored with a book, Schott would emerge from his condominium, pick up a black prostitute on Fourteenth Street, and return for a night of outrageous sex.

"Sucking, fucking, twisting, squirming, all that," he had told a slightly embarrassed Peter Neely, the DCI.

"I'm glad you told us, Ara. I can't imagine anyone having any objections." Neely swallowed.

Schott laughed. "Are you shocked, Peter?"

"Well," Neely paused.

"Yes?"

Neely grinned. "I guess my only question, Ara, is why do you choose black girls? Do you have some sort of racial preference? I don't understand."

"Black girls don't read newspapers and white girls charge too much."

"Charge too much?" Neely appreciated Schott's concern for security, but charge too much? Schott's tightness was well known but this was something else.

"The black girls are cheaper and easier to find. And no, I've never caught VD."

So Ara Schott lived alone, hoping maybe he would one day luck out and meet a good woman without having to go through a lot of time-consuming, expensive, stupid bullshit.

When Schott closed the door of his car, shutting off the sounds of the Potomac, his beeper went off.

Something was up.

6

It was clear from the face of Schott's secretary that something was up. Her name was Anna and her face telegraphed everything. She had a seemingly endless list of loony episodes of infidelity on the part of her husband, a bearded engineer who made model airplanes and chased women. "Saw your car by the Key Bridge on my way to work. If it'd been Bob, he'd have been in a van somewhere with a fisherman's wife, but you were watching the fishermen."

Schott smiled. "I think I'll take David this weekend, if I can get him."

"You'll get him and the fish'll still be there. By the way, that niece I was telling you about—she's going to be in Washington this weekend. She's going to be interviewed by a law firm. Bob says a woman like that makes him want to lick his lips." She licked her lips to demonstrate.

"And you were just wondering what I was doing this weekend?"

"I'll start lacing Bob's eggs with saltpeter. And before you start licking your lips, Peter Neely and Jackson want to see you, Code Six." William Jackson was the DCI's deputy director of plans, also called the DDP. The meaning of Code Six was known to just six men at Langley.

Schott faked a bored yawn. "Well, I suppose I better drift on over there. Anything you can't handle at this end?"

"Got it tied down," Anna said. "Bob says he'd like to play motorboat with my niece's breasts. Do you have any idea what that means, Ara?"

"I'll think about it," said Schott. It had been fourteen months since the last Code Six. There had been lots of Fours and Fives, but only one Six, following evidence that the Soviets were once again preparing to smuggle missiles into the Western Hemisphere. The President managed somehow to quash that threat with a few well-chosen words over the hot line.

Now this. Another Code Six. Ara Schott didn't waste any time getting to the DCI's office. The trouble was he couldn't act hurried.

The DCI was waiting, nervously smoking Marlboros, when Schott arrived. Neely was trim, remembered people's names, and kept a neat desk. He had retired as an Army colonel at age thirty-eight, having begun as an enlisted man when he was eighteen years old. He moved immediately to IBM after his retirement. He felt at home in white shirts and blue shirts and quickly established himself as a first-rate manager. Neely had experience in Army intelligence. When the President looked around for a good manager at Langley, he chose Neely at the urging of IBM executives who had supported his election. Most people were forced to admit he wasn't bad, although he had the personality of an elm.

Schott thought Neely was an intelligent man, prudent for the most part, but wondered how he would take the pressure when the Soviets tried to push them into the septic tank.

"Anna says we have a Code Six," said Schott.

Neely sighed. "You want to tell him about it, Bill?"

William Jackson, a freckle-faced, redheaded drinking man, was a good friend of Schott's. They had risen in the agency together. Jackson was a schemer and an optimist. Schott was cautious and careful. They were a good complement. Neely was careful always to hear them both out. "Kim Philby," said Jackson.

Schott sat in the empty chair opposite Jackson. "What?"

"Kim Philby slipped some microfilm to James Burlane at a meeting with some history professors three days ago in Moscow."

"How did he do that?"

"In a cigarette butt."

Ara Schott looked incredulous. "Kim Philby?"

"Yes."

"James Burlane?"

"Jimmy Burlane."

"The Brits, too, I suppose."

Jackson crossed his legs and scratched the ankle draped across his thigh. "Philby says just us."

"What does he want?"

Neely handed Schott a transcript of Philby's message. "This."

Schott read the message once, then again. He looked up—"KGB."

What Philby said was this:

My dear colleagues,

The Soviets have feared this day would come, I suppose. They have NATO, warm-water ports, China, and Kim Philby on the brain. In the first few years I was in Moscow, heavy-lidded types followed me everywhere. The bastards wired my flat. They read my mail. With blood flowing from cupped hands, I delivered them the liver and spleen of MI-6; still they didn't trust me. One morning in the spring of 1969, I found this little ditty scrawled on the wall of a men's toilet near my office in Moscow Center:

> Kim Philby, once turned,
> Watch his eyes
> Or you'll be b-burned.

A nice touch, the stutter, eh? And in English just for me. That little bit of poetry was gone the next day—washed away by the janitor—but it should give you an example. When I was still at Cambridge squeezing pimples and dodging public-school queers, I thought these people were our saviors. They were going to deliver us from the Fascists taking over Europe. What have I found? A nation of ignorant shits! Swine who cheat at international athletic competition. People who throw poets in labor camps. Murderous, lying, bullshit-believing, line-waiting, vodka-swilling sons of bitches! And bloody winters you wouldn't believe.

But I could not go back. The wages of sin, etc.

I am, after all, the Lucifer of MI-6—the man who made C and the Brits look ridiculous to their American cousins. From your standpoint, those bloody assholes in MI-6 had half the Cambridge University alumni association turning over secrets to the Soviets: British secrets, your secrets, everybody's secrets. And one of us was Guy Burgess, a man who reeked of garlic, let farts in polite company, and showed everybody pictures of his nude boyfriends. I betrayed more than King and Country, you see—I betrayed good blood, a stiff upper lip, obligation, and all that. I was a proper chap of good family.

"Oh yes, Philby!" they said. "His father was old St. John. The Arabist, you know. Eccentric chap. He was a bit soft on the Nazis for a while but came around proper."

It was that kind of thinking that made it possible for MI-5 to put off asking serious questions about my background. Incidentally, if it gives you any pleasure, I can tell you

that I have a dreadful case of arthritis, that
and an enlarged prostate, which needs an
operation. Even as I write this I am interrupted by the necessity to void a mere
thimbleful of urine with what is known, in
the lingo, as a "weak flow." I am tired of the
cold; I am tired of the Russians. It just hasn't
worked. The Russians are such bloody in-
grates. Last year, for example, I requested a
modest increase in the size of my flat. I
waited—that's something else that's getting
to me; the Russians spend most of their time
in line—and waited. It took them eight
months to say no on an official form. It must
be that no one remembers me in the West
anymore, so I hardly count. For you I am an
embarrassment of the past; for them I am a
coup of another generation. My knowledge of
you and MI-6 decreases each year. I am no
longer a prize. Philby? A larger flat? *Nyet!*

I am contacting you rather than the British
for two reasons. The first is that the British
loathe me with such a passion that the mere
mention of my name must bring on neurotic
symptoms. I just don't know what I could
offer them that would make them listen. The
second reason is that I have something of
interest to you alone, really—something that
should more than atone for my having spent
eighteen months giving the Soviets everything you intended for British ears alone. I
think what I have to offer you in penance is
more than adequate. A pawnbroker would be

pleased at the interest. I will only tease you
here; I'll give you a name but not the details—they're my ticket out of this ice.

What I know is this: you have, in the United
States, a very highly placed and influential
American—influential in the extreme—who
is an agent of the KGB. He is at this moment,
with the connivance of the Soviets, working
his way confidently into the aorta of your
government. I was nothing compared to him.
He is in a position to strangle both you and
those poor bloody sods at MI-6.

I must say here that I learned of this
entirely by accident. Knowledge of this man
is supposed to be secret from me—as a
matter of fact from most of us here in Moscow Center. I have no need to know, certainly. A certain Colonel Boris Strega of the
KGB, a fool somehow connected to the Premier on the mother's side of his family, told
me at a cocktail party that Moscow Center
had recruited a young man at Berkeley in
1964 who is now rising spectacularly in
American politics. Strega said he was amazed
at the resemblance of the case to the manner
in which I was recruited at Cambridge. He
was drunk and thought it was funny. The
Americans were being just as stupid about
the 1960s as the British were about the 1930s.
Please don't laugh. Ask Mr. Schott. It isn't
funny. I asked Strega who the agent was, of
course, but he just laughed. I have no need to
know.

I didn't say anything more, but I was curious, nevertheless. That was six years ago. As you gentlemen know, I'm a practiced listener. I learned, shortly after my conversation with Strega, that there apparently exists in Moscow Center a secret of secrets—namely an exquisitely placed, powerful KGB mole in the West. This agent is better than I was. Well, that hurt my ego, but I guess even legends must someday die. I got the impression, through a number of gossipy booze sessions, that this man is not in intelligence, but rather politics.

I have been given, in the twilight of my years, the task of reading files on your British and American radicals with the hope of finding potential Kim Philbys. This is boring work. I really hadn't had the heart for it, but after Strega I had new energy. Maybe there was a way out. One of the benefits of my job is that I have access to most of the library at Moscow Center, without anyone peering over my shoulder. I felt at first that my quarry's dossier would not be in the files. I began to construct my own dossiers of student radicals from magazines edited for the young. I tried to spot an obvious mark who had no KGB dossier on file, someone on the rise.

That got me nowhere.

Then it occurred to me that Center would not be so obvious as to remove their man's file entirely; after all they have dossiers on all public figures who could conceivably have an impact on public policy. They seem to dote on people with a radical past. Beyond watching people who might one day be favorable toward the Soviets or Soviet client organizations in the United States, there is another purpose for the dossiers. If the chairman of a House Armed Services Committee should die of a heart attack one morning and be replaced by an obscure congressman from Pennsylvania, the KGB wants to know how this man is apt to fall on crucial issues. They pull his file to see what he has said and how he has voted in the past. You have dossiers for similar reasons.

So what I did, gentlemen, was reread the dossiers looking for one that was somehow inadequate to the task, one with information missing—not in a conspicuous sense, but missing just the same. I found such a dossier and the tidbits of gossip I picked up—and which I am withholding from you here—fit.

I had my man.

His name is Derek Townes.

Derek Townes is an agent of the KGB. It took me six years but I can prove it.

As I said, in return for proof of my allegations against Townes, I want to spend my remaining years in more pleasant circumstances. Any warm, civilized part of the United States would do; the provinces are fine by me. I do require a garden. I want a small pension so I can have kippers and broil-

ed tomatoes in the morning, tea later on, and
a good bottle of Scotch and a book at night. A
color telly would also be nice, and an airmail
subscription to the London *Times*. I'll
require a new identity and your pledge of privacy, of course. The British are not casual
murderers but, as you Americans would say,
I think this should be between you and me.

I have been granted a holiday at Yalta on
the Crimea for three weeks beginning
October 1. It's not the best of times, perhaps,
but the Soviets moved very quickly on my request. I had to wait only eight months. That
should give you an idea of what I mean by
lines. I am aware that should Townes lose his
presidential bid in the conventions, I'll have
lost my ticket out of here; but judging from
what I read in the papers, I don't think he
will. In anticipation of this happy circumstance (I have been watching your presidential aspirants elbow and spit at one another
for several years now), I have been playing
the role of an insomniac for more than a year.
I have been to the doctor frequently and have
been prescribed all manner of sleeping pills.
They don't work, of course, because I don't
need or take them. I have developed the odd
habit of taking late-night walks around the
block. Comrade Konsomov was curious and
suspicious at first. I was followed every
night. In the end, however, they were convinced I was an eccentric and gave it up: let
the old man have his walks. These walks last

from about midnight to 1:30 or 2:00 A.M. Kim Philby, the spy who cannot sleep, walks.

I wish I could promise to bring with me data on Soviet missile and submarine performance, etc., but I cannot. I have no need to know of such matters. From the beginning of my tenure here I was put to work scheming new and ingenious ways of penetrating American and British intelligence services. Even that was a concession on their part; I've been watched carefully, as I said.

Now then, at Yalta I will be staying in a white, Oriental-looking resort hotel called the Tartar Palace. It's just to the west of town, overlooking the sea. There is a golf course there and a nice path available for my walks. You can't miss it. All your man has to do is appear from under the gorgeous poplars there and say, "Guy Burgess ate garlic the way some people eat peanuts."

If everything is okay, I'll say, "Bloody sod."

It was signed, "Kim."

"KBG," Schott said again. "My God, why did they have to choose Jim Burlane of all people?"

"Shit, you can say that again," Neely said. Burlane was close to being certifiable—even the Company's shrink said that. But he was an ace in the field, so they kept him on.

7

There were those who said Ara Schott could smell the KGB like one smells onions being fried for Lions Club hamburgers at a county fair. From the moment his bleeper went off on the Potomac, Schott had known something extraordinary had happened, even before he knew the Company was faced with a Code Six. It was spooky. There was no way ordinary employees at Langley could have heard about Philby's message. There were only three people who knew: Neely, Jackson, and James Burlane. Yet Schott was spooked from the first. Maybe it was the stars, the pull of the moon, or the ghosts of guardians past calling out, giving warning. Maybe James Angleton was giving emanations and vibrations from retirement.

Neely reread Philby's letter. It was his fourth time through. He sighed and looked at Schott. "I don't know, Ara. Why would they want to smear Derek Townes?"

"He's a Pentagon man like the President, a domestic liberal but a military hard liner."

Neely thought about that. "We've had hard liners run for office before. Even if they start out soft they end up hard line. That won't do. *Why Townes?*"

Schott looked at his fingernails. He said nothing. Nobody said anything for a full two minutes. It was two minutes that seemed like two hours. This was the great fear that nobody talked about: the possibility that an overachieving Soviet mole might one day be elected President of the United States. An open political system is vulnerable; it always leaves itself open to penetration. One of the great liberal propositions is that in the end the wisdom of the people is sound, that truth put to test against falsehood will win out. And with the exception of a handful of Presidents most schoolchildren can easily name, the system had worked out fairly well. It had not worked perfectly by any means, but the country had persevered.

Schott and James Burlane had once talked about just this possibility. What would they do if they found the Soviets had sponsored an ambitious, bright mole who was able to work his way to the top of American politics? This was a taboo subject. Langley had a contingency plan for almost every political misfortune imaginable. But Schott had never heard of a plan to cover the possibility of a mole being elected President. He doubted if one existed. What if word of the plan ever got out? The conspiracy theorists would go nuts. They would turn on the Company like dogs.

Members of the press would be right after them. It was unthinkable.

Just as men do not dwell on the possibility of having cancer—the odds are sufficiently remote—so did the men of Langley choose not to consider this possibility. Americans left that kind of thinking to colonels in banana republics. There, military men were free to select or reject candidates for public office. But what could American intelligence experts do? They couldn't withhold defense secrets from an American President for four years; that was impossible. Neely and Jackson couldn't expose Townes publicly. What *would* they do? Leak word to the publisher of the *Washington Post*? The *New York Times*? Go to the Joint Chiefs of Staff? What? The hurrah that would follow any of those courses would be devastating to the public. Richard Nixon had been damaging enough. The country didn't want to believe he was a liar and a felon; if he hadn't taped his conversations he would have gotten away with it.

This was different. You couldn't just go on television one night and tell the American public that the Democratic party had just nominated a KGB agent as its candidate for the presidency.

Derek Townes! Who says so?

Well, Kim Philby says so, folks. We know he's a traitor and all, but we've checked what he has to say and it makes sense to us.

That was impossible. Do that and the country would turn on Langley. Ever since William Colby gave Congress the Inspector General's report on

CIA activities in 1975, the public was suspicious of Langley. It was all there. Colby had given them everything: the agency's bizarre attempts to murder Fidel Castro; its attempt, with the complicity of ITT, to prevent the election of a Marxist President, Salvador Allende, in Chile. Colby gave them everything, and it had almost destroyed the Central Intelligence Agency. In the furor that followed, it was even fashionable to publish lists of CIA officers operating out of various embassies. But the public was confused and angry; all this conniving and plotting did not square with simpleminded notions of how the United States does business in the world.

If the CIA suggested Derek Townes was a KGB agent, the public would turn on Langley. Of that, Schott was certain. "Did you tell the President?"

Neely shook his head. "We serve the President. There are some things it's simply not smart to tell the President. There are some things he shouldn't know for his own good, just as there are some things we are better off not putting on paper. Put them on paper and you give an asshole like Colby the opening he needs. There are understandings between DCIs and Presidents. They're unstated but there. I think we have to handle this one ourselves."

"I agree," said Jackson.

Schott reread Philby's message yet another time. "It's possible what Philby says is true."

Neely sighed. "It's possible for the Jets to win a football game. Can we check Townes out ourselves without bringing Philby back?"

"Good question," Jackson said.

Schott looked skeptical. "If we go prying around asking the kinds of questions we have to ask of a man who's running for President, it would almost certainly get picked up by some jackal of a reporter. Running background investigations is the FBI's job anyway; we get involved and we're in deep shit from the first step. On top of that we'd need bodies to do the job."

"Need would get out of hand," said Neely.

"Precisely," said Schott. "Philby knows we can't do anything with what we have here. We have to know the rest."

"I suppose we have to decide whether we think this is genuine or Konsomov's idea of a little fun."

"For starters we might ask why the Soviets would want to scrub Derek Townes's campaign?" Schott paused and continued without waiting for an answer. "The Democrat most likely to win the nomination is Senator Corder." Bert Corder was chairman of the House-Senate Joint Intelligence Oversight Committee.

"Oh shit," said Neely.

"Let's assume for a moment that Corder is the mole. Would the Soviets risk Corder's discovery with a Philby gambit?" Schott looked at Jackson.

"They'd simply murder Townes," Jackson said.

Schott smiled. "That's what you'd do in their shoes. But supposing, just supposing, they had a mole here, in Langley, someone who couldn't help but know if we planned an operation like that. All they'd have to do is leak word that we murdered a candidate for President and we'd be finished. On top of that they'd have their man Corder in place for a shot at the presidency. Who'd believe us?"

"Maybe it isn't Corder they want to help. Maybe it's Ridgeway," Neely said. "Townes will beat Ridgeway; there doesn't seem to be much doubt about that." Langston Ridgeway, the front-running Republican, was governor of Pennsylvania.

"A Corder-Ridgeway race?" Schott asked.

"There's always the possibility that Philby is telling the truth," said Jackson. He turned his back to one side and seemed to withdraw like a turtle.

"Or none of the above," Schott said. "Maybe he's just old and tired like he says, willing to take his chances after he gets out."

"So what do we do, leave him there?" Neely asked.

Schott paused. "We bring him out. We hear what he has to say. We don't have any other choice."

"I agree," Jackson said.

Neely looked at Schott. "You're in counterintelligence, I know. You're not a field man. Jim Burlane speaks Russian, which Jackson here doesn't. I think you and Burlane should go to Yalta and bring Philby back if you can. We'll hear what he has to say."

"And if there's smoke?"

"If the smoke is convincing enough, Ara, you're going to have to sit down with Derek Townes and have a long, long talk. We can't take any chance of turning the American government over to a KGB mole."

Jackson laughed. "Kim Philby may turn out to be a hero."

"Shit," Neely said. "Bill, I want you and Burlane to come up with a plan of some kind to retrieve Philby from Yalta; get whatever equipment you need. Do not, under any circumstances, expand need. If we have to do this, we just have to do it, that's all. There's no sense putting it off. I want you to keep it as simple as possible. Don't get cute. Don't take chances if you don't have to. Just get Philby."

Schott walked slowly back to his office. Anna Humboldt was gossiping on the telephone with another secretary. He closed the door to her office and the reception area outside. Alone, Schott considered Philby's story. The Central Intelligence Agency was neither chartered nor intended to make policy. Its sole purpose was to serve the President—to give the President and his secretary of state the information they needed to run foreign policy. The agency's record was mixed. Its U-2 flights over the Soviet Union were brilliant. It had failed miserably in the Bay of Pigs, an ill-considered, stupid, impossible operation conceived by men Schott thought were idiots. It had done well in October 1962, when U-2 reconnaissance planes photographed Russian missiles in Cuba. It had not done so well in Operation Mongoose, a Kennedy-inspired program to assassinate Fidel Castro. The Mongoose people had considered, among other things, exploding cigars, poisoned cigars, an exploding seashell on the ocean floor rigged to kill Castro while he was scuba diving, and the gift of a wet suit intended to give Castro tuberculosis and a malignant skin disease. It was insane. The agency did well in the Arab-Israeli War of 1967, predicting Israel's quick victory almost to the hour. The CIA had done its best in Vietnam, but the Pentagon and the people surrounding Kennedy and Johnson wouldn't listen.

But this story of Kim Philby's was different. Ivan Konsomov had just possibly moved pawn to Queen's bishop four and was waiting there, in Moscow Center, for Ara Schott's reply. This was the moment Schott had, in effect, been training for his entire adult life. Only a handful of taxpayers who had invested in his training and career knew who he was. Schott's neighbors didn't know what he did; neither did his relatives. He was not a spy who rode the *Orient Express*, making a rendezvous at Budapest and Istanbul. He did not know karate. He had not fired enough handguns to become good. He was a man of the desk, a keeper of details. He was a linear man, tracing with relentless logic the permutations of truth. Truth was all that mattered. Confronted with a G, he looked for an F, then an E, a D, a C, a B, until he found A. He was, in the end, an epistemologist, a man concerned with the origin and nature of human knowledge. He knew how to ask questions, and weighed the answers carefully, like a jeweler divvying gold.

Finally, Ara Schott believed committed Marxists were the most conniving assholes ever to walk the face of the earth.

And the truth? The truth in the matter of Derek Townes lay with Kim Philby, who would await them at Yalta on the Crimean peninsula, 175 miles across the Black Sea from Cape Ince on the Turkish coast. Yalta! Ara Schott smiled at the ironies. Kim Philby must be smiling too.

All they could do is wait until October. They were cutting it tight, but if Philby was correct, they would still have time to do what they had to do. All they could do now was wait. And hope.

8

Leon Trotsky slipped off his loafers to rest his feet. He opened a can of Schlitz. Whether it was a national or regional brand, all American beer tasted the same to Trotsky. It was thin and bland, like the people. Trotsky had read somewhere that there were communities of German immigrants in the nineteenth century who made good beer. The current stuff was inflicted on the public during Prohibition, it was said. By gangsters. Trotsky had to smile at that. Gangsters! It was appropriate. The uniformly tasteless beer stayed on after the repeal of the Volstead Act because it was cheap to produce. Trotsky turned on the television set.

Sesame Street was a kids' program designed to teach children their letters and numbers. There they were, a black man, a Chinese woman, an old man, short and tall, thin and fat, all races, together with a menage of puppets that were frogs and birds and whatever. All of this coming in zip, zip, zip takes designed to keep the kiddies staring. It was all so wholesome and natural—kids hanging around garbage cans singing songs. Trotsky felt as if he were going to puke. Look how much fun it can be living in a slum! They didn't have television in Marx's time; it was too bad he hadn't had a chance to see how the real opiate of the people worked.

But Trotsky was luckier. He was able to see it all now. He had been given a second chance. He was reborn. He had been reborn at a crossroad: a place that mattered, a place that could change things, a place where vows might be met and destinies fulfilled. There would be those who would call it madness, he knew. But they were wrong. The truth was simple enough if people could only see it as he saw it. There were times when he *was* Trotsky. And there were old scores to be settled, lots of them.

Trotsky remembered the serfs the best. His father owned a 250-acre estate which he bought from a Colonel Yanovsky, who rose from the ranks of the Imperial Army to become a favorite of Czar Alexander II. The Czar rewarded Yanovsky with a grant of a thousand acres. Trotsky could still see the serfs herding cows into the barn to be milked. He could see the stanchions where bovine necks were locked into place come milking time.

The peasants had no protection against their masters. Nor did the masters have any protection against the whims of the Czar, the bureaucrats, or the Imperial Army. The peasants were little more

than beasts themselves. They slept in the fields.
They used to wallow on their stomachs in front of
Trotsky's father's house, groaning for more tasteless gruel. Trotsky remembered the bottoms of
their feet on such occasions; they were crusty,
broken hunks. There were landowners—neighbors of Trotsky's father—who maintained serfs
were distinguished from beasts only in that they
walked upright and spoke a rudimentary form of
Russian.

Trotsky remembered the serfs. That's why he
became a revolutionary.

As befitting a revolutionary, Trotsky lived his life
according to an abstraction. The ideal was all that
mattered to Trotsky, the notion that social and
economic classes might one day be eliminated,
that officer and enlisted man, professor and
student, foreman and worker, might stand side-by-
side as equals. Since most young men are enlisted,
students, or workers, it is an easy argument to advance. It is difficult for anybody but the most
callous to argue with the beauty of the proposition. It is easier to quarrel over the question of
whether or not it will work, thus leading to
metaphysical discussions of human nature.

Trotsky loved the righteousness of it all, although he didn't look at it that way. Such ideals
were grand for stirring speeches. Those who dis-
agreed with him were by definition hard-hearted
and, in their unwillingness to believe in a perfect
world, blind as well. You were with Trotsky or
against him; there was no middle ground. There
couldn't be. You either loved him as one loved the

Messiah or you rejected him and chose the Prince of Darkness. Being a revolutionary was like being a saint. Trotsky didn't care about sex or material possessions. He never owned much of anything his entire life. He needed only books, paper and pencil, and a bullhorn or microphone. He lived only for the passionate, dazzling beauty of the ideal. Trotsky spent time in some thirty jails, prisons, and labor camps in his life. That didn't bother him especially; prisons were for saints and martyrs. Besides, being in prison gave him time to think and write inflammatory polemics.

For Trotsky the future had no details. Details would come later, after the perfection of a classless society. Details are for journalists who report yesterday's events for today's readers or for novelists who create their own worlds. The abstract is suited to dreamers and revolutionaries and to professors who feel insecure without neat schemes and categories to outline on the blackboard. But looking back, he remembered only the details.

The details of the prisons he remembered clearly, especially his first prison at Nikolayev near Odessa and his later experience at Kherson, thirty-five miles away. In Nikolayev, he was thrown into a room with thirty prisoners, one brick stove, one small window, and no furniture. He was there three weeks before they moved him to Kherson, where they put him in an isolation cell in an attempt to break him. For six months he slept on a stone floor. The only light came from the slit of a window. He received no books, newspapers, or anything to read. There was no light to read by anyway. He had rye bread, water, and salt for breakfast, prison stew for lunch, and rye bread, water, and salt for supper. For six months he picked lice and paced.

Where other men might have been broken, Trotsky only became determined. His time came in 1917.

He remembered the details of those November days in Petrograd with a clarity that was extraordinary. He could still feel the cold of his bare room on the third floor of Smolny, the Bolshevik headquarters in Petrograd, on the night of November 10. On his orders, the Red Guards quietly seized the railroad stations, the state bank, the telegraph office, the post office, and other institutions that were essential to the Provisional Government of Alexander Kerensky. And at 2:00 A.M., November 12, Vladimir Antonov-Ovseyenko, a former officer of the Czar's army, burst into the Malachite Room of the Winter Palace to arrest Kerensky's ministers. Antonov-Ovseyenko, who had red hair to his shoulders, wore a wide-brimmed hat pushed to the back of his head. The ministers sat around a table lit by a single shaded lamp. Antonov-Ovseyenko told Trotsky the ministers seemed relieved.

That ended the only three months of political freedom in the history of Russia.

It began the process of replacing the Czar with a Marxist dictator. It led to the establishment of the Cheka under a murderous Pole named Felix Dzerzhinsky; the Cheka was said to be worse than the

awful Oprichnini, the black-coated palace guard
of Ivan the Terrible. The Cheka's duty was to provide enemies to be executed, prisoners to populate
the hundreds of prison and labor camps in the
seemingly unending reaches of Siberia. The taking
of the Winter Palace led to the replacement of the
Imperial Army with an even more repressive Red
Army.

Trotsky was always hazy about the details of the
Kronstadt rebellion of March 1921. Sailors of the
warship *Petropavlovsk* and the workers of Petrograd were foolish enough to believe that the
soviets, intended to represent the will of the
peasants and workers, might actually do just that.
Even more foolishly they said as much, on paper,
and were forced to defend the *Petropavlovsk* on
the frozen Gulf of Finland. Trotsky put an end to
that nonsense in a series of attacks from March 10
to March 12, 1921. More than ten thousand rebels
were killed or sent to prison to be executed. There
were so many dead that the Finnish government
sent a note to the Soviet government demanding
that it pick up the thousands of bodies lying on the
ice, bodies that would otherwise be swept onto
Finnish shores come the spring thaw.

Then there was Stalin. There were details in-
volving Stalin that Trotsky would never forget,
never. Trotsky's last address in the Soviet Union
before his final exile was the Hotel Jetysa, Gogal
Street, Alma-Ata, Kazakhstan. From April to
October 1926, Trotsky wrote more than eight hundred letters and sent more than five hundred telegrams to his political followers from the hotel.

The letters and telegrams were of course read by
the GPU, Stalin's secret police. The names were
dutifully recorded. Beginning in 1935, Stalin set
about taking care of these people. Some were the
subjects of well-rehearsed spectacles called trials
—after which they were shot in the back of the
head. Others were spared the fuss of public confession to crimes they did not commit and were
simply shot in the back of the head. Some of these
were dreamers and visionaries like Trotsky,
others innocents he had hoped to recruit.

Trotsky had one enduring memory of Stalin.
Stalin had gas and it embarrassed him. He used to
rattle a glass of water on his desk to mask the
sound of farts. Trotsky was convinced that for
Stalin the letting of a fart was of more conse-
quence than the murder of a human being. Stalin
murdered ten million people. Ten million! Stalin
didn't do the actual killing himself; others did
that. He murdered by putting his initials on a
piece of paper.

Trotsky, remembering Stalin's farts, turned off
the television set.

YALTA

Schott's Time

9

The Turk's name was Emil and he had begun as a gun smuggler, ferrying automatic rifles to Turkish guerrillas at Larnaca on the southern coast of Cyprus. The Greek Navy put a stop to that. Later, he smuggled heroin from small towns on the southern Turkish coast to ships waiting offshore in the Mediterranean night. Much of the heroin ended up in New York, via Marseilles, hence the term "French connection," which inspired a movie with a great automobile chase under an elevated train. The movie in turn inspired an international expression of shock and dismay; so the Turkish Navy had to interrupt Emil's heroin work.

However, the Turks didn't feel called upon to halt his smuggling of automatic weapons to partisans fighting the oppressive Greek colonels. That was more than ten years before, but Emil stayed

in business. When the Greeks got straightened
out, he earned money pretending to be a nincom-
poop fisherman blundering into gatherings of
Soviet vessels. He blundered into Russian ships,
putting British agents on board with their gear.
He blundered into Soviet vessels on behalf of the
CIA. When the Soviets—shouting at him through
bullhorns—tried to bully him into retreating, Emil
pretended to be ignorant, unable to understand
Turkish or Greek spoken with a Russian accent.

Emil grew up in an orphanage in Tbilisi, in
Soviet Georgia; he had a facility for languages and
in the course of his adventures became fluent in
English, Greek, and Turkish, as well as Russian,
his mother tongue. Emil did not discriminate
among men; religion meant nothing to him; he
thought politics was foolish. There was just one
thing Emil insisted upon.

That he be paid promptly and well. The pay depended on the danger involved. Emil knew about
danger.

As to running the Soviet patrols on the Black
Sea, well, Emil had never done that. The man
seated across from him in his home had said
Yalta. Yalta was on the Crimean peninsula.
Mother of God! "Bibble? Lance Bibble?" Emil
laughed at the man taking a hit on the bong.

"It's Lawrence Bibble, actually," Burlane said.
His lungs were filled with smoke. He was pissed at
Jackson for assigning him such a dumb-shit name.
Lance Bibble!

"When you were here before you were Burlane,
I think." Emil grinned. "Where did you come up

with Lance Bibble? Makes you sound like a queer."

Burlane sighed and exhaled. "I was never very good at picking names." He was irked at not being able to blame Jackson by name. It was true obtaining a new identity was not like buying a six-pack of Budweiser at a 7-Eleven. Jackson's men had established all kinds of identities based on the birth certificates of dead babies. The only one available who would have been born roughly the same time as Burlane was named Bibble.

"Tell me again what you want me to do?" Emil asked.

"I want you to take me and another man to Yalta to pick up a Russian. No big deal."

"Fuck too." Emil looked at Burlane like he was nuts. He bent to take a turn on the pipe. He dripped some amber-colored hash oil on the marijuana and took a hit, watching Burlane's eyes. "Yalta? You're not serious."

Burlane nodded his head yes. He knew Emil would have to be crazy to take on a job like this. The Company's list of potential employees in the area was disconcertingly short. What if they couldn't hire anyone? The election was a month away.

"The Black Sea. We have to do it."

Emil shook his head. "Have you got any idea what that entails?" He saw Burlane watching Esmeralda, a sixteen-year-old prostitute who was Emil's, the take of a dice game in a brothel. "She's nice, isn't she? Mine for a month." Emil looked proud. Esmeralda shifted slightly at the mention of her name, but said nothing.

Burlane looked out the window at freighters on the Sea of Marmara, waiting to be unloaded. It took effort not to stare at the girl. "We only know it has to be done," he said. "That's why I'm here."

Emil grinned. "I'm the best you'll find in Istanbul, that's true. But I'm not sure I'm ready to die for the CIA."

"I didn't hear anybody say anything about the CIA." Burlane always felt self-conscious going through a routine like this.

"You're just a tour guide."

"Whatever," Burlane said. He found himself staring at the girl again. She was wearing a gauzy, translucent top. She had pointed breasts and he could see her nipples. He felt himself getting an erection. Oh shit, he thought to himself. He didn't want to embarrass himself in front of Emil.

Emil scratched the gray hair on his broad chest. He was fifty-three years old. There were few jobs he was afraid of. This was one of them. "You must want him pretty badly."

"We want him," Burlane said. He slipped a hand into his pocket and tried to tuck the damn erection under his belt.

"The Russians have a submarine pen at Sevastopol'."

"I know," Burlane said. The girl's nipples rubbed against her translucent blouse as she moved.

"We Turks fish the Black Sea, but we have our limits. The Russians don't like us. Neither do the Bulgarians or Rumanians. They're touchy, the

Soviets. The Bosporus is their only year-round access to warm water."

Burlane nodded.

"We need a good boat, a fishing boat. Get caught off the Crimean coast with a fast boat and we'll wind up in a labor camp. We have to slip in and slip out in a fishing boat. We need a boat with Turkish registry. We can use Turkish ID that will peel off the hull. I can get Russian numbers that are registered in Sevastopol'. Paste 'em on, peel 'em off."

"Where do you get the numbers?"

Emil smiled. "I can get them."

"And the boat?"

"I can get a boat, too, one the Russians will believe. You have to look like a Turkish fisherman. I can think of one right now, thirty-two feet long, single diesel that will go eight, maybe nine knots. That's not fast, but you can't rush something like this. You have to do it right. You have to be patient. Do you know your geography, Mr. Bibble?"

"You mean the Black Sea?"

"Uh-huh."

"We studied it some."

"How far from Cape Ince to Yalta?"

Burlane paused. "About a hundred seventy-five miles, something like that."

"Eight point three knots is about nine miles an hour. Figure seven gallons of diesel an hour. That's maybe a hundred forty gallons one way. The boat I'm talking about has two seventy-five gallon tanks. You'll have to pay for two more tanks under the fish."

"We'll pay for the tanks."

"The fish too. You'll have to buy a cargo of mackerel. If you're going to play fishermen, you have to have fish."

"We're good for the fish," Burlane said. The girl's nipples were dark brown and large for the size of her breasts.

Emil looked at the girl. "She's nice, huh? This'll have to be cash up front."

"How much cash?"

Emil closed his eyes. "Under these circumstances, I can probably rent the boat for maybe eight thousand dollars. If we lose it, one hundred thousand dollars. Boats are hard to come by."

"Done," said Burlane. Then he added, "These'll have to be people who don't ask questions."

"It'll cost you a couple thousand bucks for the tanks. You're paying premium money for fast work, no questions."

"I understand."

"I know a Turkish boy who speaks fluent Russian. Fifteen hundred for him."

"Fifteen hundred?" Burlane said. He needed Emil and the boat too much to haggle over a few hundred bucks.

Emil paused. "No, twenty-five. He's a good boy and could be killed."

"There will be one other man coming with me."

Emil shrugged. "It's his hide. I'll need wet suits for the two of you plus the man in Yalta."

"Wet suits?"

"So you can wait it out under the boat if we run into a Soviet patrol boat."

James Burlane said, "Shit!"

"Esmeralda is lovely, isn't she, Mr. Bibble? It's her tits that do it, I think."

The girl smiled. Burlane swallowed. "Yes, she is lovely."

"If we make a deal you must take her." Burlane started to protest, but Emil stopped him with his hand. "I insist. Esmeralda!" He motioned with his hands that she should take her blouse off; Esmeralda obeyed. "Make yourself moist, girl. Now then, Mr. Bibble, you get your man here. We'll travel to Ereğli on the coast, as I said. I can send word ahead for the extra tanks. We should fill our tanks and put out from Sinop at Cape Ince, a little over two hundred miles east of Ereğli. It's about twenty-two hours by sea to Sinop."

Burlane felt his cock throbbing under his belt. He looked out at the boats on the water. "A long way."

"Can you get word to Yalta for an exact rendezvous?"

"Yes," Burlane said. He thought of Philby taking his nightly walks at the Tartar Palace.

"Fine, then my fee will be fifty thousand dollars."

"You don't come cheap."

"I risk my life," Emil said. "We'll spend two nights at sea, one going, one coming. If the Soviets stop us, we'll piss and moan and say we're sorry and won't they please let us go; we'll say the fishing is lousy off the Turkish coast. Come here, Esmeralda." Esmeralda came. "I want you to take care of this man's hard-on. Off." Esmeralda dropped her skirt. She was naked. Emil put his hand between her legs. "Ahh, she's nice and moist, Mr. Burlane. I'll go call my friend in Ereğli so you can fuck Esmeralda."

Burlane started to say something but Emil stopped him.

"Don't worry, I won't use your name again. I know how to keep a secret; it's how I stay in business." Emil stopped at the door. "Do whatever you want. I have her only a month, then I have to give her back. It's a shame not to use her."

Burlane was a bachelor; he had tried marriage twice and found it not to his liking. Still, he needed sex. He took the girl, Esmeralda, on a mattress in the corner that Emil used as a bed. The girl had a thin, hard body. She had not shaved under her armpits. She watched him with large, brown eyes, her lips slightly parted. When she thought he was ready to come she twisted under him. Afterward, Burlane helped himself to some of Emil's Turkish wine, a vile red. He propped his feet on the windowsill to watch sailboats in the distance. Urchins and sidewalk vendors competed for survival on the crowded street below. Istanbul never seemed to change.

Burlane wondered if it was on a day like this in 1945 when the KGB man, a short, stocky individual who identified himself as Konstantin Volkov, strolled into the British consulate and offered to make a deal of sorts. Volkov, the Russian consul of five months, asked for a high-ranking British diplomat whom he thought, mistakenly, was the area SIS officer. The Brit, who was in Istanbul for the pleasures of the Bosporus and to escape the terrible heat of Ankara, heard him out.

In return for 27,500 British pounds plus refuge on Cyprus, Volkov was prepared to offer Her Majesty's Government certain invaluable counter-espionage information. The diplomat was out of his area, but the Foreign Office had given him and others like him explicit instructions what to do in such a case. The diplomat was to hear him out until an SIS specialist could be contacted for help. What was it, exactly, that Volkov had to offer?

Volkov smiled and handed over a pile of hand-written notes and sketches, the gist of what he had to peddle. The material consisted of a list of Soviet agents in Turkey, together with their contacts, ad-dresses, and descriptions of the Soviet secret service headquarters in Moscow—including de-tails of burglar-alarm systems, key impressions, and guard schedules. Finally, Volkov offered "names of Russian agents operating in govern-ment departments in London."

The British official told Volkov to wait, and went to see his ambassador, Sir Maurice Peterson. Sir Maurice was pissed; he didn't like his embassy being used as a base for SIS operations. He told his subordinate to remain in contact with Volkov, and to work through London. Volkov agreed, but said the British diplomat must correspond with London via handwritten memos; there was a Rus-sian agent inside the British embassy, he said. He did not want the diplomat's notes to London typed by someone else. Volkov made arrangements for contact and told the diplomat there must be a de-cision within twenty-one days. If he had not heard from the British by the twenty-first day, the deal was off.

The diplomat stayed up all night preparing a handwritten brief for London. He then waited. One week. Two weeks. Nothing.

On the morning of the twenty-first day, an agent arrived from London to announce that he, personally, was to take charge of any deal to be made with Konstantin Volkov.

The man was Kim Philby.

The diplomat heard nothing more of the affair and later, after the summer season was over, returned with the embassy staff to Ankara. It was sometime shortly after that that a Russian military aircraft made an irregular, unscheduled stop at the Istanbul airport. A car raced to the plane. A heavily bandaged figure on a stretcher was lifted onto the plane. The plane took off.

Burlane poured himself another glass of Emil's harsh wine. This run was too much.

10

Emil's Volkswagen Beetle was originally green, but it had so much gray primer spray-painted over hastily sandpapered dents and scrapes that it resembled some mad colonel's idea of camouflage. Or so Schott thought, anyway. The chassis looked as if someone had tried to make crumpled tinfoil smooth again. Schott sat in the front seat opposite Emil, who apparently had no last name—anyway, one was never mentioned. Emil drove with abandon, only his left hand on the steering wheel. He gestured constantly with his right as he told old war stories and pointed out landmarks on the impoverished Turkish landscape. Schott listened halfheartedly, leaning to one side so he could see past a crack in the windshield. Burlane, his legs wrapped around scuba-diving equipment, sat in the back getting ploughed on Greek beer.

The boy, Hasan, who didn't look like he was

more than nineteen or twenty, also sat in the back, fingering a scar on his left cheek and watching the fields go by. Emil let a great fart, laughed, and reached back for a bottle of beer. When the beer was opened, he lit a thin black cigar to go with it.

"Beautiful, eh?" he said. "This is one of the nicer areas of Turkey."

"Lovely," said Schott. He looked at the Black Sea on their left. That could just as well be Lake Michigan or Lake Ontario, he thought.

"How long you used the name Dennis?" Emil asked.

Schott laughed. "Not long. I'll get used to it." He had never been in the field before; he couldn't believe that the future of the greatest representative democracy in the world should be riding with this crew. The group was commanded by the Turk, Emil, who was apparently willing to do anything for anyone if the price was right; he was either drunk or high on hashish, and talked incessantly of screwing young girls in the anus. The young Turk did as Emil told him and sat, saying nothing. Then there was Burlane. It was Burlane, Schott could not forget, who was Philby's contact. An improbable meeting, Schott thought: a chance bumping into Philby, surrounded by KGB agents; the passing of the cigarette. He watched Burlane laugh at one of Emil's jokes and open another bottle of beer. What if there had been no move by Philby? What if Burlane were the KGB man, returning home? Schott felt a flutter of anxiety, returning home with the CIA's head of counter-intelligence. He looked at the Black Sea once again. Across the water, about two hundred miles away, sat the Union of Soviet Socialist Republics, a police state that stretched from the Black Sea to the Bering Straits.

Emil slowed the Volkswagen for a small village. "I fucked a girl in the butt once here. In a chicken coop by that house up there in the poplars."

"Oh," Schott said. He looked at the trees in the distance.

"She loved it, twisted and squirmed in the dirt. The chickens got all excited, too; ran around flapping their wings and shitting." Emil laughed. The boy, Hasan, grinned.

It began to sprinkle slightly, then stopped. The rain left streaky blotches on the dusty windshield; the Volkswagen either had no windshield washer or it didn't work because Emil made no move to clean the mess. They passed a pathetic field of wheat and later one of barley, but mostly there was nothing save barren earth sloping gently to the seashore.

"I'll bet you're afraid, huh, Dennis?" asked Emil.

Schott knew he couldn't lie about that. "A little."

"Have you ever been out of your office before?"

Schott said nothing.

"They're tough, those Russians. Mean."

"Yes, they're said to be."

"If you get caught by the Greeks or Cypriots, you can buy your way out. The same is true for the Syrians or Lebanese. I've got a stash for just that purpose. But with the Russians it's different.

Russia is just one large prison. If I got caught by the Russians, I'd kill myself."

Schott looked at him. "How?"

Emil laughed. "I have a small pistol, but it'll never happen."

"Never?"

"Never. I won't get caught. I won't allow it. What do you say, Hasan?" He said something in Turkish.

Hasan smiled.

Schott too had a way out, a capsule in an artificial tooth where he had once had a molar. He could remove it with his tongue, then all he had to do was bite down. He had no reason for one; he had never been sent covert into a police state. But Schott took his business and his knowledge seriously. What if, he once asked, someone pulled a snatch on him while he was out to buy a bottle of Scotch at Pearson's. To humor him, the Company gave Schott a capsule. Before this mission, Neely had taken him aside and said he might have to use the capsule. Did Schott understand that? Schott didn't resent the question; he had never been in the field before. He said yes, he understood.

As they neared Ereğli, Emil began to tire of telling stories and was quiet except for an occasional foul eruption of gas. Each time he blamed Hasan, who grinned at the allegation. "We'll be dealing with a man named Erzurum," Emil said as he slowed for a herd of goats on the outskirts of Ereğli. Schott saw there was a small bay, a lovely thing lined with fishing boats and protected from storms by a promontory. "That'll be Cape Baba on the far side," Emil said.

"Ahh," Schott said. "Nice."

"This man Erzurum has a niece who lives with him. Great butt. Erzurum promised her to me next time I did him a favor." Emil grinned. "That's why I overcharged you people for his boat." He slapped Schott on the knee. "What the hell, everybody does it to you Americans, eh, Dennis? You expect it."

Erzurum's boat surprised Schott. The boat was newer than he had expected. Its white paint was leached and bleached by the sun; it needed cleaning, but the vessel—with *Bolu* painted carefully on the bow—looked like a solid, capable boat. That made Schott feel better about Emil. He may have had his eye on the niece with the great ass, but he wasn't about to gamble his life on a boat in poor repair.

"Bolu?" Schott asked.

"The name of a river and a small town," said Emil. "Erzurum was born on the banks of the Bolu. He thinks it brings him luck."

The Black Sea, if one thinks about it, resembles nothing so much as a dog's head. The dog faces east. At the far southwest is the dog's neck, where the Bosporus, the Sea of Marmara, and the Dardanelles separate Europe from Asia. It is this narrow passage, with Turkish territory on both sides, that is Russia's sole egress from its warmwater ports on the Black Sea, and one source of its paranoia about being trapped year round by ice. Moving north and northwest from Istanbul is the back of the dog's head, Bulgaria first, then Rumania. At the top of the dog's head—he appears to be a terrier of some kind—are two floppy ears: the first leads to the industrial port of Odessa; the second, the Sea of Azov, leading to Taganrog and Rostov and the mouth of the River Don.

Between these two watery ears is a diamond-shaped peninsula that is the Crimea. At the very bottom of the diamond is Balaklava, scene of the British Army's famous charge of the Light Brigade. Balaklava is flanked on the left by Sevastopol, and on the right by the smaller resort town of Yalta. It was at Yalta in February 1945 that Franklin D. Roosevelt and Winston Churchill corroborated in what Schott believed was a post-World War II giveaway to Joseph Stalin, in addition to agreeing on voting procedures in the proposed Security Council of the United Nations.

That narrow strip of seashore along the lower-right facet of the Crimean diamond holds a particular fascination for the Soviet people. Protected from the north by mountains that rise from the water, it is the only part of Soviet Russia that may be considered subtropical. There are grapes there, and vineyards, picturesque inlets, villas with red-tiled roofs. The Crimea was once Tartar, but the Soviets scattered the Tartars and replaced Tartar places with their own. It is at Balaklava, Yalta, Alushta, Sudak, and Feodosiya where the deserving comrades—chess masters, champion athletes, the Premier, and others—go on holiday.

Yalta, of course, is the gem. It was naturally at Yalta where the deserving Kim Philby was granted a holiday.

After the Crimea and the right dog's ear—the Sea of Azov—comes the dog's snout, pointing directly at Soviet Georgia, Armenia behind that, and finally Iran. The underside of the dog's snout and neck is the north shore of Turkey. At the point where neck becomes the underside of the snout lie Cape Ince and the coastal village of Sinop. The latter was the jumping off place for the Turk named Emil, his boy, Hasan, and their two American passengers. It is a bit over eight hundred miles from the back of the dog's head on the Bulgarian coast to its nose—the Georgian city of Batumi. It's not nearly so far from Sinop to Yalta.

Were it not for Soviet patrol boats operating out of Sevastopol', the run from Sinop to Yalta would have been nothing for the good ship *Bolu*.

"So!" said Emil, gesturing grandly at dockside. "Isn't she a beauty?"

"Helluva boat, Emil. Helluva boat," Burlane said. He looked to Schott for approval.

"Is it large enough?" Schott asked. He remembered going over charts of the Black Sea with Burlane.

"Hah! Plenty large," Emil said. "Find yourself some shade. I'll get us some food. Erzurum says he has her filled with diesel—that'll cost a little extra—and she's ready to go. We've got mackerel waiting at Sinop."

The idea that Schott could find some shade was curious. Aside from a few locusts, there were no trees; the sun blazed from high noon. Schott and Burlane sat on the dock by the water; Emil returned in a half hour loaded with balls of white cheese and crusty loaves of dark bread. Hasan followed carrying two cases of Turkish beer in tall brown bottles and a case of red wine.

"The boy'll fetch a couple more cases of beer and some more wine and we'll be on our way," Emil said. "Come on below, Lance Bibble. You, too, Dennis; it's too late to turn back."

When they were on board with a sufficient quantity of beer and red wine, Emil started the diesel; Hasan got the gear stowed and they were under way. "Erzurum is pleased," said Emil. "He says if I bring his boat back in one piece I get his niece for a night." He winked at Schott. "Erzurum doesn't think she's had it in the ass."

Schott watched Cape Baba fade into the distance as the *Bolu* followed the Turkish coast east by northeast, bound for Sinop.

They were an hour out, Schott on deck drinking Turkish beer, Burlane trying to nap in the cramped bunk of the *Bolu's* tiny cabin, when Schott felt a wave of anxiety sweep across him and clutch at his stomach. Was there something happening to him that he hadn't anticipated? It wasn't too late to turn back. He had a pistol; he could force them if necessary. He wished he could sleep like Burlane. How could he sleep like that? It wasn't natural. Schott didn't trust him. Burlane was behaving curiously. Schott didn't understand exactly what it was that bothered him about Burlane. He thought about it but wasn't sure. But Schott did envy Burlane his ability to sleep. Schott needed to rest.

11

At three minutes after 6:00 A.M., the edge of the sun appeared over the Black Sea to the east of Cape Ince. The sun was preceded by a lovely softening of the darkness, as it had an hour earlier over Soviet Georgia, and before that above the Caspian Sea, Uzbek, and Mongolia. Ara Schott was still tired from the long grind from Ereğli; the *Bolu* had spent most of the day and night at sea. The marine air was cold as Schott took a short stroll on the docks. He had been to Europe, but was not an especially well-traveled man; the village of Sinop looked like it was fresh out of the pages of *National Geographic*.

Hasan was busy refilling the *Bolu*'s tanks with diesel. Emil, intent on getting even more beer and wine, strode up the single main street that led to the docks. He paused to ask a question of a small boy carrying a large bucket of water. The boy sat

the bucket down and answered Emil's questions.
Emil gave the boy a friendly whack on the butt and
continued up the street with great purposeful
strides.

The *Bolu* would be leaving Sinop in about fifteen minutes for the nineteen-hour run to Yalta. If
all went well, they would be under cover of darkness the last five hours in and the first five hours
out; the sun set at roughly 8:00 P.M. and rose again
at 6:00 A.M. At 1:00 A.M., or shortly thereafter, they
hoped to rendezvous with Kim Philby in the
shadows of the Tartar Palace.

If they left with Philby at 2:00 A.M., they would
have, they figured, until noon—or ten hours—before Philby was missed at the resort. He would
miss breakfast, but that was no cause for alarm. It
wouldn't be until later that his absence would be
discovered by a maid or housekeeper. The head
start would put them just over the Turkish half of
the Black Sea, where the hammer and sickle on
the *Bolu*'s bow would be replaced by the Turkish
crescent and star.

That's if they weren't walking into a trap of
some kind. They left the dock at Sinop at 6:18 A.M.
to find out.

When the Turkish coast was a pallid gray on the
horizon and the *Bolu* was alone, plunging deter-
minedly ahead, its diesel throbbing and shuddering below, Schott motioned for Burlane to come
below with him to the tiny cabin. Schott cut a
hunk of sharp Turkish cheese with his pocketknife
and poured himself a half glass of red wine.

Schott steadied himself with his feet, his back

wedged into a corner, and waited for Burlane to get settled. "I have a few questions," he said.

"Oh?" Burlane cut himself some cheese and opened himself a beer, which foamed over his hand. "Shit!"

"I want you to tell me again about your meeting with Philby."

"Fucking stuff." Burlane dried his hands on the thigh of his trousers. He took a bit of cheese. "This is good cheese. Can you imagine what you'd pay for it in Washington? That's why you guys can shove your desk jobs. If you spent your whole life at Langley with air conditioning and secretaries who wear underpants, your mind would rot. Lucky you got away once." Burlane swayed as the *Bolu* struck a swell. "I was attached to the embassy in Moscow, detailed to accompany a group of lefties from the American Historical Association. I put all this stuff in the report I gave Jackson."

"I talked to Jackson. I want to hear it from you." He watched Burlane's eyes.

Burlane sighed. He felt like eating cheese and getting a buzz on, maybe smoke a little hash to make the hours go faster, he sure as hell didn't feel like putting up with Schott's squirreliness. Schott was a desk man. In the field you had to trust experience and instinct. Schott was a technician. Burlane had to put his cock on the block. It was hard for Burlane to be patient. He'd told the story three or four times already!

"You were there as an embassy host," Schott said.

Burlane nodded. "That's it. Helluva host, too. I

can suck up a lot of vodka."

"So the Soviets know you're Company."

"They know all the Company people assigned to the embassy."

"They know, so they have reason to watch you."

Brilliant, Sherlock, Burlane thought. He said, "That's it. If you'll excuse me for a minute, I gotta take a leak." Burlane made his way to the chemical toilet.

When Burlane returned, Schott said, "The KGB watches Philby, I assume."

"They watch him," Burlane said. "There was a guy standing right there beside him. Another guy followed me into the can like I said. Bastard stared at me like he was queer or something."

"So tell me again about Philby's approach."

Burlane thought for a moment. "Well, we were at a reception for the good professors. The Soviets want to impress the professors so they'll go back to America and tell their students how great socialism is. This reception was given by trade-union people. We were being given a chance to mingle with the workers, the backbone of the motherland and all that. Philby was there at the request of a guy from Temple, a fireball who's writing a stacked history of the cold war. We were originally scheduled to have him at another reception, but he couldn't make it then for some reason."

"He?"

"Philby. As they said, though, it doesn't make any difference; everybody is equal in the Soviet Union; there are no distinctions between workers and Philbys. They're all heroes." Burlane laughed.

"Okay, okay," Schott said. "Tell me about the room itself. I need some details."

Burlane couldn't imagine what for, but then this was Schott's first time out; he was no doubt anxious. "It was the ballroom of an old hotel, built in Czarist days, I imagine. There were fourteen of us on the trip; I can't recall all the names, but they're there in my report to Jackson. The trade unions had a long buffet set up with nuts, cheese, ham, vodka, and wine. The wine was from the Crimea, incidentally. That morning, we had toured a factory which makes aluminum irrigation pipes. I mingled with the workers and listened to their stories about how marvelous production was, their success at communal irrigation projects, and so on. I had been a few minutes late getting to the reception. Philby had been introduced to the gathering at the beginning, but I would have known who he was anyway. Suddenly there was Philby standing by the beer and vodka. I introduced myself and told him I was pleased to meet him. He acted like he didn't know I was with the embassy. When I told him who I was, he said he thought I was a professor. I complimented the trade unionists on their nice spread. He offered me a cigarette."

"I thought you said the package was unopened."

"It was. He opened the seal with his KGB tail standing there watching him. I took a cigarette and . . ."

"Philby said it was English and was harsh if you smoked it all the way to the end."

"Yes," Burlane said. "He said the Soviets provided him with English cigarettes and the London *Times* so he could keep up with the cricket scores. I felt a nub at the end of the cigarette. I told him it was pleasant meeting him."

"Then you got a beer."

"Yes, I got a beer."

"Why?" Schott asked.

Burlane laughed. "Because I suddenly realized Kim Philby was trying to send a message to the West through me. My life was in danger. When that happens my mouth gets a trifle dry."

"You got thirsty."

Burlane was still laughing. "Yes, thirsty as hell. The Soviets were buying. I also had to decide what to do next."

"And you decided?"

"I didn't decide anything actually. My bladder did."

Schott looked momentarily confused. "What?"

"I had to take a piss. I went to the toilet and this KGB asshole followed me. I pulled the tube of microfilm with my teeth and swallowed it. I squeezed the end of the butt and threw it into the bottom of the urinal in one motion."

"The KGB man was watching you."

"From the next urinal. Comrade Queer."

"Then what?"

"Then I pissed on the butt to scatter the tobacco."

"When did they search you?" Schott asked.

"Not then. I'd been with the professors for a few days and we were buddy-buddy. The Soviets didn't want the professors to know Communists are such pricks. They waited until the reception was over and grabbed me on my way back to the embassy."

Schott shifted from his right buttock to his left. "How did they search you?"

"They stripped me. They get their jollies that way."

"Did they X-ray you?"

Burlane shook his head. "No."

Schott considered that. "Now tell me about your contact with the man up there." Schott gestured topside.

"Emil?"

"Yes."

Burlane scratched his head. "The Company's done business with Emil for maybe ten years now. If he says he can do something, he can do it. He speaks four languages fluently: English, Turkish, Greek, and Russian. He has a lot of contacts. He knows how to get things done."

"So you went to him saying what?"

"That we wanted to retrieve a Russian from Yalta."

Schott looked at the back of his knuckles. "Then what?"

"He thought about it for a bit, then outlined what had to be done and how much it would cost. He jacked the price up, of course; we're Americans. As I said, he's done business with us before." Burlane remembered Esmeralda's breasts.

"He knew who you were?"

"What do you mean?" Burlane asked.

"I mean that you're from the Company."

Burlane sighed. "Ara, Italian travel agents don't retrieve customers from Yalta. I have to be either American or British. Do I sound like a Brit?"

Schott cut himself a hunk of cheese. "But you had never met him before?"

"Not that I know of. Hell, he even knew my real name."

Schott looked surprised. "James Burlane?"

"That's my name."

"How the hell did he know that?" Schott was alarmed.

Burlane shrugged. "I don't know. But just because I can't recall having met him doesn't mean I haven't. I've been involved in four rather complex clandestine operations in this part of the world. That's too damned much. People have to check your bona fides before they have anything to do with you. People put their asses on the line, they want to know what they're getting into. These types have their own underground wireless. The line on Emil, and I think it's straight, is that he does only one job at a time. In the past he's worked either for himself—smuggling guns or heroin—or for us or the British. His loyalty is to his employer; that's how he stays in business."

"I can't believe that's how they train you people to operate—hire a guy who knows your real name?"

Burlane looked Schott straight in the eye. "Out in the field, Ara, we get the job done any damned way we can. There are risks. We're not school-teachers or shoe salesmen. What you may regard as a battle of wits back at Langley is war out here. If you ask me, I think we're luckier than hell to get anybody to make this run."

"Still . . ." Schott wasn't satisfied.

"Smuggling weapons and people is what you would call one of your esoteric professions. It's a matter of on-the-job training, Ara. Despite the impressions you may have gained from the movies, there's precious damned few people who actually do it."

"I'm sorry," Schott said. "I didn't mean to second-guess your judgment."

"No, no, that's okay. I understand your concern. Look at it this way: Emil has a practice of sorts, like a doctor or lawyer. His income depends on his reputation. He might know who I am, but he has no idea in hell that we're going to Yalta to pick up Kim Philby. He has his eye on fifty thousand bucks for a couple days' work." Burlane was finished. He'd had it with Schott's questions. He drained his bottle of beer in one long pull and went topside.

Schott remained below. The pitching and yawing of the *Bolu* was tiresome; Schott knew he would need some rest. Emil and Hasan, even Burlane, were able to take the Baltic sun topside, but Schott knew he was better off below. Besides, he was troubled by doubts and unanswered questions.

Burlane was a professional, Schott knew that, yet he was still troubled. Philby's passing of microfilm to Burlane, at great risk, had gone too easily. Was it luck, Schott wondered, or was it the

skill of two men who knew what they were doing?
And Burlane, the many-lived Burlane—was it possible even after years in the field to be so casual
about Emil's having known his real name? Schott
couldn't see how. Ara Schott was on the *Bolu* for
one reason: someone had to debrief Kim Philby
immediately after he was on board. A debriefing
of that sort would take hours, something they
would have with luck. It was a debriefing—one
that could determine whether a future American
President was an agent of the KGB—that Schott
would trust to no man but himself. If they were
overtaken by a Soviet patrol, Schott would have to
send a yea or nay to Langley. His decision, sent by
a transmitter small enough to be clipped to his
belt, would be intercepted by an American station
in Turkey for relay to the United States.

A wrong yea could condemn an innocent man to
death. A wrong no could put the free world in the
hands of the Soviet Union.

Schott needed to sleep but couldn't. He was exhausted. He had a headache. He ate a couple of
figs Emil had bought in Sinop and joined the
others topside, beer in hand. Burlane was reading
one of several paperback thrillers he had brought
with him. Hasan was whittling the figure of an
animal with his pocketknife—it looked like the
beginnings of a donkey. He stood up at Schott's
appearance and kicked shavings into the sea with
his bare feet.

"Joining the world, eh, Dennis?" said Emil, who
was at the helm.

"This is hard on me. I'm not used to it."

Emil laughed. "You lead a soft life, eh?"

Burlane looked up from his book. "You'd have been better off leaving the debriefing to me."

"I'll make it. All things have to end someday," said Schott.

"You should smoke some hashish," Emil said. "It'll help you to rest; you need your rest. We have a long night ahead; you won't be worth a pinch of shit the way you are."

Schott shook his head. "I'm afraid I don't take drugs."

"Drugs? Hah!" Emil said. "Hasan, get the man a pipe."

Hasan grinned and scurried below. He returned moments later with a bamboo bong.

Schott looked hesitantly at it. "It'll help me sleep?"

Hasan grinned.

"Do as the boy says," Emil said.

Burlane put his paperback down and watched Hasan inhale a long, smooth draw on the bong. "I need to be alert later," said Schott; he looked at Burlane.

"Do it," Burlane said.

Schott did and minutes later was staring out at the Black Sea under the mellow, glowing warmth of hashish. They were right; it was relaxing. The sun above them was warming as well. The boy, Hasan, went below and returned with a broad-brimmed straw hat which he gave to Schott.

"Thank you very much," Schott said.

"You're welcome, sir," Hasan said, in such perfect English that Schott was momentarily startled.

It was the first time he had heard Hasan utter a
word. Hasan had laughed at Emil's jokes and
nodded his head yes or no, but he never said anything. Schott heard Hasan speaking Turkish to
street vendors in Ereğli and to the man at the
diesel pump in Sinop, and Emil said he spoke
fluent Russian. Hasan's textbook English seemed
not to bother Burlane or Emil, but Schott looked
at him with renewed interest. Hasan had pale-
brown skin and almond-shaped eyes with the hint
of a Mongoloid eye fold. Schott wondered if the
boy might not be older than he at first had
thought. On second thought, Schott concluded
Hasan could be as old as twenty-one or twenty-
two. Until he had a satisfactory answer for the
English, it would worry and eat at him. How could
Hasan not bother Burlane?

But the matter of Hasan's English didn't cause
Schott nearly as much anxiety as what he spotted
on the horizon not five minutes later.

"A boat, there, there on the horizon," Schott
shouted. He stood up, pointing in the distance
with his finger.

"You have the eyes of an eagle, Dennis," Emil
said.

Burlane laughed. "Yes, sir, that man has a real
fine set of peepers."

"What are they talking about?" Schott asked
Hasan.

Hasan grinned but said nothing. Emil relit his
cigar and answered for the boy. "He's been out
there all morning, Dennis."

Schott felt a wave of anxiety wash through his

stomach; he lurched as the *Bolu* buckled in a trough. "Jesus Christ! All morning!"

"A fishing boat like ours; the Black Sea is heavily fished, Dennis," Emil said.

Burlane shaded his eyes with his hand and looked in the direction of the boat on the horizon. "You didn't think everyone was going to pull out of the Black Sea so we could have it all to ourselves, did you?"

"I think I'll go below," Schott said and paused. For years he had been convinced that the tales of unshakable suspicion and anxiety reported by men in the field were romantic fiction. Now he wasn't sure. He looked at Burlane, who stood and massaged his deck-weary buttocks without taking his eyes off his paperback. He had been told it took a special nerve and a certain reckless masochism to covert in a Communist country. Schott knew Burlane had done so in the Soviet Union several times, each trip more dangerous than the one before. How did he do it? How could he see a boat on the horizon, agree with the optimistic conclusion that it was just another fishing boat, and calmly return to a paperback thriller about an ex-Nazi plot to take over the world. How? Schott crawled into the tiny bunk and, in the aftermath of the hashish high, fell into a deep, dreamless sleep.

He awoke, hours later, and went on top. The sun was setting over Bulgaria beyond the horizon. The wind, which had been blowing steadily all day, eased with the setting sun and oranges and reds twisted and swirled on the silken sea. Schott did not read poetry—he read history mostly—but he was deeply affected by the great beauty of the sunset.

"Lovely, isn't it?" asked Emil, as though he could read Schott's mind.

Later, a rested Schott sat cross-legged on deck with Burlane and ate supper. They had fruit and sharp cheese, washed down with Turkish wine. Then the stars came out. Schott looked for lights of the other boat, but couldn't see any.

"Is that boat still out there?" he called to Emil at the helm.

"I'm not sure," Emil said.

"I can't see any lights," said Schott. He took a sip of wine and was suddenly overwhelmed with a new sense of dread. Something was wrong besides Emil's knowing Burlane's name, Hasan's English, and the boat on the horizon. He felt dislocated somehow, confused, out of place. He knew intellectually where he was: in a thirty-two-foot Turkish fishing boat in the middle of the Black Sea. But there was more to it than that. Something else. Something wasn't right.

"Something's wrong," he said to Burlane.

"A lot of fishing boats on the Black Sea; you think too much about that one and it'll drive you crazy."

"It's not that."

"The kid's English bothered you. Emil says the kid was brought up in a Catholic orphanage in Istanbul. The nuns were convinced their students' futures depended on their being able to speak English. They drilled them on it every day."

Schott smiled. "His English did bother me. But

there's something else I can't put my finger on."

Burlane scratched his armpit, thought a bit, then grinned; he gestured to the sky. "The stars, Ara."

"The stars?"

"You've never traveled. When you're in a different hemisphere at a different latitude, the stars are different too. People usually don't pay any attention to the stars; I know I don't. I can't name the constellations, none of that. The only thing I recognize is the Big Dipper."

Schott looked at the sky. "You're right; the stars are different. Look at them."

Burlane nodded in the darkness. "We're surrounded by stars out here. It's jarring, I know."

Schott took another nap after they ate supper. Later, he was awakened by Hasan shaking his shoulder. Schott noticed immediately that the boat wasn't moving.

"Yalta," Hasan said. He turned in the darkness and scrambled topside.

When you're running covert in the Soviet Union, there is no relief from anxiety, from the suspicion that your presence is known in advance, that you are doomed to spend the best years of your life at slave labor. That is the horror. Visitors are routinely watched. You sweat and, fearing even the odor of perspiration will betray you, sweat all the more. Your mouth is dry. Even your breath stinks from fear. Anyone or everyone may be the many-headed hydra: cut one head off and it will be replaced by two. The most innocent Russian may be KGB: a child, an old woman. At any moment you may be selected. The moment may come with a small gesture, a polite request. You wonder what you'd do, shrug, run, what? However it comes the result is the same: there is no returning save at the leisure of the Soviets. Notions of justice are quaint in trials for spies. Such trials are theater staged for the outside world. The outcome is determined in advance, if not the precise punishment: a camp on the tundra, perhaps, at a latitude where it never thaws; ten years taken from your life. Foreign service officials may protest, but what can they do? Langley will have nothing to do with you. You know the dangers going in. No one knows how much human agony was sparcd by the development of satellite reconnaissance and the discovery that photography from space is in most respects superior and more reliable than the cumbersome and dangerous deployment of human beings in Soviet territory. Still, there are some things satellites can't do.

Human beings must still enter the country of fear.

12

He was a handsome man, his face of indeterminate Asian stock. He was Tartar possibly, or one of the other races indigenous to the Caucasus east of the Black Sea: Georgia, Armenia or Azerbaydzhan. He could just as easily have come from still farther east, from one of the Soviet provinces east of the Caspian Sea and north of Iran, Afghanistan, and China: Turkmen, Uzbek, Tadzhik, Kirghiz, or Kazakh. His foot had gone to sleep. He cursed softly. He shifted his weight so the blood would flow again. Once more he scanned the slopes of the golf course with his infrared telescope.

They would be coming across the golf course. He was sure of that; if they chose to come from the Yalta side of the resort, they would risk being discovered by a patrol. He turned his sight in the direction of the lone figure strolling on the walking path that encircled the hotel, swimming pool,

and tennis courts. He thought the figure there
walked rather briskly considering the loneliness
of the hour. The Asian didn't mind waiting. He had
been trained to wait. He was patient, a heritage
perhaps of his race. He scanned the golf course
again. He poured himself another cup from his
thermos, an expensive Czechoslovakian model
that was hard to come by. The coffee was Turkish,
its bitterness mellowed by milk and sugar. He un-
wrapped a piece of cold fish he had brought along
as a snack. He had a dip in a paper cup covered
with a lid. He removed the lid and dipped the fish
into the sauce, which reeked of garlic, ginger, and
hot pepper. He took a bite of fish and grinned; it
was good.

The Asian looked to his left at the lights over
Yalta at the edge of the Black Sea. A white moon
emerged from a part in the clouds. He could see
Yalta clearly and, below the town, fishing boats in
the small harbor. It was a long way from the Turkish coast; the Asian admired the Americans'
courage. He had been on a similar mission once
himself. The fear, which had been overwhelming
at first, abated as he had gone farther into the
enemy's heartland. In the end, he recalled, the fear
had been replaced by a calmness that he could not
explain. It was as though at the moment of truth,
when there was no way out, the human intellect
had a curious way of accepting the inevitability of
death. That was his first mission.

The Asian helped himself to some more fish. He
loved the sauce and wished he'd brought more, although it could have used more ginger. He ran his

hand along the smooth stock of his rifle. The Asian had not chosen his profession for ideological reasons. It was true that he had been taught the proper truths, repeated again and again and again until there were no other realities. He was the product of a time and place. It was his fate to become a hunter, watching if he must, pursuing if he must. He did not question. It was not his to question. He had had the best instructors and was, possibly, one of the best shots in the world with an infrared telescope. He wouldn't have looked at it that way, however; that would not have occurred to him. He merely felt lucky that he had not been condemned to repetitious work on an industrial assembly line. His work had its dangers, but it had its pleasures as well. He got to travel and if he wanted a little cold fish with a good dip for a snack while he waited, he could have it. If he liked Turkish coffee, well then it was his, together with a Czech thermos to keep it hot.

13

When Schott got topside he heard the gentle slap, slap, slap of waves against the *Bolu*'s hull; he felt a sudden need to urinate. There were lights in the distance, stretching up from the shore. Schott urinated off the port bow and looked at the lights. He felt stiff from sleeping in the cramped bunk. It was as though he had just gotten off a bus at a small town in the middle of the night.

"That's Russia, Ara," said Burlane from the darkness behind him.

Ara Schott had devoted his adult life to preventing the penetration of the CIA by agents of the Soviet Union. Schott read history late at night when other men ate popcorn and watched television with their wives. He knew about the awful purges of 1938. He knew about hundreds of thousands of political prisoners starved, humiliated, and beaten in awful camps across that vast nation.

He knew of the tortures ordered by Stalin; he knew of Beria and the rest. Schott had read Alexander Solzhenitsyn. He read newspapers: people were not lined up to get into the Soviet Union; they fought barbed wire and AK-47s to get out. Writers there could not write—or more accurately could not get published. Scholars could not think, save within the stifling confines of party orthodoxy.

Looking back, Schott would have been hard put to define the nexus of the struggle between the Soviet Union and the United States. The cold war was one of those things men could not stop. They could not desist even if they wanted to. The American President and the Soviet Premier knew that, as did Peter Neely and Ivan Konsomov. Ara Schott knew that also. Still he fought on, a passionate believer. He was a professional counterintelligence man; he was paid to be suspicious. He could not trust; to trust was to invite treachery.

Schott looked up at the subtropical underbelly of that great Soviet colossus, a vast land imprisoned by ice, barbed wire, and the Red Army; it was an awful blackness. Schott had to smile at the simple streetlights shining in the warm night over Yalta. He might well be looking at a small town on the California coast. "What time is it?" he heard his voice asking.

"A quarter after one, Dennis," Emil said. "We're running a few minutes late."

Burlane squatted on the deck beside him. "The Company has good maps. The Tartar Palace is over there, on the left. See it?"

"No," Schott said.

"Okay, trace along the docks to the west until the lights run out there. Now go straight up; that bright area there is a complex of government buildings. Now go to the left and down slightly until you come to dim light, bright light, dim light."

"I think I see it. Do you have the map?" Schott's eyes adjusted to the darkness and he was able to make out rough relationships on the map. "You're right, Jim. That's it."

"Hasan and I will get him. I think you and Emil should remain on the boat. Okay?" Burlane started to struggle with the dinghy that served as the *Bolu*'s lifeboat.

"No," said Schott. He was this close to the Soviet Union. He wanted to go ashore. He was a desk man. He wanted to know for himself what it was like.

Burlane looked at him in the darkness. "That's what we agreed on."

"I want to go. I'm no safer here than there. I have a capsule."

"Fuck!" Burlane said. "Okay, you want to come, you come. But when we're on shore I'm in command, got that?"

"I understand," Schott said. "Thank you."

"My life is on the line out there," Burlane said.

"You're in charge," Schott said.

Burlane motioned for Hasan to join them. "You two say nothing. You keep your mouths shut unless I ask you something. Hasan, if we get into trouble, I want you to run up the hill and to the west. Draw them with you if you can. Do you have some identification?"

Hasan nodded his head yes.

"If that happens now, you're on your own."

Emil came up behind them and embraced the young man. "When we get back you'll be paid twenty-five thousand dollars, Hasan."

Hasan said something in Turkish and Emil had to stifle laughter.

Schott looked back at the Black Sea. "Did we lose that boat out there?"

"I didn't see it," Burlane said.

"Neither did I," Emil said.

Burlane started releasing the dinghy. "It'll hold four people but it won't be fun." They were west of the harbor lights and about 150 yards from shore.

Emil helped them get the dinghy afloat and they were off, Schott fore, Hasan in the middle rowing, and Burlane in the aft steering with a hand rudder.

Hasan rowed steadily, taking deep bites with the oars. He stared past Burlane at the sea as his slender body stiffened against the pull of the oars. Soon they were on a rocky beach at the foot of a limestone bluff. Burlane jumped into the water and began pulling the dinghy ashore.

"The Tartar Palace is about a half mile up and to our right," Burlane whispered. "Follow me."

They followed Burlane up the bluff, across a gravel road, and between rows of grapes in a well-tended vineyard. The red soil reminded Schott of nothern California. When they moved out of the

vineyard and into a stand of junipers, he had the
feeling of having been there before, or someplace
like it. After the junipers they came to a golf
course with rough greens and a terrible downhill
lie. Beyond the golf course there were stately poplars surrounding some white buildings with red-
tiled roofs shining under spotlights: the Tartar
Palace.

Here Burlane stopped and motioned Hasan and
Schott close to him. "If Philby is on the level and
hasn't compromised himself, the Russians should
have no reason in heaven to suspect foreign agents
to be prowling around out here. This is a resort
town. They make wine here, not nose cones. You
two follow me and keep quiet. I'll give the code to
Philby, Dennis; when we get back on the *Bolu*, he's
all yours. Hasan and I are gonna smoke hashish
and drink Turkish beer all the way to Sinop."

The three of them, bent low, moved swiftly
across the golf course. When they got to the trees,
they saw there was a main building flanked by two
smaller annexes. The resort was surrounded by
formal gardens. And there, not ten feet in front of
them, was a gravel walking trail built for Czarist
ladies to exercise their limbs in the shade of
poplars. The trees were the outer perimeter of the
resort, the trail was next—covered with red gravel—then the gardens, a parking lot, and the hotel
itself. In front of the Tartar Palace were gardens, a
fountain, and a swimming pool, but no trees; trees
would have destroyed the picturesque view of the
fishing boats in the harbor and the Black Sea
beyond that. There were tennis courts in the rear.

"On the ground," Burlane motioned with his hand. "We wait here."

The three of them lay on the cool ground beneath the poplars, whose broad, dark leaves rustled in the breeze coming off the water. They had been there no more than ten minutes when Schott saw the figure of a man strolling casually toward them in the darkness of the path. Schott's mouth felt dry but he was alert, seemingly more alert than he ever had been before in his life.

Burlane stood up and walked out to meet the man. "Guy Burgess ate garlic the way some people eat peanuts," he said.

"Bloody sod," the man said. His words seemed to linger in the salt air.

"Come with me," Burlane said. "There are three of us here."

"Thought you'd never c-come," said Philby. He followed Burlane to Schott and Hasan, who were squatting on their haunches under the poplars.

"Quickly, quickly," Burlane said. The four of them began to walk swiftly back across the golf course. They were halfway to the other side when Schott felt a tap on his shoulder. It was Hasan.

"Mr. Dennis, Mr. Burlane, behind us."

"Down," Burlane said.

They went down; Schott could feel Kim Philby breathing heavily beside him. He was an older man and out of shape. Schott looked and saw a man running after them across the fairway. The man suddenly twisted and went down.

"Come on," Burlane said. He was up and sprinting the remaining sixty yards to the stand of junipers. Philby trailed, half pushed, half dragged by Hasan and Schott. When they were in the junipers, Burlane—with a remarkable sense of direction— retraced their exact route up from the vineyard. The vineyard came next, and the road, and finally the limestone bluff.

The dinghy was where they left it. They boarded hurriedly, with Philby and Schott up front, Hasan in the middle, and Burlane at the rudder again, looking over his shoulder at the dark slope behind them.

"What happened back there?" Schott asked Philby. That was the first of many questions he wanted to ask—assuming they made it out alive.

"KGB," Philby said. He gasped to catch his breath. "He either twisted his ankle and went down, or one of his colleagues shot him by accident."

"I thought you said they got tired of following you," Burlane said from the rear of the boat.

"They haven't been," said Philby.

Burlane was enraged. "Shit, that's just grand, you asshole. We've got a hundred seventy-five miles between us and the Turkish coast and a fishing boat that goes nine miles an hour."

Philby said nothing.

Hasan put every bit of strength he possessed to the task at hand.

Schott looked at his wristwatch. It was 2:15 A.M. at Yalta.

14

/

It was 3:15 P.M., Pacific Standard Time, in the President's Suite of the Los Angeles Marriott. Derek Townes was not yet President, but he would be. There didn't seem much doubt about that. There was no doubt at all of Townes's feelings about Langley.

"I want to establish my authority over the military and the CIA right from the start, Irv. The generals would like to fight a war all the time if they have their way—good for promotions and lets them try out their toys and theories. The CIA can get a President in a whole lot of shit without him knowing it. I want to know what those people are doing, when, why, and how. Covert stuff gets my okay or it doesn't go."

"It won't be easy, Derek," Irv Cohn said.

Townes twirled the ice cubes in his drink. "I don't think we can take a chance on unnamed and

unknown red-hots getting us involved in things we
shouldn't or don't want to get involved in. We'll
need people who are willing to see that's done and
done right. The Constitution says I'm Commander
in Chief, and that's what I damned well intend to
be."

"You'll need a big win to throw that kind of
weight around."

Townes smiled. "Isn't it beautiful?"

He was right. He would get a big win. The polls
showed Townes to be a prohibitive favorite in New
York, Ohio, California, Texas, Illinois, Michigan—all the states that counted. He even had a
shot at Pennsylvania, Langston Ridgeway's home
state. Ridgeway was an honorable man and hadn't
been a bad governor. But he was finished. The
first to make the conclusion, of course, was the
press. Reporters like to cover a presidential
election like a horse race, only this wasn't much
fun. Ridgeway was hopelessly behind so they con-
centrated on Townes. The public inevitably comes
to think as does the press. Derek Townes was
going to be elected President, with a dying James
Burack at his side when he took the oath of office.
That's the way it was going to be, had to be. If they
had made a movie of it in the 1940s, James Stewart
would have gotten the part. Townes was just a tad
polished, a trifle eager for the role but no matter.

"We don't wait until next month to plan our
government, Irv. We do it now. It's ours and we
know it. We want a government that serves the
people for a change. I want an administration in
place and ready to hit the ground running when I

take the oath of office. I want an administration that can work with Congress, not one that fights it. If you can get Donna in here to take some notes, I want to get some ideas on paper."

"Not *we*, Derek. *You*."

Townes ignored him. "Just get Donna."

Cohn shook his head. "We've been through that already."

"No, we haven't."

"We have, Derek. I've come this far with you, that's more than I expected under the circumstances. I'll get your people lined up for you and quietly go my way. We'll make a little announcement and that'll be it."

"You're going to be my chief of staff."

"No."

"You are, Irv. You're not going to be Vice-President. Tom Eagleton was running for Vice-President when they found out he had had mental problems."

"Please, you know it can't be."

Townes waved him quiet with his hand. "Yes. H.R. Haldeman wore a crew cut for God's sake. Ham Jordan was accused of spitting ice cubes down a woman's boobs in public and of tooting coke."

"No, Derek."

"Look, if we can have a gay mayor and women generals we can have a chief of staff with some mental problems in the past. We simply hold a press conference and tell the truth. Times are changing, Irv."

Irv Cohn stood up and put his hands in his

trouser pockets. "Not that fast. I don't think you really understand, Derek."

"Give them a chance, Irv. I'm willing."

Cohn shook his head. "The thing is I saw things. I imagined things, imaginary people. I talked to people. This isn't just a minor emotional problem we're talking about. I was loony, don't you see? Nuttier than a fruitcake."

"But it's over."

"Yes, it's over. For me it's over. But we're talking about the American public here."

Townes sighed. "No, we're not. We're talking about you, Irv Cohn, a good and decent man. We're talking about honor."

Cohn sat down. He looked like he was ready to weep. "I wish it could be that simple, Derek. I really do."

Townes got up to pour himself another drink. He put his hand on his friend's shoulder. "We can talk about it later if you like; we've got lots of time."

Cohn bit his lip. "I just don't know. Remember Walter Jenkins."

"Johnson's man."

"He propositioned a cop in a men's room or some damned thing and that was it."

"So?" Townes grinned. "They had a joke after that, don't you remember? Why is it Lyndon Johnson swims nude in the White House pool?"

Cohn looked momentarily blank.

"He was trolling for Walter Jenkins."

Cohn couldn't help but laugh. "Dammit, don't you see, Derek, it's hopeless."

Townes shook his head no. "Only if you look at it that way. Walter Jenkins was twenty years ago. Tom Eagleton was in 1972. Times have changed, Irv. We lay it on the line after the election. Reporters may be assholes sometimes, but I think they're too civilized these days to take you down for something like that. We'll tell them you're cured but will get monthly checkups or whatever."

"Then we wait out the Napoleon jokes."

Townes laughed. "Then we wait out the Napoleon jokes."

15

Emil had the *Bolu*'s diesel idling when Schott and Burlane returned with Kim Philby. Hasan had not yet secured the dinghy on deck when Emil began easing the *Bolu* out to sea; a mile later he put the diesel on full throttle and set a course south by southeast for Sinop.

Schott took Philby below into the tiny cabin. "We must chat, I think. Is that how you English chaps would put it? We may not have a lot of time."

Philby held onto the edge of a cabinet for support, then sat. He was tired and cold. He was hungry. He looked at the seconds on his digital wristwatch blinking crimson in the darkness. Schott's watch noted the passing of time in a cool, mint green. The thief, red, cop green. It should have been the other way around. Philby smiled. "This is it then: the Turk, the young man, and you two?"

"Just us," Schott said.

"What did you do when B-Burlane gave you my message?"

"We talked about it."

Philby laughed. "D-Did you tell your President?"

"No."

Philby sat on the tiny bunk. "I don't imagine you did. I know I w-wouldn't until I was satisfied." Philby began to tremble; his eyes began to water. "I think I'm going to break down and cry on you, Mr. Schott. I'm sorry."

Schott said nothing.

"I know you must be very worried about the Soviets, Sevastopol' b-being so close to Yalta and all." Philby wondered, near the end, if he were going to finish the sentence.

"We couldn't risk anything dramatic like helicopters or a jet boat. The reason I'm here is if we can't make it across."

"The decision is yours then?"

"If we run into trouble, I have to decide then and there. It'll be my decision, yes."

Philby's jaw trembled involuntarily. He remembered long Moscow nights and the radiator hissing in his flat. He was on a fishing boat where people spoke English. Philby had never gotten used to Russian. He spoke fluent Russian but his dreams were still in English. It was the awful irony of his life that he couldn't stand the bloody Russians to whom he had betrayed Great Britain and the Americans, including the one who sat across from him now. "Marine air is hard on me. I have ar-ar-thritis."

Schott coughed. "The sun will be coming up in a

few hours. We'll be warm then."

"You must forgive me, M-Mr. Schott, but I have to tell this story my way, I think. I must take my time. Please, we spies don't have p-priests like the Catholics. But in a way we do, don't you think?"

"Mr. Philby?"

Philby laughed softly. "It is the duty of the priest, if I'm not mistaken, to preserve and protect the Church and its doctrine. A priest must b-believe, in his heart, in the institution of the Church and the value of its doctrines. He is G-God's soldier; he remains vigilant. It is his d-duty, just as it is yours, to hear me and decide, if necessary. I would like to confess, Mr. Schott."

"Confess? I'm not sure I understand."

Philby leaned forward. "I've had to bear this awful b-burden alone now for more than a quarter of a century." Philby struggled hard not to be overwhelmed by emotion a second time. "If I t-tell you about me, you'll understand why I'm certain about Derek Townes. You have to l-l-l-l . . ." The word was stuck; it wouldn't come.

"I'll listen," Schott said.

"Thank you. B-bloody stutter." Philby fell silent for a moment. Both men listened to the rattle of the *Bolu*'s diesel.

Schott looked at his wristwatch. He said nothing.

"I guess I should get on with it."

"Start with yourself if you like. But you *should* get on with it; we may not have much time, judging from the incident on the golf course."

"If the S-Soviets are on us, you'll need enough to make a d-decision."

"Yes."

"I understand. Over the years I've come to the conclusion, Mr. Schott, that undergraduates are largely a-adolescents in adult bodies. They have a love of the abstract, the ideal, and the theoretical. They're impatient if the world doesn't b-behave like they think it should. This infatuation with the a-abstract comes with pimples. In fact that's what the Russians call them, the Pimpled Ones. The ideal of equality is an ennobling one, Mr. Schott. The Soviets understand its attraction. They indoctrinate children in grammar school, but with the coming of p-pimples, the Soviets have their problems also. The young aren't stupid; they can see for themselves the inequalities of the system. They see p-party officials being chauffered about in limousines. In the United States the educated young rebel against institutions at a-age twenty, just as they rebelled against their parents five years earlier. Young people m-match the reality around them with the whitewashed versions they have been taught in grammar school. The grammar school versions never hold up, of course. They feel cheated, l-lied to."

"You were a Pimpled One at Cambridge," Schott said.

Philby smiled. "You should re-remember it was 1931, 1932; the economy of Great Britain failed just as it did in the United States. We were told by our radical professors that o-oppressive capitalism had failed from 'internal contradictions,' whatever that meant. We could see for ourselves great wealth a-amassed by a privileged few. We could see the class system; we were p-part of it.

Then, in 1933, I went to Austria and witnessed for myself the fascism that was then overwhelming the Continent. I saw the in-ineffectual Social Democrats crushed by thugs and goons from the far right. I ended up marrying a Communist girl named Litzi, partly to get her out of there.

"I came to the conclusion that fascism was the future of Great Britain as well as the Continent. And, in retrospect, if Hitler hadn't been so in-indecisive in 1941, that would h-have come to pass. One has, I suppose, finally to choose between freedom and equality. I chose equality and the Soviet U-Union. What better place to fight the Fascists than in the secret s-service?"

"It w-wasn't a commitment to the Soviet Union, you see? I'd never been there; the language and the people were foreign to me. It was a commitment to an ab-abstraction, an idea. The a-awful part of it was I didn't see it as an ab-abstraction. I saw it as something men could a-achieve." Kim Philby interrupted his monologue with a bitter laugh. He stood to stretch.

Schott said, "So tell me about our Mr. Townes."

Philby sneezed. "Could I have a d-drink of something, please? My nerves are a trifle edgy, if you know what I mean."

Schott poured them both a water glass of Turkish wine.

Philby sipped the vile wine. "That's almost as b-bad as the stuff we get in Moscow. There are striking similarities between Cambridge during our years there from 1929 through 1931—by our, I include Burgess, Anthony Blount, and Maclean—

and Townes's experience during the late 1960s. Our economy was going to hell; the Nazis were be-beginning to stir in Germany. Communism was first fashionable in political clubs; later, anyone who wanted to c-call himself an intellectual had to be a Communist. Intellectuals and Communists were thought to be the same thing.

"You know recently they did a l-long study in Great Britain, in 1980 I think it was, to see if there had b-been any real changes in social and econom-ic mobility in the last fifty years. Mind you, this is after all manner of reforms in education, hiring p-practices, and so on. There was no change. None. The old Edwardian upstairs, downstairs is still there, if in a modified form. We were Cambridge men, the backbone of the British establishment; it was we who had built the Empire and we who lost it as well." Here Philby paused.

"Tell your story, please."

Philby, whose eyes were adjusted to the dark-ness, could begin to see Schott's face clearly for the first time. "Look at yourselves. After JFK's m-murder there appeared cracks in a world that seemed, really, to be so solid in Ike's time. Derek Townes was an undergraduate at Berkeley. He was there with bright, arrogant kids who c-con-sidered themselves a vanguard of sorts. Your re-reporters praised them. They were thinking. They weren't apathetic. They did something besides d-drink beer at fraternity parties.

"And in 1967, he was a graduate student at the barricades with Mark Rudd at C-Columbia. He was KGB by then, I'm convinced. He was perfect.

He was b-bright. He came from an influential family, a family that had served Presidents. The connections were always there for the asking. His father and grandfather both had taken time out from business to s-serve their country. It's all there in his dossier—except for his recruitment. Few libraries match Moscow Center's.

"Derek saw blacks burn down their slums in 1965. In 1966 and 1967, he saw h-his country stupidly commit itself in a civil war in Indochina. The United States was maintaining puppet regimes in Saigon; any fool could see that. It was fashionable in Townes's circles to think in terms of blacks and whites, of the dreaded Establishment, of the com-complicity of Du Pont, Dow Chemical, and the arms manufacturers. Townes saw an arrogant country that just w-would not give up; no matter what the cost, no matter how many young men lost their lives, Johnson persisted. The C-Communist world, of course, identified with Ho Chi Minh. There was this small Asian country, North Vietnam, fighting a war machine g-gone mad. Mario Savio, Rudd, Jerry Rubin, the Students for a Democratic Society, the Y-Yippies, and the rest saw themselves romantically as guerrillas aligned with blacks in the slums, w-workers in Prague, and peasants in Hanoi. It was p-pathetic.

"Is it any wonder, Mr. Schott, that we were successful in our ef-efforts? We offered Townes the o-opportunity to become a real guerrilla, not a pretend one. Join the KGB and he could be a part of a struggle that was or-organized and would win in the end, not just a bunch of rag-tag kids with marijuana and headbands. You people humored them with excessive coverage in the press. We offered them the real thing. A young man like D-Derek Townes, without the maturity to go with his education, why, he was m-made to order, just as I was in my time." Kim Philby looked tired. Few Americans would hear what he was saying. Maybe Schott, but precious few others. Vietnam was an awful, bitter episode in their national life.

Schott coughed. "In a situation like this, I need more than circumstance."

"I understand, Mr. Schott. The th-thing is when you agree, when you sign on with the Soviets, there is no turning back. The Soviets won't h-hear of it. For all the violent, conspiratorial fiction that's popular these days, we both know the British and you Americans have no t-taste for cold-blooded m-murder. That's not true with the Soviets; murder for them is nothing. They learned it from the Cz-Czars."

Schott blew into cupped hands. "A trifle chilly down here, don't you think?"

"D-Damned cold, I'd say," Philby said.

"You were saying how you couldn't go back again."

Philby smiled. "Not once you've made a c-commitment. This is Faustian, Mr. Schott. We're dealing here with Mephistopheles. You think I'm j-joking? Listen. I believed passionately that the Soviets were the only alternative to a future under Adolf Hitler. Derek Townes, I'm sure, b-believed that the American government—operating with

the complicity of corporations and a-arms manufacturers—had gotten completely out of hand."

"You're saying it tore the country in half."
Schott sighed.

"So much so that thousands of young men were
willing to g-give up their homeland for Sweden or
C-Canada. Being a deliberate expatriate is one
thing; you can always go back. But this was different; these y-young men were willing to give up
everything: their family, their friends, their
future. In Sweden the language and food are
strange. That's not easy; I can tell you from
experience. With me it's cricket; even the Soviets
understood that. They arranged to have the
T-Times flown to me so I could keep u-up with the
scores."

"I understand what you're saying. But what I
need in the case of Derek Townes is something in
the way of facts."

"If you l-look at Townes's college transcripts,
you'll find he took six courses from Dr. Nicholas
Ostrov at Berkeley. This was to the exclusion of all
other economics professors. W-Why would he do
-that?"

"He liked Ostrov's classes."

"Ostrov's a Marxist e-economist."

"We have Marxist economists in most decent
state universities."

Philby shook his head. "Not Marxist economists
wh-who are agents of the KGB."

"What?" Schott swallowed.

"For more than twenty years."

"That doesn't mean he recruited Derek
Townes."

"Townes appears on your FBI records, Ara, as having been a regular guest at p-parties in Ostrov's home for almost three years."

"FBI records?" Schott looked startled.

Philby turned up the palms of his hands. "We Russians are everywhere."

"I take it that information is not in Townes's dossier."

"No. The transcript was, but not the out-of-class information. That was elsewhere; when I found it I knew I h-had my man."

"Circumstantial," Schott said.

"Circumstantial?" Philby smiled. "Yes, I suppose. Townes's code is Boris."

Schott stood up and held onto a cabinet. His mouth tasted sour. "You know that for a fact?"

"The code at Moscow Center for its secret of secrets, a mole working his way into the heart of your government, is Boris. I've spent the last five years of my life in a paper chase. Derek Townes is Boris."

"Boris," said Schott. It was such an ordinary, harmless-sounding Russian name. "Boris the mole."

"Yes," Philby said.

"What I would like to know, Mr. Philby, is why Boris, if that's who Townes is, was pushed into politics. Why wasn't he steered into the intelligence service as you were, and Burgess and Maclean?"

Philby ran his fingertips down along his jaw and across his throat. "The SIS has been around a lot longer than you Americans, Mr. Schott. If you'll recall, your m-man Henry Stimson was opposed to

the establishment of an American intelligence
service in the Second World War. He said gentlemen d-do not read other people's mail. The CIA
was not formed until immediately after the war,
and opportunities for its penetration were not
well developed until my involvement with Burgess
and Maclean was well known in Washington.
Really, everybody knew I was a Russian spy. The
British w-were embarrassed and didn't want to
admit it, but you people knew. You were l-lucky.
You learned a lesson early, at the expense of the
British."

"Better security, you're saying."

"Almost from the first. And then you had
A-Angleton who was suspicious of everything. I
know there were those at Langley who didn't like
him, but he w-was what you needed: a paranoid.
Intelligence people have to survive polygraph
examinations and trial by sodium p-pentothal or
whatever drug is fashionable. Your people have
the right to elect whomever they wish."

"But you just don't chart the career of a man to
the presidency the same way you worm your way
into the bureaucracy."

Philby laughed. "Heavens no! Of course not.
Townes's success was fortuitous, there's no doubt
of that. The usual g-goals are the Armed Services
committees in the House and Senate and the Intelligence Oversight c-committees. As far as we're
concerned, a staff m-member on one of those committees is as good as a member of Congress."

"And the Pentagon?"

"Careers in the military offer more p-problems.

The most successful officers come from the service academies where they receive sufficient b-brainwashing and advantages to put them off limits to us."

"I want to know how it was done. Townes is charming, but no Kennedy."

"The moles were pointed in different d-directions: some trained at Johns Hopkins or Columbia and entered the foreign service; others went into politics, hoping for a good committee a-assignment."

Schott said, "Put your money on enough moles and if just one of the many manages to score, then it was worth it."

"Ahh," Philby said. "Exactly. The greater the n-numbers the greater the chances one of them will emerge in a critical position. We can't control time and c-circumstance."

Schott sighed. "They'll send a poet to a labor camp for mild satire—everybody knows that—and still the Soviets recruit young people. I'll never understand it."

"I wish I could do more to help you with your d-decision, Mr. Schott. The details of Boris's success are known only by his handler and by a select f-few at Moscow Center. I'm not of that group. I wish I could find you the names of other agents, but I can't. My need doesn't include details. I advise the Soviets on the weaknesses of the liberal imagination, on the w-workings of democratic elites, on the pressures and dangers of being a mole."

"Assuming that Townes is Boris, could Ostrov

be the handler?"

"I doubt it. He's too openly a M-Marxist to be entrusted to handle Boris. He'd be the first man to be suspected in something like this. I think he recruited Townes and turned him over to another operative, possibly a man ensconced in the Washington political establishment. It would have to be a m-man whose contacts with Townes would be normal and frequent. There would have to be a l-legitimate reason for them to have contact over the years. I think you can rule out KGB people working out of embassies."

"Ostrov wouldn't know who he is."

"No, Townes would have been introduced to his handler by a third agent, removing O-Ostrov entirely from Townes's future. They would sever contact, which did happen by the way."

"Where would you begin, Mr. Philby, assuming for the moment I agree there are grounds for suspicion?"

"I would begin with a c-covert background investigation on Townes to e-establish his circle of friends and acquaintances over the years. I know it's the FBI's job to do those BIs, but I think I would do it myself in this case."

Schott's eyebrows raised in the darkness. "Not the FBI?"

"No. Heavens!" Philby laughed. "The FBI is as easy to penetrate as a p-pack of cub scouts. Get a kid a law or accounting degree and the Soviets have a ticket. I don't know for a fact that the S-Soviets have people in the Bureau, but if I were you I wouldn't chance it!"

Schott knew Philby was right. This was something Langley would have to take care of itself.

Philby coughed softly. "So you start with what you know, Mr. Schott, a fact here, a revealing bit of information there. You act quickly yet carefully. You do what you h-have to do."

Schott poured himself and Philby some more wine. He looked at his wristwatch: it was 3:30 A.M. on the Black Sea.

16

Ara Schott was hungry. "What do you say we go topside? Maybe I can get the boy to come down and fix us something to eat. They'll be hungry too. We have a long day ahead."

"Thank you, Mr. Schott. I'm very tired and b-breakfast would help." Philby followed Schott topside out of the diminutive cabin.

The *Bolu* was working its way through a thick bank of fog that had settled on the Black Sea. Visibility couldn't have been more than a hundred feet. It was daylight but they could see nothing.

"Ahh, good morning, Dennis!" Emil greeted Schott and Philby with a crooked grin. "How do you like the fog?"

"Good or bad for us?"

Emil shrugged. "Good. Can't see us by plane or by boat."

"Nice," said Philby.

"This is Mr. Shevchenko. Emil."

Emil extended a hand. "Pleased to meet you, Mr. Shevchenko."

Philby smiled and shook Emil's hand. "Solid little boat you have."

"I was wondering," Schott addressed Hasan, "if you might fix us some breakfast. I see there are potatoes and onions that might be fried, along with some fish. Mr. Shevchenko here also has a fondness for tea, a habit he picked up years ago on assignment in London."

Hasan nodded yes and went below.

Thirty minutes later, they were sitting squat-legged on the deck eating their breakfast and drinking hot, strong tea when it came.

Burlane heard it first. He cocked his head and stared into the fog.

Then it was on them with a hollow, throbbing rumble of diesels.

A sleek patrol vessel flying the Russian flag emerged from the fog as though it were a ghost. Sailors on the deck of the vessel stood poised with automatic weapons. They were Soviets, unreal figures in the mist.

"Oh, fuck," Burlane said softly. There was no need to shout. There was nothing he could do. Was it time? His time? He took another bite of fried potatoes.

A man with a bullhorn in his hand shouted instructions at them in Russian.

"He says anyone who moves will be shot," Emil said. He took a sip of hot tea and watched the Russian with the bullhorn. "Believe me, I had no idea," he said by way of apology.

Apologies did no good, Schott knew. He moved his tongue up to his molar. He had failed. How had this happened? How had the Soviet vessel found them in the fog? It seemed impossible. The *Bolu* couldn't have been spotted from the air. How? He looked at Burlane who continued to eat, his jaws working steadily as he stared at the Russians.

The Russian shouted something again over the bullhorn.

Emil killed the engine of the *Bolu*.

The patrol boat pulled alongside the fishing boat and the Russian captain reduced his own engines to a malevolent, loping idle.

Schott started to rise from the deck.

"*Nyet!*" shouted the man with the bullhorn. He glared at Schott.

Schott stayed where he was. He freed the cyanide capsule and tucked it under his tongue. His transmitter was in the cabin. He couldn't get to it. A beginner's error, he realized. He should have had it with him. Neely and Jackson would have to decide for themselves about Derek Townes. Schott couldn't believe the patrol boat existed. It was like being in the movies; he must have seen a scene like this in the movies.

The man with the bullhorn shouted something in Russian again.

"He says they want Comrade Philby," Emil said. He looked at the man who had been introduced to him as Mr. Shevchenko. "That must be you, eh?"

Kim Philby took a sip of tea and pushed his breakfast away. He rose slowly to his feet, tears in his eyes. "Your breakfast was very good," he said to Hasan. He walked to Schott who rose to meet him. "I didn't make it," Philby said softly. "Such a terrible world. How did this happen?"

"I don't know, Mr. Philby."

"What I told you about Boris is true. Derek Townes is your man."

The Russian shouted at them over his bullhorn. Sailors scrambled about the deck of the patrol boat.

Philby stepped back from Schott and turned to face the Russian sailors. He said something in Russian.

The Russian officer answered without using his bullhorn.

"He says I m-m-must go," said Philby. He turned and shook Schott's hand. "Good luck, Mr. Schott."

The Russian officer spoke again.

Philby looked at him and half smiled. "*Nyet*," he said.

The Russian laughed.

Philby followed the instructions of the Soviet deck officer. Twenty minutes later Kim Philby was standing on the deck of the Soviet vessel. He seemed stooped with age as he stared at his feet. The Russian captain backed his vessel away from the *Bolu*. Four sailors manned the single gun mounted on the bow of the patrol boat.

To Schott the Russian vessel looked unreal floating beside them there in the fog. Burlane cupped his hands around his mouth and called something in Russian. The Soviet sailors grinned and looked at their officer, who laughed and called back something in Russian.

Burlane shrugged his shoulders. "I tried," he said in English.

"What's that?" Schott asked.

"I asked them if they took credit cards or blue jeans," Burlane said.

Schott started to say something but was startled by two quick shots fired from the Russian deck gun. The *Bolu* shuddered with each boom. It took Schott a second to realize the *Bolu* was suddenly without a bow. The Russian captain didn't bother to watch the *Bolu* slide under. He gave them a wave, put his engines into all-ahead full, and disappeared into the fog.

"Everybody aft," Emil shouted. In four or five giant strides he was at the dinghy, unfastening the canvas straps that lashed it into place. Nobody said anything as they launched the tiny boat. Hasan took the oars and backed them away from the *Bolu*; they watched in silence as it slipped beneath the water and was gone.

Schott felt suddenly cold. "How far?" he asked of nobody in particular.

"Maybe a hundred miles, something like that," said Emil. "You people owe a man a new fishing boat."

Schott glared at him.

"No need to get upset, Dennis. A deal's a deal is all."

"He'll get a boat," Burlane said.

"What?" asked Schott.

"I said he'll get his boat."

Schott looked into the fog. "Amazing how they

found us so easy. They couldn't possibly have seen us from the air."

"Luck maybe," Burlane said.

"Bullshit."

Emil coughed. "No need to wear yourself out, Hasan. Wait'll the fog lifts and we'll take it from there."

"We should've grabbed some wine to go," said Burlane. He seemed unconcerned at his predicament.

"Why didn't he shoot us?" Schott asked.

"Figured sinking us would do it, I suppose." Burlane picked at his lower teeth with a thumbnail.

"Well?" Schott asked of Emil.

"The fog's starting to burn. Well, what?"

"Was sinking us as good as shooting us?"

"If a storm blows up out here we're dead."

"And if the weather holds?"

"I don't know," confided Emil.

"You don't know?"

"We'll take turns at the oars and head south."

Schott sighed. The KGB was well on its way to placing a mole in the White House and here he was stranded in the middle of the Black Sea. "We don't have any water," he said.

"Rains almost every night out here," Emil said.

Schott said nothing. He watched as the fog thinned. A half hour later it had burned off. The sun felt warm.

Hasan suddenly stood, grinning. "Look, Mr. Dennis," he said in his perfect English. He pointed at the horizon.

There was a boat out there.

"Hah. Look there, gentlemen," Emil laughed.

Schott saw it also. "That's the same boat that was there yesterday."

Emil shook his head. "Lots of boats on the Black Sea." He removed his shirt and began waving it. "They see us. They're coming this way."

Burlane looked relieved. "I don't give a shit who it is!"

"It's the same boat," Schott insisted.

"Could be, I guess," Burlane said.

"These boats all look the same from a distance," aid Emil. He put his shirt back on.

"No, this is the same boat," Schott said. "The roof line is the same."

Thirty minutes later a fishing boat flying a Turkish flag pulled alongside. Two mates helped them aboard and the captain uncorked a three-liter jug of red wine. Emil was animated. There was much backslapping and laughing among Emil, the captain, and the two mates. Hasan grinned and looked pleased. Schott and Burlane watched, drinking coffee mugs of wine.

Emil put his arm around Schott's shoulder. "This man's name is Gamal, Dennis. He wants to know if we were on the boat that was off his starboard all day yesterday."

Gamal grinned, waiting for Schott's response.

"Gamal said he thought we were following him," Emil said.

"Tell him we'll all get drunk when we get back to Turkey," said Schott.

Emil translated for Gamal, who listened, watching Schott. He gave his reply to Emil. "He said you're on, Dennis. We're headed for Zonguldak. He says he knows women there who'll fuck us till we're blind."

"Well, I don't know," Schott hesitated. He looked at Burlane, who was pouring himself some more wine.

"Tell him hell yes, for God's sake. Don't be a pussy."

"Sure," said Schott to Emil. He immediately felt guilty. They had work to do.

Burlane knew what he was thinking. "Patience, my man, patience. When you're in the field you give thanks for small favors. All gods are equal. And when someone saves your ass you celebrate properly. We might have to do business in this part of the world again." Burlane spread the palm of one hand like he had it between a woman's legs; he grinned and worked at the lady with his middle finger. "No, I amend that. *I* won't be doing business in this part of the world again. You might, but not me. This is my last run. I've had it." He hesitated. "But we still celebrate."

TROTSKY

Burlane's Turn

17

Trotsky adjusted the goatee on his chin. The wire-rimmed spectacles were tight on his nose. He took them off and put them in the palm of his right hand, widening the spread with his left thumb. He tried them again. They fit. Trotsky smiled. He left the toilet stall and threw the paper bag in the waste basket. Head up and with an arrogant, purposeful stride, Trotsky walked across the carpeted lobby to the heavy glass door that led to the street.

The tires of the taxis on the street made a hissing sound on the wet pavement. Trotsky turned his back on the wind and coughed once. No one had seen him; he was sure of that. No one knew who he was. He turned his head against the rain and turned in the direction of Times Square. Trotsky wanted to see for himself the Western decadence he had read so much about. It was 12:30 A.M. The night people, high on pot, brains buzzing with coke, were on the street looking for sex and adventure.

Trotsky felt good. He had been denied his place in history once. Now that he was being given another chance, he would prevail. He was certain of that. He would prevail in the name of the workers and of his friend Lenin. World War I had not led to revolution in the West as he had predicted. Nor had World War II. Instead, the Soviet Union had grown and prospered in the awful fashion of Joseph Stalin. Trotsky walked past department stores, elegant fashion boutiques, banks, law offices, publishing houses—pausing only to wipe the moisture from his spectacles. A storm front had hovered over the East Coast for several days now, refusing to go away. Trotsky was tired of the wind and rain.

Trotsky was careful when he walked past darkened streets. He knew about crime in New York. He understood its causes. It was a symptom, he knew—the stirring of revolution. The time would come, he believed; the impoverished of New York's poorer boroughs would rise, in the name of the workers, and in one grand, sweet moment abolish the wild inequities of wealth and status. The Soviet Union would have to be brought down too—a matter of honor and revenge.

At the corner of Forty-third Street and Broadway, Trotsky was approached by a young man wearing a baseball cap, tattered sneakers, and a blue nylon Windbreaker. He grinned at Trotsky and pushed a pamphlet into Trotsky's hand.

Trotsky looked at it, squinting slightly through

his spectacles. "Paula's Pago Pago Nights," the pamphlet said. "For the most exotic night in Manhattan." There was a photo of a slender young woman on the glossy paper. She was nude except for a gold chain around her waist. The pamphlet gave a West Forty-sixth Street address. Paula's was open twenty-four hours a day, the pamphlet said.

Trotsky felt suddenly nervous. His hands began to tremble. It was uncivilized, he knew, but Trotsky couldn't help himself. He took the next right and began working his way toward Paula's.

He walked past it twice before he found it. Paula's was nothing so much as a door on a nondescript block with a small, neatly lettered sign above the door: PAULA'S PAGO PAGO NIGHTS. Trotsky opened the door and stepped inside. He found himself in a small foyer. There were potted plants in three corners, helped by pinkish-white Plant-Gro lights that gave the small room an eerie, sensual quality. There was a calendar on the wall with the dates superimposed over a photograph of a woman's breasts.

A pleasant-looking young woman in a trim business suit sat behind a desk in front of him. A sign on the desk said Paula's accepted both Visa and Master Charge.

Trotsky's breath quickened. He wanted to see this place. He had known labor camps in Siberia. He had known exile. He had commanded an armored train in the pursuit of the White Russians. He would know this. He cleared his throat, uncertain of what he should say.

The young woman helped him out. "We have a flat fee of fifty dollars, sir. That entitles you to spend as much time as you would like watching the dancer next door. You may have as much to drink as you like; the drinks are part of the flat fee. When you're ready, you pick one of the young ladies and she will give you a massage in a private room."

Trotsky was slightly embarrassed. "The dancer?"

"Yes, you may open the door and take a look if you would like."

Trotsky hesitated, then opened the door. He saw a small room with a dancer in the middle to the right of a short hallway. Other dancers in scanty costumes watched from chairs around the floor.

"May I?"

"Certainly," the young woman said.

Trotsky walked down the hallway and opened another door. He caught only a brief glimpse of a young woman dancing in the nude when he closed the door. He checked his goatee to ensure that it was well in place and returned to the foyer. Trying his best not to tremble, he pulled two twenties and a ten from his wallet and gave it to the woman. His breathing quickened.

She smiled and gave him a ticket with a number. "Give this to the attendant when you go in for your massage. There'll be a locker there for your belongings."

Trotsky found that the room with the dancer was small and surrounded by chairs on all sides. Five men and three women dressed in G-strings

and nipple cups watched the girl dance. The
dancer wore a garter belt for tips; for five bucks
she would show some pink or bend over and let
her butt do what it wanted. The other women were
bored, but the men stared, not blinking, their
blood pressures high.

The girl with the garter was enough to make any
man's blood race.

Trotsky took a seat and watched as one of the
other men took a bill, folded it neatly lengthwise,
and held it at his crotch for the dancer to retrieve.
She did and without using her hands. She worked
herself rhythmically against him for a long
minute. She turned then and spread her backside
for him as she removed the bill. She winked at
Trotsky and slipped the folded bill under the garter.

One of the other young women watching rose
and came to Trotsky. "Would you like a drink?"
she asked.

"Vodka, please."

"Straight vodka?" The girl, a small blonde, looked surprised.

"Yes, please," Trotsky said.

The girl went into an adjoining room and returned shortly with a shot glass of vodka. "When
you're ready for your massage just select one of us
in here and we'll go to a private room. You can
stay here as long as you like and drink as much as
you want." She paused, then added, "Within
reason, of course."

"Certainly," said Trotsky. He adjusted his
spectacles.

The dancer set Trotsky's hormones racing. He knew he wouldn't be able to wait through another drink. He chose a slight brunette who for some reason reminded him of his second wife, Natalie, when Natalie was a young woman. There was something about her mouth. She had an expressive mouth like Natalie. He walked over to the young woman and smiled, feeling foolish. "I think I've had enough of the dancer," he said.

The girl stood and scratched her breast, which was covered with a transparent bra of a shiny, silky material. "You go in the next room and take a shower. There'll be an attendant there who'll assign you a locker. I'll meet you in room six, which is down the hall inside there and to the left. You can't miss it. When you finish with your shower you go to room six. If I'm not there, I'll be along shortly."

Trotsky gave her the empty shot glass and did as he was told. He went next door for his shower. Another man was there dressing. He said nothing to Trotsky, who undressed in silence. The attendant was a black man who watched an Elvis Presley movie on a tiny black-and-white television set. The sound was turned down to a barely audible murmur as Elvis sang songs and impressed young women by the side of a pool.

Trotsky showered quickly and dried himself with a towel given him by the attendant. He stored his clothes in a metal locker and walked down the hallway, a fresh towel around his middle, his wallet in hand.

Room 6 was a fair attempt to come up with a

South Pacific decor in a Manhattan sex shop. The
floor was an indoor carpet of a sand color that
went to the very edge of a small pool. The concrete
underside of the pool was painted dark blue. The
walls and ceiling were pale blue. Planters around
the edge of the walls featured tropical-looking
plants kept alive by lights overhead. Soft clouds
were painted on the ceiling. The room was warm,
which surprised Trotsky somewhat—he expected
it to be cold—and was fed humidity artificially,
giving the air a moist, tropical quality. Love songs
accompanied by ukulele were also piped in.

The big feature, however, was the bed, which oc-
cupied center stage—blue Pacific stage left, beach
beneath, lush tropics stage right. The bed was re-
cessed into the floor, an attempt to make it blend
with the beach scene.

The young brunette arrived a couple of minutes
later. "Did you want another drink? I can get you
another drink if you like." She had a tray of
cigarettes, lotions, and ointments.

"No, thank you, the one drink was fine."

The girl gave him a look that was half tease, half
question mark. "Say, you're not a cop are you?"

"No, no," Trotsky laughed.

"I didn't think so. Cops are pricks. You can spot
'em right off. You're kind of crazy looking, but
you're no cop."

Trotsky stiffened slightly at the word *crazy*. He
had been one of the meanest cops on Earth at one
time in the cause of revolution. He wanted to tell
her that. He remembered his armored train. His
word had been law. "What's your name?"

The girl smiled. "Rose," she said.

"My name is Leon Trotsky." Trotsky turned his chin at a proud angle; his hand at his goatee.

"Oh! You're a Polack, I'll bet."

"No, not Polish." Trotsky looked serious. He remembered the towering figure of the indomitable Trotsky, master of Kresty Prison.

"No? Might as well take the towel off; you would have surprised me. Would you like oil? I wouldn't recommend it. It sounds horny, I know, but it's a pain to get off."

Trotsky removed the towel. "What are you going to do?" he asked uncertainly.

"What are we going to do?" Rose skinned the pasties off her nipples with her fingernails, then popped the G-string with her thumb. "I'm going to give you a massage unless you have something else in mind."

"Well, I do, sort of."

Rose began rummaging through the tray as if intent on finding the correct lotion for a massage she knew well she wasn't going to be giving. "Anything extra you negotiate with me. The girl tell you that out there?"

"Yes, she did," Trotsky said. It was hard not to stare at her crotch. He felt himself getting an erection.

"Straight sex is sixty bucks. Head'll cost you another thirty, but they say I give great head. Best head in St. Paul."

Trotsky thought of being inside her mouth and wanted to go for the latter but he didn't. He said, "Straight sex, I think."

"You think?" Rose laughed. "Don't you know? You got a wife that doesn't do anything?"

Trotsky's lips tightened. "Straight sex," he said. He stopped then added, "But I don't just want to jump on. I want to talk first." He gave her an affectionate pop on the butt.

Rose looked at her wristwatch on the tray. "Sure, we can talk some. Only I ain't got all night. People'll be wonderin' what's going on out here. This is a business, you know."

"A business?"

"I just ain't got all night is all."

"You're from St. Paul, you say. What state is that in?"

"Minnesota. It's right by Minneapolis. Say, could you do a girl a favor? If you want to talk, you could do me at the same time." Rose lay back with a bored look on her face. She opened a package of chewing gum from her tray, then arched her spine and spread her legs. "You could sort of come up from time to time for air and whatever it is you want to talk about. I get some real talkers in here." She started chewing gum lazily.

Trotsky smiled, something at which he'd never had much practice. "I don't see why not. Is your father a worker in St. Paul?" He lowered his head.

"Oh thanks, that's nice. No, he drives a beer truck. Not very exciting but I read where truck drivers make more money than schoolteachers, a lot more. Yes, that's it."

Trotsky paused and looked up through the thicket of black pubic hair. Rose tasted sweet-sour. "The other girls who work here, are they from working families?"

Rose ran her tongue around the inside of her mouth. "We don't talk about families much," she said. "If your mouth is getting dry down there, you can work on my tits if you want, but after that we gotta get on with it."

"Do they beat you?"

Rose began to stiffen. "Faster with the tongue. There. Yes." Rose twisted at the waist. "Not since I moved in here. When I was on the street my old man used to work me over once in a while. Now I just ball and do drugs. Man with a tongue like yours'd make a helluva salesman." She laughed at her little joke.

Trotsky grinned on his way to her nipples. He started with thumb and forefinger then moved in with his lips. Her nipples tasted salty.

"Not too hard now, Leon."

Trotsky backed off.

"That's it. That's just fine." While Trotsky worked at her nipples, Rose picked up her wristwatch and checked the time. "It's getting a bit late, honey. I think you should get inside me now."

"What if I want the other?"

Rose knew what he meant. "Thirty bucks more."

Trotsky pulled three ten-dollar bills from his wallet and handed them to her. "A regular capitalist."

Rose shrugged. "A girl's gotta live. Sex don't come cheap. You can pay me now and get your rocks off, or spring for a divorce lawyer next week."

Trotsky rolled over on his back. He remembered

the Russian girls who had wanted to sleep with him after he had led the revolt of the Petrograd Soviet in 1905. He hadn't had time for sex then—or later for that matter. All he could think about was politics.

Rose grabbed a handful of balls and massaged them gently. "Now you come whenever you feel like it, honey. Don't you worry about me."

Trotsky's mouth felt dry. "Tell me, Rose, what would you be doing if you weren't here?"

Rose paused just above the head of Trotsky's penis. "I don't want to be no fucking secretary if that's what you think."

"But you do want to get out of here?" Trotsky looked down his body at Rose's face.

Rose glanced up at him. "I don't know what I want. This is okay for now I guess. Fuck all night and toot coke with the girls all day."

"It must be awful," Trotsky said.

"Oh, I don't know." Rose took Trotsky's cock in her mouth.

Rose began working her hand up and down at the base of Trotsky's cock. She had already given him too much time. She worked on him with determination, her cheeks sucking rhythmically. Rose paused in her labors and looked up at him, her lower lip drooping slightly. "I do a lesbian act Friday and Saturday afternoons at a place called the Pink Sappho. You might want to check it out if you're in town long enough."

"Thank you," he said. He wanted her mouth down on him again. It was so warm he could hardly believe it.

Rose knew he was anxious. She brushed her lips against his cock, then lowered her head all the way and finished him off.

18

Neely was startled by a sudden clap of thunder directly overhead. The tops of alders twisted and whipped in the distance. Neely took another sip of coffee. He watched the lightning dance and bounce across the Potomac. Beyond the river was the capital city. Thunder moaned and grumbled from the direction of the lightning. Wind ripped sheets of water across the parking lot outside. A bolt of lightning popped the tops of trees not a hundred yards away. Neely was waiting for it but was still surprised by the crack of thunder that followed. It was an awesome *crrracckkk* trailed by a hollow boom that shook the windows. Neely took a sip of coffee. He had drunk too much coffee and his mouth tasted awful, but he couldn't stop. Neely lit a Marlboro Light, and looked at Jackson and Burlane. "So that was it," he heard himself telling Ara Schott. Schott had gone over this twice, step by step, detail by detail.

"Yes," said Schott. Schott liked storms. He remembered driving through Utah once, or maybe it was Wyoming, in an electrical storm that had been genuinely frightening. The clouds had come first, he remembered, black clouds that rolled and billowed from the west. Then it turned dark. Then the lightning came. Schott remembered clearly his anxiety: there was no place to stop, nowhere to go, nothing to do but drive on through the rain. The lightning touched ground close by and turned the darkness a bright, startling white.

"His story was he did it because he thought the Fascists were going to overrun Europe?" Neely poured himself some more coffee from the insulated stainless-steel pot on his desk.

"Yes," Schott said again.

"These storms are something else," said Burlane. "Bastards hang in there and won't go away. Raining in New York yesterday, same as here. You got any whiskey, Peter?" He gestured toward Neely's teak liquor cabinet.

"Help yourself," Neely said. He rested his forehead in the palm of his hand.

Burlane retrieved a fifth of Old Bushmills. "Ahh, Irish. A dollop do you think? We need it."

Jackson and Neely smiled. Schott held up his cup. Burlane spiked their coffee. They sat quietly, the four of them, watching the lightning. They listened to the thunder pop and crack. They watched the trees bend under the wind. When they finished their Irish coffee they made more—two-thirds whiskey to a third coffee.

"Whenever I see lightning like this I remember Galveston, Texas," said Jackson. "I used to go down there to see my grandfather when I was a kid. Storms come in off the Gulf you wouldn't believe."

Neely laughed. "Charlottesville for me." Neely had grown up in Charlottesville. His father had been a professor of military history at the University of Virgina. "Jim?" He looked at Burlane.

"For me it was a storm near the Czech border. I was supposed to be debriefing a defector, a queer who may or may not have been a double." Burlane shook his head.

"Oh?" Schott asked.

"Well, he was or was not a double depending on whether he was or was not a double." Burlane looked disgusted; he ran his tongue over the front of his teeth. "It was at Hainburg on the Danube."

"For me it was Utah, or maybe Wyoming, I can't remember," said Schott.

"I remember the queer had these great big brown eyes and he looked at me like a woman. I've always been a straight diver and it scared hell out of me," said Burlane. He had never admitted that to anyone. The allegation that Derek Townes was KGB was like a death in the family. This was no time for bullshitting.

Schott held his cup up for a refill. "There was nowhere to go. I was alone on the road. There was no place to stop. That was when I owned a Renault. The lightning was everywhere, twisting and ripping down from the blackness just like it is now." That said, Schott jerked upright at another crack of thunder directly overhead.

"So in the end the country relies on us," said Neely. He looked at Schott.

"I suppose it does." Schott stood up. "I have to take a piss."

"When you get back, I suppose we'll have to go over it one more time."

Schott sighed. "I suppose."

They waited, saying nothing, until he returned.

"Now then," Neely said.

Schott loosened his tie. "As I said, there were several things that bothered me. One was the Turk's knowing Burlane's name."

Burlane looked disgusted. "Christ, how many times do I have to explain that? You people've been reading too many paperbacks. How many people like Emil are around to do jobs for us do you suppose? The truth is we deal with people who know one another. It's an underground of sorts. You send me in there three or four times, my name gets around. It can't be helped."

Schott was still skeptical. "Then there was the kid with his perfect English. You want to tell me how a kid who speaks English like that winds up running intelligence agents across the Black Sea?"

"Emil said he learned it from nuns. It's possible. That was a last-minute proposition, Ara. You have to take chances. Sure, you could check the kid out and Emil too, but it'd be like issuing invitations to Konsomov."

Schott fixed himself another Irish coffee.

"Okay, Jim, nuns it is. You want to tell Neely and Jackson here just how it is that a man follows us across the golf course? The guy twists and goes down. We don't hear anything but he's down there nevertheless."

Neely interrupted. "And still you make it to your boat and escape into the darkness."

"Until sunrise," Schott said. "I'm given plenty of time to debrief Philby when a Soviet patrol boat overtakes us. The captain retrieves Philby and his gunners blast a neat little hole in our bow. They did a nice neat job, like surgeons."

"Leaving you there," Neely said.

Schott nodded. "Leaving us there. He could have had us cut in half with machine guns. He could have hung around to watch us drown. He didn't. Forty minutes later we're picked up by a Turk." He looked at Burlane for an answer.

"Beats the shit out of me," Burlane said. "How was he supposed to know there was a Turk fishing the next block?"

"He seemed to know right where to find us," Schott said.

Burlane shrugged. "Fuck."

"You have to admit it was a bit of coincidence. We were fogged in. We couldn't see more than a couple hundred yards. They couldn't possibly see us from the air, yet there they were."

"Dammit, Ara, if it was a Konsomov play, do you think he'd be so obvious as all that?"

"Maybe he made it obvious to throw us off."

"Jesus Christ!" Burlane was losing his patience. "Okay, now we're told Philby's back in Moscow like nothing happened. He's got the same apartment, the same wife, the same privileges. He still spends a few hours a day at Moscow Center. There're no rumors, nothing. Anybody here want to explain that?"

"It doesn't make any sense to me," said Neely. He looked at Burlane.

"What can I say?" Burlane said.

Jackson coughed. "There was a twister reported south of Fairfax this morning."

Schott looked at Neely. "Our people in Moscow report no unusual rumors about Philby at all?"

"None," agreed Neely. "Philby had a holiday in Yalta and returned when his time was up. That was it. There is no suggestion that anything unusual happened. The only thing is he's knocked off his late-night walks, which makes Konsomov's people happy."

Schott considered that. "If this was a Konsomov play, he'd kill Philby."

"We'd expect it," Neely said.

"I agree," Jackson said.

Neely flinched at a clap of thunder. "Maybe Philby's still working for the Brits."

Schott shook his head. "He'd never be able to do that. The Soviets catch him and they'd skin him with pliers."

"What do you think happened?" Neely asked Jackson, who had said little.

Jackson ran a hand down the side of his broad face. "I don't know."

"The thing is," Schott said, leaning forward in his chair, "the thing is I believed him. He sounded right. I believed his confession. I believed his reasons for doubling against the British. I believed he wanted to get out of Moscow. I believed it all. I believed him about Ostrov. There in the boat, face-to-face, I believed him."

"Then we have to find out," Neely said.

Schott waited for a great, lazy roll of thunder which was punctuated by snaps, booms, and jarring cracks. "I think so."

"Despite the fact that Philby's back in Moscow like nothing had happened?"

"It's an instinctive thing, Peter. I believed him. He was telling the truth; I'm certain of it. Kim Philby believes in his heart of hearts that Derek Townes is KGB. Just what in the hell is going on over there I don't know."

"We have to find out."

"Certainly we have to find out. In the meantime we have to do what we can about Townes before he's nominated for President."

"Without the FBI?"

"Without the FBI. Philby was clear and adamant on that point. He says the Soviets have a well-placed man in the Bureau and I believe him. We do it ourselves."

"You do it."

Schott looked at Burlane. "You up for a little burglary, Mr. Burlane."

Burlane smiled, "Name it."

"We need to use the Bureau's computers. We'll need their access codes."

"It can be done, Ara. A little burglary there too. You know how to use the things I take it?"

"If you can get us inside, I can use the computers."

Neely stood and looked at the lake that had been a parking lot twenty minutes earlier. "You two can keep in touch with me through Jackson. He has reason to see me every day. There should be no records kept."

"No notes, nothing." Jackson looked at Schott.

Schott closed his eyes and sighed heavily. "We'll need the computer."

"You'll need that," Jackson said.

"We need to find Townes's control," said Schott. "That should be someone he's known from the beginning, since he was recruited. That means he's going to be in the FBI data somewhere. If he's there, we'll find him."

"Sure," Burlane said.

Schott tried to be patient. "I repeat, if he's there, we'll find him."

Burlane turned in his chair. "We've got days, not months, Ara."

"Your problem is you haven't joined the twentieth century, Jim. The computer finds him, not us. Cloak and dagger would take months, I agree. The FBI data is good, first-rate stuff. We simply steal the dossiers of everyone ever connected to Townes and tell the computer what attributes would most likely describe our man."

"Oh yeah, just like that." Burlane dug at his crotch, staring at the ceiling.

"You've got it. I'll write a program that'll do just that. You find a way for me to get that data from the Bureau without those people knowing about it, and I'll give you a list of names in a half hour. If you want I can program the computer to give us odds on the top three."

"Okay, sport. I'll get you your data somehow." Burlane walked to the window and flattened his nose against the pane. "Fucking rain."

Schott wondered briefly if he shouldn't check Burlane's dossier while he ran his paper chase of Townes's control.

19

Schott parked his Toyota in the underground parking lot of the Thornton Motor Hotel and walked across patches of oil stain to the elevator. The levels were distinguished by colors rather than numbers. He was on the green level; there was a yellow level, a blue level, and a red level. They were primary colors, at least, not apricot, avocado, and persimmon. For that Schott was grateful. It was a culture that was bored, a fact that once bothered Schott. But elevator levels identified by color no longer concerned him. His job was to ensure that the proprietors of the Thornton Motor Hotel had the freedom to mark their elevator levels in Sanskrit if they chose.

The above-ground levels were numbered. He punched number twelve and stared at the artificial wood grain of the elevator wall until the door slid open. He was met there by a Secret Service agent who accepted his identification and allowed him to continue down the carpeted hallway. He walked past an alcove with a low table, an ice machine, and a soft-drink machine, until he came to number 1216. He paused and punched the door-bell.

"Just a moment, please," a woman's voice called from inside.

Schott waited. If he had his choice, he wouldn't be talking to this or any other woman under these circumstances.

The door was opened by a tall, striking woman with shoulder-length blond hair set in soft curls at the end. Susan Townes had large, green eyes, an aquiline nose, and an expressive mouth that now grinned at him sardonically. She wore tight black slacks and a gray blouse that was undone to her sternum. The First-Lady-to-be wore no bra. The bare breast that confronted Schott had a hint of freckles on its upper reaches and a nipple that startled him with its nakedness. He felt a sudden pang of envy for any man who had this woman for a wife.

"Mrs. Townes?" he heard himself saying.

"You must be Mr. Schott." Susan Townes took a sip from a highball glass. She gave him a lazy, crooked grin. There was a momentary silence.

"I'm with the Central Intelligence Agency," he said needlessly.

"We did have an appointment, didn't we?" She laughed.

"Yes, ma'am," he said.

"Chasing spies and all that."

Schott was overwhelmed by the presence of Susan Townes. He could smell her perfume. "Well, yes and no. This is more in the order of a fail-safe measure. As you know, the Secret Service is assigned the responsibility for protecting you and your husband. The FBI runs routine checks of potential cabinet appointments in the event your husband gets elected."

"So Derek won't be embarrassed. You look to me like you're the one who's embarrassed."

"Well, yes, I guess I am a bit." One part of Schott wanted desperately to see Susan Townes's breast again, another told him to keep his gaze high. He let his eyes drop for the briefest of seconds. When he looked up again, Susan's green eyes met his with a disconcerting directness.

"Well, I . . ."

"Good. There's no reason this has to be unpleasant." She turned her back on him and spilled some ice out of an insulated plastic container into a water glass. "I have expensive whiskey and expensive whiskey," she said. She poured Schott three fingers of Wild Turkey. "One of the perks of being Mrs. Townes; visiting governors don't drink Jim Beam. Would you like water?"

"A little, please," Schott said. He found himself staring at her ass as she bent over.

"Here you go. Please help yourself when you want more. The whiskey tonight's on a man who wants to be ambassador to the Court of St. James's."

"Thank you."

"Please, have a seat."

The living room of the Towneses' suite was decorated in chain motel golds and browns. There was a sofa, a matching loveseat, an easy chair, a small wet bar, a color television set, and a coffee table. On the coffee table there were news magazines and the latest editions of the *New York Times*, the *Washington Post*, *Los Angeles Times*, and the *Wall Street Journal*. There was also an issue of *People* magazine with Susan's picture on the cover. The headline said, SUSAN TOWNES, AN INTIMATE LOOK AT A VERY PRIVATE LADY.

Schott settled on the loveseat. "As I was saying, Mrs. Townes, the FBI is assigned by statute the responsibility for domestic counterintelligence, keeping us secure from penetration by the Soviets and others. The Pentagon has an organization called the Defense Intelligence Agency assigned the task of domestic counterintelligence—mostly near military bases—and for gathering intelligence in foreign countries."

"Which leaves you the responsibility for collecting intelligence overseas." Susan Townes took the couch.

Schott cleared his throat. "For the President and for the Department of State. Normally background investigations are conducted by the Secret Service or the FBI—except in extraordinary circumstances."

"I don't imagine the people at the FBI are very happy about this visit."

"They're not," Schott laughed.

"But you're still here."

Schott took a sip of whiskey. "We insisted."

"You must have been persuasive."

"Just because we're asking questions about your husband's past doesn't mean we believe he's done anything wrong. I don't at all wish to be Joe McCarthy reincarnated. But you do have to understand our position here: we're charged ultimately with protecting the security of the United States government. It isn't easy, I assure you."

Susan Townes laughed. "You don't have to go through all that. I understand."

"Really, I would like to finish. We've had our ups and downs over the last ten or fifteen years. Sometimes we've gotten ourselves involved in some episodes we'd have been better advised to avoid."

"Well, there's the Bay of Pigs, Chile, and Angola that I can think of right off."

Schott found himself wanting Susan to turn so that her blouse would open again. "There are those, certainly. We have a problem of being a secret organization in an open society. We have to be careful that we follow our charge as closely as possible. In the short run we serve Presidents; in the longer view we serve the public."

"Which is it here, Mr. Schott?"

"The public, Mrs. Townes. I would like to stress that President Burack knows nothing of this inquiry. He's ill. If nothing comes of it there is no reason that he needs to know."

"My name is Susan. Could you please call me Susan?"

"Certainly. You should call me Ara. We're both here for the truth, nothing more."

"You don't mind if I stretch out, do you?"

"Oh no, go ahead."

Susan Townes slipped off her light shoes, using the toes of one foot to push on the heel of the other. She lay back, resting her weight on one hip, her elbow over the arm of the couch. "I don't make a very good politician's wife. I don't feel comfortable giving speeches written by somebody else. I get tired of all the Machiavellian plotting. I get bored standing at Derek's side smiling all the time. It makes my cheeks ache. I like privacy. I like ordinary pleasures."

"I want you to understand that I'm not here as part of any crazy plot to ace your husband out of the nomination."

"Ask what you have to ask." Susan hesitated, then added, "Will you tape us?"

Schott shook his head. "That won't be necessary."

"Whatever." Susan shifted her weight causing her blouse to part once again.

The nipple was a soft pink—velvet pink if there is such a thing. Schott swallowed. "When did you meet your husband, Mrs. Townes?"

Susan closed her eyes. "Let me see, that would be in 1964 at the University of California."

"At Berkeley."

"Berkeley, yes. But I can't imagine you don't know that already."

"I suppose we do have most of everything on paper. And Derek?"

Susan Townes moved slightly and the lovely nipple was gone. "Derek was a student. He had a sex drive in those days. We used to smoke pot and make it in artists' lofts." She shook her head. "Oh well. He was studying for a second degree, in political science. I was an early admit; I was only sixteen years old. He was twenty-five. He'd spent two years in the Peace Corps."

"In Nigeria."

"In Nigeria. He spent two years working with sanitary projects and teaching English at the University of Nigeria at Nsukka."

"Has Derek ever told you much about his experience in Nigeria?"

"Not a lot, really." Susan shrugged. "It was his experience in Nigeria that he says got him interested in politics. Anyway, it gives him good stories for speeches to black folks in Detroit and the District. He has photographs of the university with bicycles all around. He has some perfectly awful stories of the slums in Lagos. I suppose he went to bed with a lot of black women but he didn't talk to me about that."

"Did he make any lasting friends there, people he still sees?"

"Well, he became close to members of the Nigerian family he lived with. The family grew maize."

"But he doesn't see them any more."

"Are you kidding?" Susan smiled and got up to fix herself another drink.

"Anybody else that you can recall?"

"There's Gereben, I suppose."

"Who?" Schott leaned forward.

"Milos Gereben." She spelled the name for him.

"Who's Milos Gereben?"

"A psychiatrist in Manhattan who specializes in neuroses of the rich. His sister was married to the manager of a British chemical firm in Lagos, something like that. He was there to visit her when Derek met him at a cocktail party at the American embassy."

"A naturalized American citizen?"

"I think so."

"Was Derek especially close to him?"

Susan smirked. "I don't know if Derek has ever been especially close to anyone."

"Oh?" Schott said. "You mentioned his name specifically. I just wondered why is all. What do you know about Gereben?"

"I think he was a refugee from Hungry as a youngster."

"A refugee?"

"Yes, I remember Derek saying he had crossed the Hungarian border at night."

"I see. You say he was a youngster when he crossed. How old was he?"

Susan took a sip of her drink. "I don't know. He was a student, I think. He's older than Derek, maybe in his late fifties now."

Schott made a note on his pad. "Derek never mentioned where he crossed?"

"No."

"Or if he was debriefed on his way across?"

"No. Derek mentioned him when we first met, then seemed to forget him until recently."

"This was at Berkeley?"

"Yes. Does Gereben mean something to you?"

Susan looked interested.

Schott laughed. "Oh no, he doesn't mean anything especially. This is all routine stuff."

Susan laughed. "This isn't routine at all, Mr. Schott."

Schott felt foolish. "I guess you're right."

"Just what is it you're looking for? Maybe I can help you out."

Schott got up to fix himself another drink. Susan Townes struck him as simply a lovely woman. "We're looking for whatever," he said over his shoulder.

Susan gave him an uh-huh look when he turned around. "Okay, spook, you ask the questions."

"You said Derek seemed to forget Gereben until recently. Could you explain that please?"

"Sure. Gereben has a private practice in Manhattan. When Derek was elected senator from New York they got reacquainted. Derek and Milos have lunch together whenever Derek's in New York or Milos is in Washington."

"Ahh. I see," Schott said.

"Tell me, Ara, will this take just one session or will there be more?"

Schott considered that. He didn't want this to be one session. He wanted an excuse to see Susan Townes again. "I can't imagine we'll cover everything this evening. Can you tell me about Nicholas Ostrov?"

Susan laughed. "I was wondering when you were going to get around to the good professor. I wouldn't have believed you people were that transparent."

Schott looked chagrined. "You'll have to believe me, Mrs. Townes, when I say your husband's past as a student radical is of no particular interest. I'm not here because I believe in guilt by association or because Derek's favorite professor was a Marxist economist. Professor Ostrov emigrated to this country. He has relatives in Warsaw Pact countries."

"I see."

"Ostrov, I take it, was a special friend of your husband's?"

"They were like father and son. Derek took every class Ostrov taught. We all three smoked pot together and planned grand demonstrations."

"Have they kept in touch over the years?"

Susan looked surprised. "Why no, they haven't."

"Isn't that unusual?"

Susan scratched her thigh and looked at Schott. "I don't see why."

Schott turned a palm up. "No big deal. A lot of public officials turn to their old professors for advice when they make it in the world; you know what I mean."

"No, Derek hasn't kept any contact at all with Ostrov as far as I know. Perhaps it's because he's concerned Ostrov's reputation as a Marxist could hurt him, something like that."

"What did you say Derek studied?"

"I didn't." She smiled. "It was political science first time around. Economics when I met him. Then international affairs for his master's at Columbia."

"Oh," said Schott. He knew he sometimes struck

people as a plodding figure. Susan Townes, on the other hand, liked to have a good time. "When was the last time Derek saw Mario Savio?"

"The last thing I remember about Mario Savio was that he was working in a bookstore or something. Derek made a new circle of radical friends at Columbia; the people at Berkeley just seemed to fade somehow."

"I see," Schott said.

"Are you looking for some kind of pattern?"

"To be frank, Susan, I'm not sure what I'm looking for. This is just territory we have to cover, an unpleasant business at best. We're aware of the possible adverse consequences to the Agency; the FBI knows I'm here. We have to take the risk."

"Duty," Susan Townes said.

"Yes." Schott smiled. "There's duty, certainly, but more important than that—truth."

"I suppose you want to know about Columbia now."

"Yes, ma'am." Schott did his best to imitate Gary Cooper.

"Derek's interest in radical politics declined sharply at Columbia. There didn't seem to be any reason for it particularly; he just seemed to tire. He was at the center of things at Berkeley. At Columbia there was a clique of sorts around Rudd; the chosen ones were quoted in the press and filmed for the evening news. Mario had his group at Berkeley. Rudd had a good thing going too. They were heroes. They got a lot of attention. They didn't like strangers butting in."

"And Derek wasn't part of the clique?"

"No, he wasn't. He could have been, I suppose, but that would have required some effort on his part. He wasn't exactly welcome. His reputation at Berkeley preceded him; it was as though Mark Rudd wanted to prove Columbia wasn't some second-rate or warmed-over Berkeley. He wanted people to know this was a New York show. This was Columbia. Columbia radicals. Columbia martyrs. Can you understand that?"

"I can see that."

"I'm not sure Derek was ever committed to anything ideologically, not really. Being a radical was fun in those days. It was street theater. Anything went, the more shocking the better. I think Derek's real interest was in power. When he couldn't be in power, he didn't want to play the game. He's on top of the world right now."

"Yes, well . . ." Schott tried hard not to express any emotion.

Susan looked puzzled. "I don't think you're interested in Derek's foreign contacts at all. I think you're after something else, Mr. Schott."

Schott smiled. "Ara, remember? I'm trying to be as straightforward as I possibly can."

"You would have to be committed, wouldn't you? If you were a spy, I mean. You would have to live and die by some notion of how the world ought to be."

Schott ran his fingers down the line of his jaw. He felt heavy inside his body. "That's an interesting question, Susan. You can look at it that way, I guess."

"Derek wants power more than anything else.

He's driven by the idea of holding power. Nothing else matters. My husband and I have not had sex in more than a year, Ara."

Schott didn't know what to say. He thought Susan Townes was a lovely woman, desirable in the extrene. "I'm sorry, Mrs. Townes."

"Susan. Would you please call me Susan? Everybody calls me Mrs. Townes. When I was younger I had friends, no more. I'm not allowed the time and privacy it takes to make friends. I have people who want to see me, of course, but not for me, because I'm Mrs. Derek Townes. They call me Mrs. Townes. Are you married, Ara?"

"No," Schott said.

"Are you attracted to me?"

"Yes," Schott admitted.

"Do you go without sex?" She looked at him straight on with her green eyes.

Schott grinned. "Mostly."

"Where do you get it, Ara? Where do you get affection, someone warm to hold on to you?"

"I buy it. I sit home and read history until I can't stand it. Then I go down to Fourteenth Street and buy it."

Susan Townes laughed a great raucous laugh. "That's great. If I could even do that it would be an improvement. Do you think I'm good looking?"

"I think you're beautiful," Schott said.

"Jesus, why is a warm body so damned important? Why?"

Schott sighed. "I don't know. I wish I did."

"You know, I could be a spy, Ara. Me. Anybody could be. Did that occur to you?"

"Oh yes."

"When we're finished, are you going to tell me not to talk to Derek about your questions?"

"I don't think so," Schott said.

"Why is that?"

"Because it probably wouldn't do any good."

"Do you think I'm a fool, Ara?"

"I think if I had you and Derek Townes had a sack of feathers we'd both be tickled, and that's the truth." Schott started to get up from the loveseat.

"Derek used to tie me to a bedpost and tease me until I twisted. I loved it. Do you think you could do that?"

Ara Schott wanted Susan Townes. She was his for the asking. He decided to be a fool. "Would you take your blouse off, please?"

"Certainly." Susan's hand dropped to the remaining buttons of her blouse. "I've never done anything like this before. I've dreamed of it."

"So have I," Schott admitted.

She removed the blouse.

Schott smiled. "Oh yes."

"Will there be anything else?" she laughed.

"The slacks, I think."

The slacks came down. When the slacks were at her ankles, she slipped her panties off and said, "If we start standard, we'll stay standard. If we start with imagination, we can go from there. The beginning is important. I don't wanna be on any goddamned pedestal."

"I understand," Schott said. "You don't want standard."

"That's not what I dream about. If you're going
to do something crazy, you might as well go all the
way."

"My dreams are your dreams. Come here then."
Schott removed his tie.

She came to him and stood in front of him. "Go
for it, Mr. Schott."

"Ara."

"Ara," she said.

"Turn around."

She turned. "I want the full treatment, everything."

"Beautiful." Schott gave her an affectionate pop
on the butt. "The full treatment it's gonna be."

"Thank you." Susan Townes took a deep breath.
"It's been so damned long you just don't know."

Afterward they lay in one another's arms, enjoy-
ing the lovely, musty odor of sweat and sex.

"I've never done this with a man, not ever. I
mean go to bed with him just like that. I've never
even had an affair since I've been married to
Derek. I've wanted to but I've never had a chance."

"It was grand, I'll have to say that," Schott said.

"I don't want this to be the end of it, Ara." Susan
burrowed her face into the hollow of his neck and
shoulder.

"You're going to be married to the President of
the United States. It's impossible."

"Promise me this won't be the end," she said.

"I don't know what to say."

She started to cry. "Please say we won't lose
touch. Please."

Ara Schott didn't want to lose touch either. He

knew what he was going to say was stupid but he couldn't help himself: it just came out. "You'll have to call me. There'll be security working the other way."

"Thank you, Ara. You just can't imagine. Thank you." She clung to him tightly.

20

His name was Doug Emery. He was twenty-four years old. He was a Maryland boy, born and raised in Laurel, located on the old highway between Washington and Baltimore. His father was a trainer at the trotter track in Laurel. Doug was a good student. He earned a bachelor's degree in information systems management from the University of Maryland. In his senior year he married a mulatto girl named Alice McNeese, from Cumberland, Maryland. That upset Doug's mother but she got over it. Doug's father didn't mind; he had an eye for beautiful women and Alice had liquid brown eyes that took your breath away. He understood. A year later Alice gave birth to a daughter, Cora, a lovely little thing. Alice's mother-in-law thought Cora was just gorgeous. That face she shared with Alice. The two of them became the best of friends. They were inseparable, in fact.

All that was fairly easy to learn with a discreet question here and there. Doug wasn't a drunk. He was faithful to his wife. He paid his bills. He was a registered Democrat. He was a member of the Army Reserves, attending monthly meetings at Fort Meade just outside Laurel.

There was no easy way to bribe or blackmail Doug Emergy. He was level-headed, well liked, and—with his knowledge of computers—had a future ahead of him in a Washington bureaucracy that couldn't function without computers.

It had been fairly easy for Emery to land a job with the staff of Senator Walter M. Bower's Subcommittee on Privacy. Senator Bower, a liberal Democrat from Michigan, was a ranking member of the Senate Judiciary Committee. Most of Bower's campaign money came from political action committees organized by Detroit labor unions. In the course of events some of the leaders of these unions—suspected by some of having Mafia connections—became concerned about the manner in which the government seemed to know everything about everybody at all times. This information was stored in computers working on behalf of federal agencies and organizations, which seemed to appear almost weekly in Washington. So it was that Bower asked for $200 million of the taxpayers' money to study the issue of privacy and federal computers.

The chairman of the Judiciary Committee was initially reluctant to spend that kind of money on yet another study. But when Bower agreed to sponsor a measure providing federal money for a coal-fired power plant in the chairman's state—

North Carolina—the chairman agreed. The $200 million was a trifle, the chairman said. This was an urgent matter; what's $200 million out of a federal budet of $3 trillion?

Bower hired a staff and rented office space not too far from the Capitol. He then leased terminals that were connected to government computers all over Washington. The idea was to find out what kind of information the government was collecting, on whom, and why. The union leaders who gave him campaign money complained that if a man farts in Grand Rapids, the fact of the eruption is recorded on tape in huge, sterile rooms that roar and buzz twenty-four hours a day.

It was at one of these terminals that Doug Emery sat, good-natured, with dimpled cheeks and wavy hair, Styrofoam cup of coffee in hand, waiting for good things to come.

Schott and Burlane were disappointed that there was no way to blackmail Emery. If there had been, they could have come by the various codes, passwords, and instructions to his terminal that would have enabled them to dip into the FBI's data bank to retrieve the information they needed on Derek Townes.

It was impossible for them to tap in on the lines carrying the data from computer to terminal because that was in code—developed in 1979—and was virtually impossible to decode. If they had a hundred computers and six months of time they had a chance.

But they didn't.

Their second option was to learn the entry code

used by a particular operator at a particular terminal. If they could gain access to the terminal, Ara Schott could write a program to steal information from the FBI's computer, a program that would erase all traces that it was ever used or had even existed. That would take about two hours at the outside, Schott estimated. He knew his computers.

Normally, an entry code would have been impossible to obtain except through an egregious break in security. But due to the nature of Bower's personality, Schott and Burlane got another kind of break.

It is one of the perks of senators with seniority to head committees and subcommittees. With committees come staff. With staff comes the opportunity to hire the sons, daughters, and other relatives of potential financial backers. Some, like Doug Emery, had to be trained and highly skilled; others could be college students momentarily bored with books. Bower made good use of the perk. He was loathe to spend all of his $200 million ration on physical security—better to spend it on payroll.

The unofficial but commanding standard by which power is measured in Washington is how many bodies one has under his or her command. Bower wanted as many as possible. He wasn't a bad man, especially; he was merely using good sense. A man does not come to be a United States senator if he does not know how to use power.

The offices where Bower's staff worked observed *some* standards of physical security.

Someone like Emery was allowed to use only one
terminal. The only persons using the room where
his terminal was located were those who had a
reason to be there and were properly cleared.
Emery worked in a walled cubicle so the colleagues in his section could not peer over his
shoulder. There was a rule that he could not
operate his terminal with other people in his
cubicle, no matter who they were. To even get onto
the floor where the terminals were located, a
person had to go through a deviously designed
L-shaped room. The bulletproof doors at either
end of the L could not be unlocked at the same
time. When you stepped into the chamber to present your identification, the door locked behind
you. You were observed by a guard behind bulletproof glass.

Owing to the pressures of inflation and Bower's
determination to use as much of the budget as
possible for the payroll, there were a few needed
security alterations that were skipped. They seemed small enough. Inconsequential, really.

One of these was that a small window on the outside wall of Doug Emery's cubicle was not blocked. The subcommittee had the top six floors of the
Lawrence Building, as it was named. Emery's terminal was located on the eighth floor. The windows of the sixth and seventh floors were dutifully
blocked and workmen prepared to do the same to
number eight. But they were stopped by Senator
Bower, who noticed that expensive nonsense on
his way to the New Senate Office Building. He put
a stop to it. "Just what is the goddamned point?"
he demanded.

It would take a human fly to scale eight floors to the unblocked windows, he said. "Nobody's gonna be able to peer in on our people working on the eighth floor." He said he did not believe in Spider-Man. Unspoken was a worry that the secretive appearance of a committee working behind blocked windows would draw undue attention from the press and renewed questions about his $200 million budget.

The windows of floors eight through twelve remained unblocked.

Bower pointed out, also correctly, that the only building of like height and in a direct line of sight with the unblocked upper floors was more than a quarter of a mile away.

That was where Schott and Burlane, passing themselves off as Washington lobbyists for an imaginary farm organization, secured office space.

It was there also where they took turns watching Doug Emery working at his terminal. They watched with a telescope that enabled them to count the freckles on Emery's hands if they chose or to trace on scratch paper the engraved design on the ring on Emery's right hand.

Schott watched patiently, thinking of sex and Susan Townes.

Burlane watched with patience, thinking of sex and a divorced woman, a dancer who lived in the District.

They were after Emery's entry code. Once that was secured, Burlane would be faced with the problem of getting Schott ensconced in Emery's gray metal swivel chair for a few hours in the dead of night.

The problem was that Emery had to use both hands to enter his code on the terminal's keyboard. Schott and Burlane could record the numbers and letters entered by his right hand—their angle gave them that—but not his left. If he happened to lean back or turn his head to sneeze, they would get his left hand. But only then.

Waiting for the right circumstances required Schott and Burlane to take turns staring through the telescope custom-made for the CIA by the German manufacturers of Hasselblad cameras, the cameras that took pictures of Neil Armstrong stepping on the moon in July 1969.

Schott watched and recalled the smell of Susan Townes's hair, the curve of her hip.

Burlane's fantasies were much the same, if a trifle more acrobatic.

On the fourth day they got the break they were looking for. Emery shifted in his chair as he entered his code, giving Schott, for the first time, a brief glimpse of his left hand at the moment of truth. The only problem was that the angle of Emery's hand—and the rise of his knuckles—prevented Schott from seeing the action of Emery's little and ring fingers. The thumb, forefinger, and middle finger, yes. The little and ring fingers, no.

Schott marked the sequence.

JHI9REX

JHI9RES

JHI9REA

JHI9EZ

One of those.

There was one minor problem with two dis-

quieting circumstances. Schott and Burlane knew
the computer was programmed to shut down immediately and accept no further instructions if the
wrong code was given three times running. In that
event the computer would notify security guards
in the building an unauthorized person was using
the terminal.

They could wait and hope they got another
break, which might take weeks, months, or never
come at all, or they could go with the 75 percent
chance of entering the right code.

"The election's two weeks off," Burlane said.

Schott looked down at the street outside. "Every
damned time. He just sits there square shoul-
dered. Why doesn't he slouch like everyone else?"

"He's a numbers man. He's neat and orderly.
Numbers people are like that; they don't slouch or
fart in polite company."

"He picks his nose."

Burlane laughed. "But notice he wipes it off in
the wastepaper basket. A real slob would use it on
the underside of a table."

"Damn."

"Well?"

"It'll probably be my butt if I punch three
wrongs in a row, not yours."

"A whole lot of things can go wrong. Three out
of four isn't bad."

Schott turned from the window, defeated.
"Okay, I don't suppose I have any choice. We can't
wait here forever."

"Good," Burlane grinned.

"The question now is how we get past all that

security. The doors are locked between floors and
there are security people on every level."

Burlane put his arm around Schott. "Ara, my
man, you leave the second-story stuff to me. I'll get
you in and get you out. You just do a little computer review so you can write that program in the
time you'll have."

Schott sighed. "It won't be easy."

"Nothing ever is in this business."

Burlane took a drive through the streets of
Washington the next day to see what could be
done in the matter of getting Ara Schott a couple
of hours on Doug Emery's computer terminal.
Nothing came to him immediately, so he went to a
movie that promised action and female skin. That
done, he had a sandwich and a couple of cold
Heinekens at the Hawk 'n' Dove on Pennsylvania
Avenue, down the street from the Library of Congress. Burlane considered himself to be an artist
of sorts in matters of breaking and entering. What
he needed, he knew, was inspiration.

He drove around the Lawrence Building.
Nothing.

He followed the avenues that move from the
center of the city into Maryland suburbs like the
spokes of a wheel. Still nothing.

When rush hour came, Burlane found himself
stalled in the traffic inching its way to Prince
Georges County. It was there that the muse
paused, rather like an outrageous hooker, and
blessed him. He was in the traffic outside the
Elsevier Building. The Elsevier was an eighteen-
story structure of concrete and glass that housed

the lobbying apparatus of the multinational oil companies.

Burlane didn't like the oil companies.

He looked back over his shoulder. The Elsevier was about a quarter of a mile from the Lawrence Building.

Now as it happened Burlane had seen the movie *The Towering Inferno* on television one night between rounds with a lady named Elaine. And he had read about the tragic burning of the MGM Grand in Las Vegas. There had been helicopters circling the burning hotel in network television footage.

Burlane grinned and pulled to the curb at the nearest bar, where he had a couple of beers to celebrate having found the solution to his problem.

After the traffic had subsided, he drove to Langley, where Ara Schott awaited the results of his genius.

"We need a distraction," he told Schott.

"A distraction?"

Burlane rested his feet on Schott's desk. "A diversion. It has to be big enough to bring on police and fire department helicopters."

"Ahh," Schott said. That made sense. He waited for Burlane to provide him with the details. Burlane was a professional at such matters. He had found a way.

"We burn down the Elsevier Building." Burlane paused, watching the shock register on Schott's face. "That is, I burn down the Elsevier Building. You wait for me at a helicopter parked in the

woods a couple of miles from Capital Centre."
Capital Centre at Landover, Maryland, was where
the Bullets played basketball and the Capitals
played hockey.

"What are you talking about?"

"I'm talking about getting you time on Doug
Emery's terminal. The only way to do that is to
burn down the Elsevier Building. I can pack all the
goodies I need into an attaché case. I'll trigger it
while I'm on my way to meet you in Landover."

"Hey, wait . . ." Schott began.

Burlane interrupted. "Bet you didn't know I
could fly a helicopter, did you? Well, I can and I'm
not half bad." He was starting to get excited. He'd
never pulled an escapade like this before.

"You can't just go around burning up
buildings."

"Sure you can." Burlane sniffed. "In this case
we have to."

"We have to?"

"The security in that building is nutty in spite of
the window behind Emery's cubicle. There is just
no way for us to work our way up floor by floor
from the street. No way. All the doors are locked.
There are God knows how many alarms. There are
guards on every floor."

"There's gotta be a way."

Burlane shook his head. "You've been watching
too many movies. No, the only way we can do it is
to land on the roof with a helicopter and lower you
down with a winch to Emery's window."

"For that we burn down the Elsevier Building?"

"You don't land on the roof of a building and

lower a guy four floors with business as usual on the streets."

"There just has to be another way," Schott said.

"Look at it this way. We're faced with the possibility that Derek Townes may be an agent of the KGB. Now we owe it to the public to find out if he is or not without destroying the Company if we turn out to be wrong. We've got two weeks. The oil companies have been ripping off the public for years; we all know that. When they want a law written protecting their interests, why then it's written. They make plenty off the rest of us; they can afford it. This is a public service on their part." Burlane laughed at the idea.

"Oh shit, Jim."

"No, Ara, I mean it. What do you want to do, burn down a building owned by public employee lobbies or schoolteachers? Or how about a hotel full of old people?"

"Come on now."

Burlane shook his head. "Look, nobody's going to get killed. They have a couple of security guards on the ground floor and that's it. There won't be anyone working in the middle of the night. We're picking on people who can most afford it."

"Can you imagine what it will cost them to replace an eighteen-story building?"

Burlane tried to be patient. "Do you want time on that computer or not?"

"I want it."

"Then we burn down the Elsevier Building."

21

James Burlane sprang for a classy three-piece suit—that is, the Company sprang for it. He wanted to look right striding into the Elsevier Building. The men who worked there, lawyers most of them, were high bucks guys. They called their whiskey at lunch and had their shoes shined by old black men. A thirty-buck haircut was not a luxury but an essential if you worked for Exxon, Phillips Petroleum, Union 76, Mobil, or Gulf Oil. It was not *their* wealth they represented before the councils of government, but that of multinational oil corporations. You wouldn't have known that from looking at them. They were arrogant and self-assured; they wore the trappings of power as though wealth was their own. They were working for Arab sheikhs as well as their corporate headquarters in Texas or wherever. Money was nothing to them.

So Burlane had no second thoughts at all when he strode into the lobby of the Elsevier, briefcase in hand. He walked confidently to the elevator and pushed the button. He watched the legs of a young woman in a trim wool suit. When the door opened Burlane got in—he was alone, which he liked—and punched up the fifteenth floor.

Once there, Burlane went down the hall casually looking for an unmarked door that would likely enter into a custodian's supply closet. He found one not twenty feet away. There was nobody in the hall. Burlane stepped into the closet—which was actually a small room with shelves on three sides—and examined the contents. There were vacuum cleaners, mops, buckets, soaps of various kinds. There were cardboard boxes of toilet paper on the very top shelf. Burlane grinned and pulled down a box. He took the toilet paper out of the box. He removed the device in his attache case and put it on the bottom of the cardboard box, set the timer, and refilled the box with toilet paper. There was one layer of toilet paper remaining. He placed each roll on the floor and flattened them with the heel of his foot. He put the mashed rolls of toilet paper in his attache case and left.

Fifteen minutes later he was on the street, hiking the eight blocks to an A & P grocery store where his car was parked.

Machines that flew always seemed to be magic to Schott. Airplanes did fly; he accepted that. He saw them every day over the Virginia skies on their way to and from National or Dulles. He had flown on a lot of commercial flights himself, to visit his parents in Ukiah, California, and to Phoenix to visit his sister and her family. When he got on a plane, he lay back and surrendered himself to the soft lap of technology. The stewardesses smiled and had good legs. The pilots were steady and reassuring over the intercom.

This would be a different trip.

The helicopter that Burlane had waiting for them that night in the Maryland countryside looked like a scratched plastic bubble over two small seats. It once had been painted green but had been repainted gray. The gray paint had apparently been purchased at a closeout; it had blistered and then had peeled. The result was that the thin tubes, the stuff of the machine's chassis, looked like they'd been chewed on by a beaver. Schott peered in and examined the cockpit. The inside had been allowed to gather dust, then had either been hosed out or allowed to endure a rainstorm without the canvas flaps designed to snap on the outside. There was a fine layer of silt on the metal plate where the passengers rested their feet.

The seats—canvas webbing on a metal frame—sagged from the weight of countless butts bound on God knows what kinds of adventures.

"This'll get us there?" Schott asked.

Burlane giggled. He pulled out his cock and pissed on the ground like a horse in a field. "Providing it's got enough fuel."

Schott jumped back to avoid the splatter. "How old is it?"

Burlane tilted his head thoughtfully, replaced

his penis, and looked at the helicopter. "Eighteen, maybe twenty years, something like that. It's an old fucker." He wiped his hand on his trousers.

"Couldn't you have gotten something a little better than this?" Schott tried not to look too concerned; he was a novice in the field and didn't want to appear too nervous.

"I suppose I could have, but not without leaving some way of tracing it to me. Nobody, but nobody could possibly know I have this machine. Just nobody." Burlane looked proud.

"Why is that?" Schott was learning to expect anything from Burlane.

"Because I stole it."

"I swiped it." Burlane grinned. He gave the helicopter an affectionate slap with his hand. "I just sort of hot-wired it and flew it off. The beauty of it is the people who owned it aren't in any position to complain."

"Why not?"

"Because I think they use it to fly pot from some fields in Virginia where there aren't any roads."

Schott tried his best to look calm. "Have you ever flown a machine like this before?"

"I flew it here, didn't I?"

Schott leaned close to the engine; it was filthy with oil-covered dirt. "I mean before this."

"I think so."

Schott looked startled.

" 'I think so'? What kind of answer is that?"

"I can't remember. I may have flown one like this in Germany about ten years ago. It doesn't matter. I've flown a lot of helicopters and I can tell you this little number's a beauty. Got a nice touch."

So that was the helicopter, the comforting presence of technology.

The pilot was rather like the helicopter: capable, experienced, but slightly battered from the past. Burlane was intelligent, that was routinely accepted at Langley. He was good at languages. He had a touch with machines so he could do things like install bugs, take pictures, pick locks, and fly helicopters. His physical appearance, however, was unsettling at first sight. He had thin, sandy-colored hair that tended to show dandruff at the roots. His nose, which was too large for his thin face, was twisted slightly to one side. He drank too much. He laughed at odd moments, causing people to wonder. Burlane had caught the clap on several occasions being, as he put it, "an aspiring cocksman with all races and on all continents." He liked to dip his wick. His dossier was clear on that point.

But there was one thing he did very well: his job. Burlane had a knack for muddling through that endeared him to Company gamesmen. The sleek man in charge at Langley overlooked Burlane's disquieting appearance and manner,

Burlane looked at his wristwatch. "Mickey says it's midnight. There went the Elsevier." He had an odd, bemused look on his face. "We'll give it a half hour to get out of control and another thirty minutes for helicopters to arrive on the scene. We'll leave in another half hour and join the fun." He leaned forward and examined the instrument panel as though he'd never seen it before.

"You blew up that building?" Schott still didn't quite believe it.

Burlane cleared his sinuses and spit on the field. "That was the plan. You want to get on Doug Emery's terminal, this is gonna have to be it."

"Jesus, still . . ."

"Time we go," Burlane said. He slipped into the pilot's seat and began flipping toggle switches on and off, checking needles and dials.

"I guess," said Schott. He took the passenger's seat.

Burlane leaned out and spit again. "This business scares the shit out of me, Kemo Sabe, I can tell you that."

Schott sighed. His hands were trembling. "Me too."

"This whole thing's gotta be done by me and thee, pal."

"I know." Schott looked around for some seat belts and found there weren't any. He saw the bolts where the belts should have been anchored.

"Whether we win or whether we lose, if anybody finds out, it's our butts on the line. There are people who will not, just will not accept our explanation of all this. You talked to Kim Philby? *The* Kim Philby? Sure you did. There he is going to work at Moscow Center every day."

"So we do it ourselves," Schott said.

"You're damned right, Kemo Sabe. If this fucking thing doesn't get us there and back, then it just doesn't is all."

Schott waited, saying nothing. He looked at his wristwatch. "What do you think?"

"Time, gentlemen," Burlane said. He began flipping more toggle switches and the cockpit lit up. A few minutes later the blades overhead began making a whop, whop, whop noise overhead. After that Burlane pulled back on the stick and the helicopter rose swiftly in the warm Maryland night for the trip to the District. The Elsevier, in the distance, was in flames.

Even at quarter to one in the morning there were enough lights in the District that the city looked like a great, sprawling spider's web from above. Schott recognized the Beltway encircling the center. He saw the Washington-Baltimore Parkway, an anchor strand of the web. Burlane aimed the helicopter at a flickering torch far in the distance. There Burlane passed near the confusion and headed straight for the Lawrence where, without pause or ado, he settled on the rooftop.

Schott sat, immobile, unable to move as he waited for the whop, whop, whop of the blades to slide to a gentle whup, whup, whup, then fall silent. The sound was nothing compared to the sirens of police and fire trucks up and down the street. But the blades sounded like cannons to Schott; every whop was a whacking boom in his imagination. He looked at Burlane who stared, wide-eyed, unblinking, at the roof of the helicopter. Burlane looked as if he wasn't breathing. When the sound stopped, it was Burlane who spoke first.

"Fuck, that was loud," he said in a conversational voice.

"Ssshhhhh!" Schott put his finger to his lips.

Burlane laughed. "We're in the middle of the roof of a building twelve stories high."

"Humor me," Schott whispered.

Burlane set about unbuckling the gear. There was a portable electric winch that would be spiked onto the roof above Emery's window. There was black nylon rope for the spool. There was a seat fashioned of canvas straps. He stacked the gear in a neat pile.

He then removed a tape measure from his coveralls. "The far side, not the inside." He motioned to a wall and gave Schott the end of the tape.

Schott wanted to look over the edge and see if there were police gathered below. Burlane looked unconcerned. Schott took the tape and went to the wall as he was told.

By the time he got back, Burlane had the winch clamped into place on the runner of the helicopter. "Helluva a fire, eh? Roast those oilmen's little weanies."

"Aren't you worried about the cops?" Schott couldn't believe Burlane's nonchalance.

"Too late to worry about that now. We're inside with no rubber. Get your seat snapped on there. Got your stuff?"

"Just a sec." Schott retrieved his gear from the helicopter. Burlane had supplied him with a series of nylon bags that snapped on to his belt. He had a bag for tools, a bag for his camera, and several bags for film.

"Snap 'em on, cowboy."

Schott snapped.

"Got everything?"

"I think so."

"I said, dammit, do you have everything?" Burlane's voice had a hard edge to it.

"I do."

"Over you go then."

"What?" Schott started shaking.

"Oh my God." Burlane looked disgusted.

"I'll be okay, Jim."

"Kickoff time. Get in there and give it your best shot."

"I said I'll be okay."

Burlane took Schott by the shoulder. "We're here, buddy. All that planning you guys do over there in Virginia. All those schemes. Well, the deal is sooner or later it all comes down to this or something like this. A knot in your stomach and a dry mouth. You don't think; you just do it."

Schott blinked.

Burlane walked to the edge and peered over. "You'll surprise yourself. Afterward we'll get drunk and remember what it was like."

Schott stepped into the seat, which was a strap that went between his legs and a band around his waist. He popped the metal snap of the seat on to the ring fitted on the end of the black nylon rope.

"Down you go."

Schott kneeled at the edge. Burlane put the electric winch into reverse and backed the rope up on the spool. "Be sure to hold on to the line like I showed you. Use your feet. Don't worry about people below. Anybody there'll be watching the fire down the street."

"Okay," Schott said.

"Now when you get there, don't forget to attach the suction device first. You cut; the device'll hold the glass. Watch the edge now."

"I'll watch it."

"Got your rubber gloves on?"

"Got 'em," Schott nodded.

"Got your camera and enough film?"

"Yes."

"I talk to you in the receiver now, you pay attention."

Schott swallowed. "Okay."

"If I yell for you to come a running, you come a running; I'll let you hang and reel you up."

Schott waited for a truck to pass on the street below and, without a word, turned his back to the ledge. Seconds later he was being lowered from the roof of the Lawrence Building. He listened to the whine of the electric winch overhead. He joined those on the street in watching the excitement of the fire in the distance. "Slow," he said into his transmitter as they neared the eighth floor. "Slow, slow, stop. A little higher, please. Good."

Schott placed a circular instrument that looked like a giant suction cup against the center of the pane behind Doug Emery's terminal. He gave the knob in the center of the disc several quick twists. He then took a special tool Burlane had lifted from the Company's collection of such instruments and quickly traced around the edge of the glass once, twice, and yet a third time. On the fourth time around, the pane swung free. Schott eased himself into the room, holding on to the pane so it wouldn't smash against the building. He unsnapped himself and used the cutting tool to slice the pane in half. He brought each half inside. That done, he unfolded a large square of plastic that was impregnable by light and taped it to the area where the window had been.

Schott wiped the sweat from his forehead with the back of his arm and unclipped a lantern from his hip. He plugged it in to a wall socket and switched it from the battery to alternating current. He aimed the light at the front of the terminal.

"Okay," he said into the transmitter.

"Do your job. Don't talk unless you have to. Anything comes up, I'll let you know.

Schott wanted to say something but didn't. He suddenly felt good about himself. He placed a slip of paper with the four possibilities for Doug Emery's entry code on the table by the terminal's side.

He punched a button on the console.

One sentence appeared on the screen in pale green letters: DOUGIE, YOU STUD, GIVE ME YOUR LITTLE NUMBER.

Schott had to laugh at that. He took a deep breath and punched up the first code on the list.

TRY AGAIN, HANDS, appeared on the screen.

Schott punched up the second number without hesitating.

TRY AGAIN, HANDS, appeared on the screen.

A bead of sweat slid into Schott's left eye. He dug at the eye with the heel of his hand. He pressed the button on his transmitter. "I've missed twice. You want three or four?"

There was a pause. "Four," said Burlane. "If you miss, jump in the saddle."

Schott punched up the fourth possibility. A vertical column appeared on the screen:

```
FD  MASTER FILE
    RECORD CONTAINS 180 CHARACTERS
01  MASTER RECORD
      05 FD-NAME                         PIC 9(5)
      05 FD-SEX                          PIC 9
      05 FD-DOB                          PIC 9(9)
      05 FD-POB                          PIC X
      05 FD-SSN                          PIC XX
      05 FD-MARITAL HISTORY              PIC XY
      05 FD-PRIMARY KIN                  PIC (6)
      05 FD-SECONDARY KIN                PIC (6)
      05 FD-EDUCATIONAL TRANSCRIPTS  PIC X
      05 FD-EMPLOYMENT HISTORY          PIC XY
      05 FD-CREDIT HISTORY               PIC X
      05 FD-LCR'S                        PIC Y
      05 FD-DCR'S                        PIC X(25)
      05 FD-CREDIT                       PIC X(25)
      05 FD-DRINKING                     PIC X(10)
      05 FD-SEXUAL                       PIC X(15)
      05 FD-RESIDENCES                   PIC X(5)
      05 FD-SUBVERSIVE ORGANIZATIONS
                                         PIC X(6)
      05 FD-FOREIGN TRAVEL               PIC 9(7)
      05 FD-IN NY TIMES, WASH POST,
         LA TIMES                        PIC X(5)
      05 FD-IN NEWS MAGAZINES            PIC Y
      05 FD-PRESS NAMES, CROSS REF       PIC 9(5)
      05 FD-POL ACTIVITY                 PIC 9(9)
```

05 FD-POL ASSOC	PIC XY
05 FD-PHYSICIANS	PIC 9(7)
05 FD-SEC CLEARANCES	PIC 9(5)
05 FD-ACCESS CLASS INFO	PIC X

Schott stood up and stretched to relieve the
nervous tension. "Got it," he said into the transmitter.

"Go," Burlane answered.

What Schott had was a listing of categories of
information compiled on those people with files in
the FBI data bank. What he did not have was the
instructions to the computer necessary to call up
the data on Townes or any of Townes's listed
friends, neighbors, and associates. That would require him writing his own program, a program
that would erase itself when he was finished,
leaving no record of his having been there.

Ara Schott was one of the best men with a computer at Langley. His estimate of two hours to
write the program was way too long. In his fourteenth minute he got an unexpected break; the
program was written in the thirty-second minute.
What the extra hour and a half gave him was a
chance to call up the records on 214 people—all
those professors, acquaintances, colleagues, and
others listed in a background investigation conducted for the FBI for Townes's appointment to
the Senate Foreign Relations Committee and those
people mentioned in connection with him in
articles in the *New York Times, Washington Post,
Los Angeles Times, Time* magazine, *Newsweek*
magazine, and *U.S. News and World Report.*

Schott punched the terminal console with his left
hand and rhythmically shot pictures with his
right, pausing only to exchange film cartridges in
his camera. The camera was the most dependable
and easy to reload in the stock at Langley. Schott
had received careful instruction in its use by
Burlane.

He was finished at 4:40 A.M. He stood up,
stretched, made sure all the film was in the nylon
bags snapped to his belt. "Done," he told Burlane
through the transmitter.

"They're still pissing around with the fire but
there aren't any copters still up."

"Let's go then."

Schott peeled back the plastic over the window
and looked outside. It was still dark but would be
getting light soon. He waited for Burlane to lower
the seat, then eased into it. The nylon rope was no
sooner taut than he heard the terrible racket of
the chopper blades on the roof and they were
away. Burlane headed west by northwest, over
RFK Stadium, over the area where Douglas Mac-
Arthur had routed the Bonus Marchers in 1932,
past the trotter track at Rosecroft, past the Beltway. The electric winch had reeled him in by the
time they got to the Beltway; he pulled himself
awkwardly into the seat by Burlane, who was
listening to police chatter on the radio.

"Thought you were going to take forever," said
Burlane.

"I think I'm hungry."

"Did you get what we need?"

"I got everything we need, I think. I could use a

big breakfast with three or four Bloody Marys."

"They got the fire under control a couple of hours ago."

"Took a half hour for my hands to stop shaking," said Schott.

There was a squawk on the radio. Burlane motioned for Schott to be silent. He leaned forward and listened to a woman's voice on dispatch issuing various codes. "A security guard heard us take off," Burlane said.

Schott looked alarmed. He twisted in his seat and looked back at the lights of Washington receding in the distance.

"We're okay," Burlane said.

"You're sure?" Schott felt a flutter in his stomach.

"I'm sure."

"What are we going to do with this machine?"

Burlane grinned. "I'll take you back to the car. You want to rendezvous somewhere for breakfast? How about Annapolis?"

"What are you going to do with this machine?"

Burlane adjusted a knob on the instrument panel. "I'll get rid of it. You worry too much, Ara. There's a fish market at the end of the main drag there."

"Down by the harbor."

Burlane grinned. "I'll meet you there at ten o'clock, say, and we'll find someplace to have breakfast."

Schott was convinced Burlane was capable of anything. He closed his eyes and thought immediately of Susan Townes. She was a sen-

sational woman, both intelligent and erotic. He
thought about her and had a full-blown erection
by the time Burlane settled the helicopter at the
Landover starting point.

Schott and Burlane had their breakfast in Annapolis, then drove to Langley where they developed
Schott's film. The rest was fairly simple. Schott
gave eight keypunch operators the chore of entering the data according to a program he had written for the occasion. Schott entered Townes's data
himself so there could be no possible link to their
quarry.

Burlane and Schott waited in Schott's office,
drinking coffee, as the data was entered. At
quitting time, Schott put his people on overtime.
They remained at their terminals entering the
data stolen from Doug Emery's access.

At 8:00 P.M. it was finished.

James Burlane stood over Ara Schott's shoulder
as Schott gave the computer its final instructions.
He had asked the machine to give them the three
top prospects for the man they were after.

The computer was succinct. It gave three
names, rank ordered.

      1. MILOS GEREBEN

      2. IRV COHN

      3. SUSAN TOWNES

"Whoa," Burlane leaned forward. "This is like a
pari-mutuel scoreboard. Win, place, and show."

"Gereben," Schott said. He was thinking Susan
Townes. The computer concluded Susan Townes
was possible KGB. He thought of Susan's hands
and breasts and thighs. That couldn't be.

"Would you look at number three? Wouldn't that be something?"

"Sure would be something," said Schott. He realized that he was in love with Derek Townes's wife.

"I assume we take them from the top."

"Yes," Schott said. His mind was buzzing from the burden of responsibility and from a fantasy smashed. Susan Townes!

"He lives in Connecticut, just up from New York."

"Yes, Connecticut." Schott signed off on the terminal.

22

Burlane was in a contemplative mood as they left the Bronx past Mt. Vernon, bound northeast past New Rochelle, past Greenwich, past Stamford, to South Norwalk on the Long Island Sound. The towns on the way had a nice ring to the ear: New Rochelle, Mamaroneck, Rye. Rye, New York. Schott turned the sound over in his mind.

Schott had never been to Rye. Was it named for the grain, he wondered? No. It would be named, ultimately, for a man. It would have been for a man who made a difference, a man who gave reason to be remembered. A merchant, a man known for his accumulation of wealth? Schott hoped not. Perhaps it was the proprietor of a roadside inn? A man full of stories who drew pints of stout for weary travelers. That would be nice. Or maybe he was a politician of some sort, an administrator, a judge. Or a farmer, a yeoman, a man of the earth. That too was okay by Schott. Rye was still clean, in his mind, pure. The people who slept in distant homes were trusting of Schott. Their security depended on him. Maybe Robert or Richard Rye, or whoever, was a soldier. He could have been named John, John Rye, a soldier in the Continental Army, a young man with a bride and young son. Had he stood his ground with his Pennsylvania long rifle and there, high on danger and flush with love of country, spilled his blood for sweet freedom?

And left Rye, New York, as a legacy?

Would they have a bronze statue of him in a park somewhere, his arms outstretched on his departing? It would be a gesture the old masters understood. The local historical society would have a monograph on young John Rye in the town library. Old ladies who traced genealogy would care; no one else. A local high school would do battle in his name as the Rye Raiders.

Schott sighed. The days of heroes were gone. He and John Rye fought side by side two hundred years or more apart. But there was a sweetness to the fight for John that Ara would never know. Rye had a chance to stand fast in a green field with the warm sun overhead. Schott was about to commit a felony, breaking and entering, at the residence of a psychiatrist in South Norwalk, Connecticut.

Schott's reverie was interrupted by Burlane, who adjusted the radio to a station where men sang melancholy songs of lonesome truckers and California lovers. Burlane sang along in the soft glow of the instrument panel of the rented Chevette.

Burlane retrieved a clay pipe and a soft plastic bag from his jacket pocket. "Want to fix me a hit?" he said.

Schott held the plastic bag stupidly in his lap. "I'm not sure," he began.

Burlane laughed. "Just load the pipe; it's been seeded."

Schott took a pinch of marijuana and filled the bowl. "How long have you been smoking this?"

Burlane took the pipe. "Except for our Yalta trip, I'll bet you haven't even seen it before, am I right?"

"You're right," Schott said. "How long you been smoking this?"

Burlane lit the pipe with his cigarette lighter and took a long, slow draw. "Oh, I don't know. Six or eight years now, something like that. Jim Burlane, spook and pothead. What kind of music do you like?"

"Jazz. Not that cool stuff with dudes in sunglasses and so on. I like wide-open stuff—sweaty trombonists, a good man on the cornet."

"I'd have thought the opposite," Burlane said.

"Most people do."

"What were you thinking of back there?"

Schott smiled. "I was thinking of Rye, New York. Want me to fill that again?"

"Please. You want to try it?"

"No, thanks," Schott said.

"What about Rye?"

"I was wondering how it got its name. I concluded it might have been after a soldier, maybe, in the Continental Army, who stood his ground."

Burlane exhaled. "Thinking of what would

happen if we got caught?"

"Not exactly."

"Close maybe," Schott acknowledged.

"We could get wasted, you know. It's possible. More likely we'll just get caught. The locals would check our phony ID and put our prints onto the computer. We'd be flagged of course and the clean-up people would be sent on up."

"You'd think I'd get used to it."

Burlane lit his second hit. "This is only your third time out: Yalta, the terminal, and now. I've been doing this for years. You never get used to it. Someone cuts me in half and nobody knows me, nobody."

"Same with me."

"Sure, same with you. Only you've been inside all this time. Out here it's different."

"It's different." There were more lights up ahead. Port Chester?

"There's this singer I like, sings sentimental songs."

"Finished? Let me take your pipe."

"He's sentimental about small things: a young man getting his draft notice and knowing his days as a boy are over; a mother calling her son in for dinner, he's out there killing pretend pirates. He's got songs about wild horses and guitar pickers. There's something about those songs." Burlane's voice drifted off.

There was a small white moon out with a circle around it. "Cold out there tonight. Leaves'll crunch under our feet."

"Ara goes marching off again, hurrah, hurrah.

Ara goes marching off again, hurrah, hurrah." Ara adjusted the radio to fight the static of another station.

"This is it?"

"Uh, huh." Burlane geared down the Chevette and took an off ramp. They pulled into a toll station. Burlane flipped the correct change into the wire coin scoop.

They were soon into the country, into what was said to be one of the wealthiest counties in the United States. The white moon was low and to their right. They followed a macadam highway through the land that sloped gently to Long Island Sound. The shadows of the trees lay long on the fields between homes. The homes lay mostly in darkness, although an occasional light shone through the leaves.

The people who lived here were lawyers, executives, physicians, and others with leisure. They lived alone—they were unable to see their neighbors for the trees that gathered around the homes like centurions. They were educated people, people who traveled. They had been to the best schools. They knew what the world was about. They were sons and daughters of achievers, people who know about money and power. They were the first people to have milk in a cardboard carton, an Osterizer, a color television set, a microwave oven, and a machine that kneads, rolls, and cuts pasta. They were comfortable in restaurants; they knew how to order and tip. They knew how to pronounce Pepys and Simenon.

This was their country.

"High bucks," Burlane said, as though he had read Schott's mind.

"Live in the country by the Sound. An hour from New York."

Burlane slowed the car. "It's coming up now, a couple of bends or so."

"He is away, isn't he? I mean, we're not going to wind up in the Norwalk city jail or some damned thing?"

Burlane checked the rearview mirror. "Out with your gloves. He isn't due back until Sunday. Just do as I say and old Jimbo'll get us in and out."

"Where are we going to park?"

"In Gereben's garage. We leave it outside and we're in trouble; neighborhoods like this usually hire security types to patrol the place."

"When he leaves, he checks out; when he returns, he checks in."

"That's it," Burlane said. "The critical time will be when I'm trying to figure a way to get into his garage. You'll stay here on the side of the road. I'll go ahead on foot. When I give a whistle, you come on ahead. He'll have burglar alarms and good locks, so it might take me a while."

"And if the security people pull up before then?"

"When they ask for your identification, accidently bump the horn when you pull your wallet out. Don't do it when they first pull up. You haven't done anything wrong. Tell them you were headed for New Canaan and took a wrong turn."

"That sounds believable," said Schott. "Come on, they can't be that dumb?"

Burlane laughed. "What can they do? You haven't done anything wrong. The worst they could do is check your license and ID out on the radio. Your ID'll check out on every computer between here and Washington. They'll have to let you go."

"And you'll meet me back in New York tomorrow?"

"Just like we said. I'll be there. Remember, the horn honk has to look like it was accidental. Just a slight beep'll do. It won't take much."

"Got it." Schott absently snapped the thumb of a rubber glove.

Burlane pulled the car to the side of the road. "Gereben's house is about a quarter of a mile from here. I'll hike the rest of the way on foot." He got out and stretched, his voice coming in soft, frosty puffs. He started to walk, then thought better of it and turned, leaning down to Schott.

"You don't have to wear those gloves now, you know. Just when you're with me in the house." He grinned at Schott, who sat stiff and wooden-faced.

"Just let's get it over with, okay, Jim?" Schott was slightly irked. He felt he'd endured enough danger and nail-biting by then to qualify as a veteran in the field.

"Sorry, Ara, part of the initiation is all. You're doing fine." He looked up and down the road and took off at a trot in the direction of Milos Gereben's house.

Schott checked his wristwatch; it was 1:30 A.M. The Long Island Sound was in the trees in the distance. Schott kept the window unrolled on the

driver's side so he could hear Burlane's whistle. It
was a cold wait.

But not all that long. At five minutes past two,
Schott heard a soft whistle across the cold night
air. He turned on the Chevette and drove slowly
down the highway until he spotted Gereben's
home, a low house with a roof of cedar shakes. As
he eased the Chevette down the driveway he saw
Burlane in an opened garage waving him on. He
parked the Chevette beside a green Morgan sports-
car, a classic with a leather strap around the hood.

Schott killed the engine and sat as the electric
door opener did its job.

"Gloves?" Burlane asked.

"Got 'em."

"This place has every kind of alarm imaginable."

Schott's head jerked.

Burlane looked at Schott like Schott was nuts.
"Listen, I've got the touch with that stuff. I've
gone through heavier systems than this like I was
Houdini."

Burlane took him through rooms lined with
cedar and natural stone. Gereben liked hand-
crafted wooden furniture and leather chairs. He
had mounted water colors of Long Island Sound
scenes on the walls. The rooms exuded a strong,
masculine charm, accented by the lingering odor
of rich, sweet pipe tobacco.

Burlane led him straight to Gereben's study;
Burlane stepped into the doorway and turned with
a smirk on his face. "We'll find it here," he said
triumphantly.

"Yes," Schott said. He agreed without knowing

why. He knew intuitively that Burlane was right. They would find the answer here.

"You should see this place." Burlane began unwrapping lightproof sheets of black plastic. "Let's tape her up, then we can turn on the lights."

Twenty minutes later Schott was able to make a full accounting of Milos Gereben's study. If they had all been read—and they showed every sign of having their backs opened and their pages turned —then Gereben's books alone would have marked him for a man of intelligence and curiosity. He was a psychiatrist, not a professor, and so had no publisher's freebies to line the walls. Schott found that virtually all the books had brief notes in the margins, apparently in Gereben's handwriting: "Yes!" "Okay!" "No." "Bullshit." "He's been reading too much Jung." "What study?" "It didn't say that," and so on. The books were wall to wall, floor to floor, and in several languages. Gereben, reading Luis Borges in the Spanish, penciled his notes in Spanish. Reading Goethe in German, he made his notes in German. He had books published in Hungarian, books published in Russian. The latter surprised Schott.

"Would he have these around?" Schott pointed to a quarter of a wall filled with Russian novels and short stories in the original.

"Of course," Burlane said. "A guy like this, his ego wouldn't let him do anything else. Ask him and he'd tell you he learned Russian to read Pavlov and went from there."

"History, literature, and biography, he can't be all bad."

"Depends on how you look at it," Burlane said.

"What's that?"

"History, literature, and biography."

Schott smiled. "I see what you mean. Where do we start in a place like this?"

Burlane took a seat in the leather-covered chair behind Gereben's desk. "Well, now." He grinned. "You know how to ask a question."

What he did next seemed incredible to Schott at the time. Later, in retrospect, it still was difficult to believe. The book on James Burlane was that he was primarily a technician. He took his orders and went out there and got things done in countries where there was reason to believe you were being watched by goldfish and fence posts. He had a sense of humor given to non sequiturs, unfathomable aphorisms, and cynical asides. Hell, Burlane was even left-handed. Now, butt ensconced in Gereben's chair, Burlane revealed another side of himself. He looked up at Schott and said, "Okay, my man, I'm going to show you a trick. In addition to all my other charms and talents, I read. You didn't know that, eh? Well, I do."

Schott looked at his wristwatch.

"Listen, Ara, we couldn't possibly go through a room like this systematically. There's just not enough hours left. We'd work ourselves to exhaustion and still not find what we want."

"So what do we do?"

"Sit down."

Schott looked around the room, picked an easy chair, and sat. "I see what you mean."

"This guy reads."

"You said that before."

Burlane gestured toward a wall of books. "I mean he really reads, Ara."

"We know that," Schott said.

"But does he write?"

"Huh?" Schott looked puzzled.

"Probably some. He has a typewriter here but the ribbon looks brand new. He has this room rigged to listen to patients, if necessary. There's a machine built into his desk. He probably takes his tapes to his New York office to have them transcribed, letters or whatever. Look here, a drawer full of tapes." Burlane motioned to the desk with his head.

"You think we should start with the tapes?"

"Well, if we were to establish priorities ..." said Burlane.

"I think we should."

"Then I think the tapes, yes."

"Okay, I'll go second. I'll have to think about it."

"Now then, we can choose from the drawerful of tapes here—all marked with name and date with tape over that. Or we can check the unmarked extras in this drawer here." Burlane tapped the other side of the desk with his fingers.

Schott got up and walked around the desk to look at the open drawer of marked tapes. "There have to be seventy or eighty tapes here. It would take us all night to listen to that stuff. So go for the ten unmarked extras, you're saying?"

"Playing the odds," Burlane said. "You pick a number."

"Nine," Schott said.

"Poor number."

"Why's that?"

Burlane chose a cassette. "Because Asians think in odd numbers, Europeans in even. I say we start with number four." He popped the cassette into the recorder in Gereben's desk.

Schott later vowed that he would swear to it on a Bible if necessary, but so help him God what followed next was true. It happened. Burlane punched the Play button. What was recorded on the tape—as later transcribed in painstaking detail by Schott—was this, G for Gereben, T for Derek Townes:

G: You're asleep now.

T: Yes.

G: Are you comfortable?

T: Yes.

G: I have a number of questions for you, Derek. It is necessary for you to be absolutely honest.

T: I understand.

G: I'm told you've been having emotional problems. Can you tell me about them?

T: Emotional problems?

G: That's what I was told.

T: Running for President isn't easy, if that's what you mean. To win the presidency you have to stay right square in the middle. What pleases coal miners doesn't necessarily set well with farmers. What pleases the North pisses off the South. I've got business to think of, labor, the military, Congress. Everybody wants to go with a winner, of course. I'm lucky there. But you never know. One screw-up, one gaffe—you never know. The voters are like cattle: spook them one week before the election and it's all over.

G: A lot of pressure.

T (*laughs*): A lot of pressure! You just don't know.

G: It must be hard.

T: You've seen pictures of Johnson and Nixon. It turns you old.

G: The price for all that power, Derek.

T: You don't know about price. You don't have any idea what price a man can pay.

G: Try me.

T (*pauses*): I can't.

G: You're talking about something other than running an election campaign.

T (*sighs audibly*): I'm talking about treachery.

G: Oh?

T: Yes.

G: You want to tell me about it?

T: I can't.

G: You're talking about the Soviet Union, aren't you?

T: Yes.

G: Remember, Derek, it was I who introduced you to Nicholas Ostrov. It's okay to talk to me. I've been working for the party ever since before I crossed the Hungarian border in 1956.

T (*long pause*): I still don't know.

G: The party is worried about you, Derek. You're here at the suggestion of your control.

T: I should never have come.

G: Your control was concerned. I'm a professional, Derek.

T: I know.

G: If we talk about it, maybe we can get it resolved somehow.

T: If only Lenin were still alive today.

G (*pauses*): No one lives forever, Derek.

T: At least he died a natural death.

G: You want to tell me about the treachery.

T (*angrily, his voice changing*): I don't have to tell you about it, Gereben. You know damned well what I'm talking about.

G: You feel guilty. You feel you are betraying the American people, people who trust you.

T: What? (*laughs*) The American people! You think I'm worried about betraying the American people?

G (*pause*): I can understand that. The honor, the reverence, the trust.

T (*a hard, even reply*): You know damned well what I'm talking about, Gereben. You're one of them.

G: I'm not sure I understand, Derek.

T: Fuck if you don't.

G: I don't, really.

T: I'm talking about Stalin.

G: Stalin?

T: When I was in exile in Alma-Ata in 1928, I sent five hundred telegrams to my supporters. In the course of ten years, Stalin systematically murdered each one.

G (*startled*): What?

T: He tried to erase my name from the history of the revolution, me, who led the revolt of the St. Petersburg Soviet; me, who saved the Bolsheviks

from the White Armies. I shouldn't have to tell you
this, Milos; you're an educated man.

G: Trotsky?

T: Yes.

G (*clears his throat*): Leon Trotsky?

T (*laughs*): In the flesh, Milos.

G (*long pause*): I'm afraid I don't understand.

T: What don't you understand?

G: You're telling me you're Leon Trotsky?

T: Of course.

G: Trotsky was assassinated in 1940.

T (*angrily*): I'm afraid this conversation is at an
end.

G: Please, please sit. I was just surprised, that's
all. I do want to hear what you have to say.

T: The bastards.

G: Tell me how you came to be Leon Trotsky.

T (*laughs*): I don't know why not. You could say I
was reincarnated, but only nuts and mystics believe in reincarnation. This is the age of science.

G: You were reincarnated?

T (*interrupts*): Or you could say I am mad, a conclusion befitting shrinks such as yourself. I think,
therefore I am. Who said that? I can't remember.
Anyway, it's true. I've been Trotsky off and on now
for about eighteen months.

G: Off and on?

T: Yes, off and on.

G (*pauses*: How often would you say?

T: How often am I Trotsky?

G: Yes.

T: Well, it started every three or four months,
then it was once a month or so. It's getting harder

and harder now, though.

G: How is it getting harder?

T: Derek Townes doesn't have any privacy. It isn't time yet to go public. Poor bastard.

G: Poor bastard?

T: Townes.

G: Oh.

T: The KGB hooked him when he was just a kid really, caught up in all that Vietnam hysteria. He was vulnerable. He was a believer and they took advantage of him.

G: That's what made him want to be you?

T: They wouldn't let him off the hook. There was no turning back.

G: I see.

T: No, you don't. There is no way under the sun you could see. You grew up as a youngster to be a Communist. There has been no other way for you, not ever. You're an officer of the KGB, an agent, not a traitor.

G: Townes made a commitment to a cause.

T: What did he know about causes? He was a kid really, an adolescent in an adult body.

G: You say he didn't know about causes. What about you? If anybody in this century knew about causes it was you. Why did Derek Townes become you?

T (*laughs*: Ever the scientist, eh, Milos?

G: I don't understand.

T: Maybe he didn't choose me. Maybe fate chose me. Maybe it was the gods, whatever.

G: Reincarnation?

T: Yes.

G: I don't believe in fate, Leon. May I call you Leon?

T: Certainly.

G: I don't believe in reincarnation or the gods. I'm a man of science.

T: What does it matter? I am Trotsky.

G: Just assume, for a moment, that this is something else, something for which there is a rational explanation.

T (*laughs*): Assume that I'm crazy?

G (*concerned*): I didn't say that.

T: But that's what you mean.

G: Crazy suggests something aberrant, something deviant. All I'm saying is that there may be a perfectly normal explanation for your choosing to be Trotsky.

T: I am Trotsky. If you want this conversation to continue, you'll have to accept that.

G (*quickly*): I do. I do.

T: No, you don't.

G: Tell me, do you will yourself to become Trotsky or does it just happen?

T: You're talking about Townes now?

G: Yes, Townes.

T (*long pause*): I've thought about that. I think it was born out of Townes's hatred of the Soviets for trapping him and holding him while he rose and became successful. They helped him with laundered money, of course, but Townes was convinced he could have done it on his own, done it without their support. He could have been elected to the U.S. Senate on his own, everything.

G: He thought he could have become President

on his own?

T: There's no question in his mind. But he's working for the Soviets, betraying the system he came to admire, a system that recognized and rewarded his talents and instincts. He hated them. The betrayal was an almost unbearable burden. He drank too much. He began to quarrel with his control. But the Soviets never give up, never.

G: He was a prize. I can see that.

T: For the Soviets? Oh yes, no way they would let him go. Their own man in the White House. If he wanted to be President, if he valued life itself, he would do what he was told.

G: How did he choose Trotsky?

T: I chose Townes.

G: Could you explain that?

T: It just happened. I chose him. I took him over. I have need of him.

G: You have need of him?

T: Townes will be an instrument of the workers, but not in the way the Soviets think.

G: Could you explain that?

T: All I could do in the twenties and thirties was give speeches, write articles, and keep moving from Stalin. I had power during the war against the White Russians but gave it up after we had won. You'll remember I was Lenin's choice as his successor, but that never came to pass.

G: Stalin saw to that.

T: He hated me because I was Lenin's colleague, hated me because I was admired. He got me the first time around, but not this time. That's why I took over Derek Townes.

G: I see.

T: By himself, Townes was powerless to do anything about his situation. He was intimidated, bullied. He lacked audacity and nerve. The presidency meant too much to him. Townes loves power. That's one thing we have in common.

G: You're saying the emotional burden is too much for him to handle.

T: He's going to pieces. He's vulnerable; that's why I chose him.

G: What if he wanted you out?

T (*laughs*): Why should he? We both have a mutual hate, mutual cause for revenge. At first he tried to deny me, then he just kind of gave up. He's an intelligent man. He may be tormented by his bargain with the KGB but he's not dumb.

G: You're saying he accepts you?

T: More than accepts, he encourages me. He knows his history. He appreciates irony.

G: If Townes can't strike back at the Soviets, maybe you can.

T (*pauses*): Let's put it this way: when the American public elects Derek Townes President in a couple of weeks—and they will, there's no doubt of that now—then they'll also be electing me President.

G: President Trotsky?

T: No, no, President Townes. President Trotsky will be President Townes's little secret. (*Laughs*)

G: Tell me, what would you do if Townes permitted you to come out in the White House?

T: There are no if's involved. He's planning on it.

G: I see. But what would you do?

T: I don't know. I've given that a lot of thought but I have to admit I'm not yet certain. There are consequences to be weighed.

G: Can you give me an example, a possibility?

T: No, not now.

G: There's nothing I can do to get you to change your mind?

T: No.

G: Okay. I guess there's still one thing I don't understand about all this.

T: What's that?

G: I know you said you picked Derek Townes because you both bear the Russians a grudge and he was vulnerable. That's not enough, somehow. There has to be more.

T: Let's see. There is one more thing, I guess. (*Long pause*)

G: What's that?"

T: Both our names begin with T, there's that.

G: Yes.

T: Well, there is the fact that Townes did an honors thesis on me at Berkeley. It was a real opus, about eighty or ninety thousand words, a first-rate job. It was an original project and with a little editing he might have found a publisher. He was proud of it. It was good work.

G: I didn't know that. Why wasn't it published?

T (*sighs*): Because Ostrov and his control talked him out of it. They thought it might get in the way of his future.

G: The KGB said no.

T: It was not only a no, it was an absolute, goddamn, hell no! It was a terrible blow to him after all that work.

G: I think that's enough for this evening, Comrade Trotsky. We'll have to have another session soon. I'm going to count three now, then snap my fingers. When you awake you will be Derek Townes again and you won't remember any of this conversation.

T: I'll be back. You can count on that.

G: One, two, three. (*There is a sharp snap*)

The tape was finished.

There followed a long silence. Schott and Burlane were soldiers of the cold war. Alone and in secret, they fought their battles. For Schott it was largely a war of numbers, of probabilities and possibilities. He was counterintelligence. He was paid to be paranoid. He was surrounded by the KGB; for him there could be no other way. Even his critics in Langley conceded that, even as they resented his conclusions that virtually none of their operations produced anything but disinformation.

The first thing Schott thought was, why me? If this is true, nobody will believe me! They'll think I've lost it at last. Gone bonkers! Soviets on the brain like a tumor growing, growing until I've lost it.

But there it was on tape. "Did you hear that, Jim?"

Burlane stared into space, his mouth partly open. "I heard it." For Burlane it was largely a war of nerves and physical courage. He was convinced anything was possible.

"The English language is incapable of expressing what I felt listening to that tape."

"What do I say?"

"I think we should listen to it again."

Burlane nodded and punched the rewind button. Hadn't he always said anything was possible, just anything? They listened to the tape again, each of them staring at a wall of book spines without seeing the titles.

"Trotsky," Burlane said. "Derek Townes, and that was his voice on the tape; Derek Townes thinks he's Leon Trotsky."

"And what's more ..." Schott gestured to the tape recorder.

"What is more is he has said as much to Moscow Center via a shrink who works for the KGB."

Schott nodded. "Do you realize the Soviets have known about this since March?"

Burlane rewound the tape again. "I don't understand."

"The whole Philby episode from the very beginning was intended to let us know about this in a way that we'd believe."

"Why? I mean, why didn't they take out Townes themselves?"

Schott hesitated. "For the reason they couldn't take a chance on being caught."

"There was too much about the Yalta trip that was wrong, Jim. The Turk's knowing your name. The fishing boat on our starboard all day. The guy following us across the golf course. Hasan speaking perfect English. The Russians finding us in the fog and sinking us so cleanly. The fishing boat picking us up again."

Burlane put his forehead in the palm of his hand. "No, no, Ara. If it was KGB, why wait for so long and why put Philby back to work? To finish that play you'd have to put him in hiding. *They didn't do that! Why?*"

Schott started to speak but didn't. Burlane had him on that one. "I don't know," he said.

"Which means he is working for himself, as he said."

Schott thought about that. "Well, yes."

"Or for somebody else," Burlane said cheerfully.

"Yes, that's possible. What do we do now?"

"See if he's got another recorder around here and record this tape."

It ran their way that night, Schott later told Neely. Ten minutes later Schott found a portable cassette tape recorder in a drawer built into a hallway closet. They recorded Gereben's conversation with Derek Townes and left at 4:30 A.M., numb from the awesome responsibility that was theirs.

23

They were alone with the road and their thoughts. The radio delivered mostly static, picking up stations out of the ionosphere: from Terre Haute, Memphis, and Halifax. Schott adjusted the tuning knob. Burlane drove, alternately watching the rearview mirror and the shadows of fields in the light of the moon. Schott settled on a talk show from Buffalo, scowled, and turned it off.

"So how long do you think the Soviets have known?" asked Schott.

"Since last weekend," said Burlane.

Schott turned in the seat. "How could you possibly know that?"

"Remember Townes's campaign people made a big deal last week about how Derek Townes's doctor said he was wearing himself down with the campaign and ought to take a break?"

"Yes."

"Well, Townes said he was going to take the weekend off at his summer home."

"Oh," Schott said.

"His summer home is in the news all the time. You want to tell me where it is?"

"East Norwalk, Connecticut."

"On the other side of the estuary in front of Milos Gereben's home?"

"Maybe a two- or three-mile drive."

"They said that was his first weekend off since he settled in on Des Moines for the Iowa caucus? They said it didn't make any difference to Derek Townes if he had James Burack's blessings. That wasn't enough. He doesn't do things halfway; he plays a full court press all the way."

"His doctor wasn't kidding," said Schott.

"It looks that way."

"Even Philby seemed a little bewildered that Townes could do it. Remember, I told you we talked about more than Townes? He said he wanted me to understand why it was that he agreed to work for the Soviets, and how there was no turning back. He said it was important to him that I understand before he would tell me about Townes."

"You heard him out?" Burlane asked.

"Yes, I heard him out. I had to. He was risking his life, after all. He wanted to begin with himself for a purpose; he was convinced I had to know about him before I could understand his allegations about Derek Townes. Does that make sense?"

"Sure it does."

"He told me about going to the Continent as a young Cambridge graduate, seeing for himself the rise of the Fascists. He said he was convinced that Great Britain and the Western powers didn't have the spine to stand up to them. The only hope, he felt, lay in socialism. And for that reason he signed on. He signed on to keep the faith, to burrow into the intelligence establishment, to be in place when the Fascists took over. Only if the Socialists had people in place would there be a chance to overthrow the thugs. That's how it was put to him."

"And Philby bought it?"

"Yes, he bought it. He said for some of the same reasons Derek Townes bought it thirty years later. The logic of the times was that the system had failed. A system that worked would have found some way to withdraw from the Vietnam quagmire. Philby was young and easily attracted to the abstract. It was the same for Townes and his generation. It was fashionable to call yourself a revolutionary in 1968. It was romantic. It was okay for Philby when *he* first signed on. There was a feeling of euphoria, he said. He felt like he was joining a great and noble cause. But as time went on and he'd earned the respect and friendship of his colleagues, Philby learned what treachery is all about."

"Guilt," Burlane said.

"It was awful, he said. Both Maclean and Burgess were alcoholics, remember. So was Philby. The Soviets must have given him a liver transplant to keep him going. Philby always had a stammer. But as everything closed in around him it got worse and worse. Sometimes he could hardly get a word out. What I'm saying is that tape isn't all that preposterous if you think about the pressures involved. Townes has been hanging from the KGB pike for more than twenty years now. He's made it to the doorstep of the White House, with Konsomov's help to be sure, but more and more he's convinced it's on his own merits."

"Anyone would come to think that way. I know I would."

"If you think about it, joining the KGB is a lot like getting married. It's easy to fall in love, but sometimes impossible to live with the consequences. In the abstract communism's a beautiful idea. Bright people like Philby and Townes think they have to be part of it. And when the Soviets do the courting, it's damn well flattering. You know what it's like to be in love. Your lady turns you inside out."

Burlane laughed. "That hot feeling in the pit of your stomach; orgasms that feel like they're going to blow your balls off."

Schott shifted his weight on the car seat. He thought about Susan Townes. That's how it had been with her. She was beautiful even though he knew standards of beauty were set by fashion photographers and by Hollywood. He wanted her for himself. He could hardly tolerate not having her. "Signing on with Mother Russia is like marrying the witch of the East. It isn't until later, after it's too late, that you see her in curlers and have to endure temper tantrums."

"A fucking shrew," said Burlane. "She runs your

life. She's always there nagging, bitching, and complaining. She runs the show down to the last detail."

"Oh boy, yes."

"A demanding, one-way bitch."

"It was afterward that Philby realized how he'd blown it. He drank and stuttered but endured. Townes, now, he's another case."

Burlane leaned over to scratch his ankle. "Derek Townes quietly lost his mind. He went nuts. He wants to get the bitch, blow her fucking in half."

"If it was a wife, we'd read about it in the papers the next day, a two-paragraph story inside by furniture ads, maybe."

WOMAN STRANGLED, HUSBAND HELD FOR QUESTIONING.

The man who would be President in three days was a lunatic.

"Trotsky," said Schott. He shook his head sadly.

"Yes, sir, folks, you think Richard Nixon turned out wrong, take a look at this model." Burlane giggled and adjusted the rearview mirror.

"First Philby. Then Yalta. Now this."

"Nothing makes sense."

"No," Burlane said.

"You're wondering why the Russians let us go?"

"That and why Philby was allowed to go on his way like nothing happened."

Burlane geared down for a corner. "Born to do something all night, born to do whatever all day, doo dah, doo dah. Camptown something, blah blah day, oh doo dah day."

Schott gave Burlane a pained look.

Burlane said, "Stephen Foster."

"We've got three days, Jim."

"We'll muddle through. But I think I should say there's one unanswered question you didn't ask."

Schott looked surprised.

"Oh yes, there's another. A biggie!"

"Which is?"

Burlane gestured over his shoulder with his jaw. "Why we're being followed."

Schott twisted in the seat.

Burlane took a sharp right onto a narrow farm road. "On the way out, but I wasn't sure. Now on the way back. Look there now."

The lights of an automobile took the same turn and followed them, staying well back.

"Why didn't you say something?" Schott asked.

"I wasn't sure. I'm still not." Burlane turned left on yet another country road.

"It went on by."

Burlane shrugged. "Figured it would. We're on our way back now; they'll pick us up again on the turnpike."

"Are you sure?"

"No," Burlane acknowledged. "I've got a feel is all with some headlights here and there to fuel the paranoia. Nothing to bolt down."

"But a strong feel?"

Burlane shook his head. "Sixty percent, maybe seventy."

"Who?"

"I don't know."

"The KGB?"

Burlane shrugged. "If they're Comrade Konsomov's people, I have to admit I don't know what the game is."

"The Russians'd just take him out." Schott turned and looked out the rear window again.

"You'd think so." He slowed for the on ramp to the turnpike. "We'll find out who's back there tomorrow."

24

They finished a nice lunch of spinach salad
dressed with lemon juice and olive oil, lovely
fillets of sole poached in white wine, and broccoli
with a hint of cumin in the dressing. Neely, the
shorter of the two, liked the salad. He smoothed
the front of his mustache with the back of his
finger. Jackson was partial to the dressing on the
broccoli. They both liked the wine and Jackson,
with a slightly effeminate wave of his hand, ordered a second carafe.

Thus sated—feeling slow and sluggish—they returned to Langley in Jackson's Alpha coupe to
hear Schott and Burlane report on Milos Gereben.
They seemed rather like two large, secure toads
instead of two poor bastards who knew very well
it was midday Saturday and a President was to be
elected on Tuesday.

The responsibility for sorting out the mess was

theirs. They had no one to turn to, not the President, certainly not the Congress. It was theirs. They had to decide.

So they said the hell with it, we should at least have a full stomach. Thus prepared they arrived to hear the latest mad chapter. Jackson, on his way into Neely's office, sucked in his breath and wondered momentarily if he shouldn't be buying his pants a size larger. Not too long ago it was thirty-two, then thirty-three, then thirty-four—oh, he'd hated that one for some reason—then thirty-five, and now thirty-six. Jackson was dismayed. He didn't know if he could take size thirty-seven or not.

Neely's office was designed to be the most secure in the building. Neely pulled the blinds and sat behind his large neat desk. Paperwork on the desk sat in piles under polished agates. There was a handsome bookshelf filled with books about the intelligence business. Jackson sat on Neely's left, in Neely's rocking chair. Schott and Burlane sat in front in functional chairs with armrests. Schott sat upright, correct, and turned a pencil. Burlane dug at his crotch and sprawled, revealing brown socks that didn't quite match.

Neely turned the wedding ring on his left hand. "Now why don't you tell me, Ara, as concisely as you can, what exactly it was you learned in Connecticut?"

Schott sighed and—looking at Neely over the top of a yellow pencil—told the story as directly as he could, trying to anticipate as many questions as possible.

Jackson blinked. Neely started to laugh. "Now what is this, some kind of joke, Ara?"

Schott pulled the cassette out of his jacket pocket. "Here's the tape. The guy on this tape is either the impressionist Rich Little or he's Senator Derek Townes."

"You can take your pick," Burlane offered.

Neely glared at him and saw the mismatched socks for the first time. "Please, Mr. Burlane."

Burlane picked up the Sony tape recorder at the foot of his chair. "We brought this here machine if you want to listen." He didn't care if Neely got pissed or not; Burlane had had it.

"Leon *Trotsky*?" Neely lingered on the second word. He looked at Schott for an answer.

"Gereben is KGB. For whatever reasons Townes thought he should talk to Gereben."

"And Gereben hypnotized him?"

"Yes, sir."

"And taped it?"

"Yes, sir."

Neely looked at Burlane, who shrugged and dug at his ear. "Jimmy?"

"What he says is so."

Neely returned to Schott. "Who figured this out?"

Schott gestured toward Burlane. "He did, as I said."

"Poe and all that."

"It worked," Burlane said.

"And the tape was where?"

"Unmarked and in a box of empties, sir," Schott said. He wondered suddenly why he was sirring Neely. He had never done that before. Just as quickly he knew the reason why: he wanted it to be clear that the responsibility for the decision and thus blame for its outcome would be clearly. Neely's, not his. Schott's mind wandered briefly to the luscious memory of Susan Townes's body smell, then came quickly back to reality.

Neely looked at Jackson. "I think we should hear the tape."

"Yes, certainly," said Jackson. He too was thinking of responsibility and blame. He had fought bureaucratic battles before and occasionally bared his ass to the ax, but never, Jesus never, anything like this.

They listened to the tape, all eyes on Neely, who sat staring at the middle of his desk. When it finished, Burlane punched the tape recorder off and stood up. "I gotta take a leak," he said and left the room.

"It's Townes," Neely said. "Tom?" He looked at Jackson.

"Sounds like it to me." Jackson's instincts told him to be careful. They were going to be talking about assassination. If the angels had a side, Jackson wanted to be on it.

"Ara?" asked Neely.

"It does sound like Townes and he does apparently have mental problems."

"He thinks he's Leon Trotsky?"

"Yes." Schott didn't know what else to say.

Burlane was back from the toilet. "Well, do we shoot him or not?"

Neely looked startled. "What?"

"He's the one who thinks he's Trotsky, isn't he?

This is why we're all sitting here smelling our armpits. Our balls're on the line. It's them or us."

Neely smiled at the mention of smelly armpits. Neely was so rank he could smell himself. He oozed sweat. He smelled like a boar. But he just wasn't ready for Burlane's question. "You said someone followed you?" Neely asked.

Schott answered for Burlane. "We think so."

"If this were a KGB joke, Konsomov would have hidden Philby somewhere."

"That's the way I see it."

"No way would they follow you. Why would they follow you?" Neely was suddenly frightened. What if he wasn't good enough to be DCI? Maybe he was the wrong man to be making this decision.

"Well, I think we should find out just who in the hell was back there and why," Burlane said. "There has to be a reason; people don't follow folks across the Black Sea or southern Connecticut for nothing."

Neely couldn't believe it. He had just two days. How had this happened? It was like standing in the middle of a dream. "He still wouldn't be inaugurated until the middle of January."

Neither Jackson, Schott, nor Burlane said anything. They spoke by their silence. It was unthinkable to let Derek Townes become even President-elect. The walls of security would fall immediately. It was the first rule of protecting very important persons, as Neely knew well, that security goes up in perimeters. The first perimeter is the sweep, in which advance security people identify and locate the local crazies and politicals.

Their comings and goings must be monitored in advance. Next comes the itinerary, chosen to avoid the predictable; there must be alternate routes, chosen to allow for change at the last minute. Each perimeter of security closes in around the President: plainclothesmen watch windows with binoculars; they circulate in the crowd. Uniformed policemen block exists and intersections; they form a human barrier between the President and the public. The last perimeter is the Secret Service agents on either shoulder of the President; these men have sworn by their honor to sacrifice their lives if necessary in defense of the President.

This organization of concentric rings of protection was about the best that could be done under impossible circumstances. The alternative would be to seal off the President; there would be no more triumphant marches or parades in which to receive adulation. No man who would be President wants that. The Secret Service people once programmed a computer to give them the odds that a political nut might make it to the President, as opposed to, say, a mere crazy. The computer told them what they knew all along, namely that it is highly unlikely that any single human being could assassinate a President and escape with both his life intact and identity unknowable. It's a little easier for him if he just wants to assassinate the President, escape alive, and doesn't mind if they find out who he is. If he wants to kill the President and doesn't mind dying in the process, then there's not much that can be done to stop him. The nuts who can be identified and monitored, they're one thing. Those crazies out there whose brains are deteriorating, unknown to themselves or the people around them, those are the ones who are the worry.

Any hit on Derek Townes would have to fall under the first category. Given the efforts of the Warren Commission and the many investigations that followed, it was hard for Neely to believe there is a bit of evidence that is not somewhere, somehow, recorded. There is enough information on the assassination of John Kennedy to glut an ordinary computer. Neely knew the publications of the Warren Commission and various congressional committees took up yards of shelf space. It was all there, except possibly for the truth.

The CIA would have to make the hit and retreat absolutely undetected. Their effort would have to withstand any manner of investigation—in absolutely undetected. Their effort would have to withstand any manner of investigation—in vice of his platoon sergeant in basic training at Fort Bliss, Texas: if you get caught, escape then, right then, before the enemy gets a chance to get security in place. The same was true of the responsibility ahead of Neely. The longer they waited—and each hour counted—the tougher it would be to pull a clean hit then vanish.

Neely looked at his wristwatch. "It's four o'clock. If the polls open in Maine at eight o'clock Tuesday morning, then we've got, what, sixty-four hours left?"

Jackson shifted in his chair. "I think we should

pop the seal on one of Neely's quarts. We've got some serious talking to do."

Neely got up for the bottle and glasses behind his bar. "No notes," he said.

"No tapes either," Schott said.

"Amen to that," Burlane said. He got up to help Neely with the whiskey.

"No tapes." Neely opened his small refrigerator for some ice.

"Anyone says anything about this conversation again, ever, is a dead man," said Burlane. He stood up and looked at his companions over a glassful of whiskey and ice. "Listen, that's the only way it can be. We have to accept it and live with it and keep our fucking mouths shut."

"So what would you do, Jim?"

Burlane helped himself to some more whiskey. "You were thinking of a hit?"

"Yes."

"If we hit him with a weapon it would have to be stolen and have a telescopic sight. I'm the best shot here, so I'd have to do it. But it would be stupid. Measles is the smart way."

"Measles?"

"We kill him in a way that appears to be an act of God, a heart attack maybe, or a killer disease. Go after him with hardware and we're gonna get burned."

Jackson said, "You still have the same problem, Jim. Each hour we wait the harder it'll be regardless of whether we use hardware or try to dream up a measles scheme. Killing a President with the measles is as hard as shooting him."

"You have to contend with an autopsy," said Neely. "I was thinking of hardware because I didn't have any time to plan anything that elaborate. The same rules apply: we can't do anything where we'll be traced."

Burlane turned to Schott. "The computer dossier on Townes said he had several draft-resister friends who fled the country. Any who didn't come back?"

Schott leaned back in his chair, thinking. "Yes, several."

"I'm talking about close friends now, people who smoked dope with him and got carried off in paddy wagons with him."

"Yes," Schott said.

"Now then, are there any who remained incommunicado? Someone isolated?"

Schott smiled. "Nathaniel Aldeburg. He now owns a movie theater in Stockholm and by all accounts hasn't spoken a word of English in ten years."

"Any contact at all with Townes in that time?"

"Not that we know of. It seems unlikely."

"If I asked you to answer yes or no as to the possibility that Aldeburg and Townes took drugs together when they were students at Berkeley, how would you answer?"

"Well, pot probably."

"What else?"

Schott looked puzzled. "I don't know. Townes has always valued his mind; I doubt if he'd mess around with LSD."

"Uppers, downers, speed, what?"

"None of those, I wouldn't think."

"Coke? Would he have tooted coke?"

"What are you thinking?"

Burlane looked at Neely. "Okay, assume you've just been elected President. It's the night of the election. You've swept the country. What do you want to do?"

"I'm not sure," Neely began.

Burlane looked disgusted. "Shit, man, that's why you'll never be President. You want to celebrate, right?"

"Right." Neely looked foolish.

"You'd want to celebrate all that power. The most powerful man on earth from at least one pole of reckoning. You've got a real shot at history. As President you can change things."

"Yes, yes, of course," Neely said. He started to say something else but was interrupted by Burlane.

Burlane was on a run. He wasn't about to be stopped. "It's *the* night of your life, *the* moment. There'll never be anything like it again and you know it. You *know* it. The inauguration with all the balls and so on, that's anticlimactic. God damn it, when you've got it, flaunt it. This is your night to howl. Am I right?" He turned and pointed a finger at Jackson.

"You're right," Jackson said.

Burlane poured himself another drink. "Townes doesn't want to miss a minute of his big night, does he? The networks are busting their asses to get details on the landslide. It's his. He won. It's a moment that will shine always. He wants to make sure he'll etch it in his mind so that later he'll be able to think back and savor the details. He wants it to last forever; failing that he at least wants to be clearheaded the morning after. Yes, sir, this is *his* night. Tell me, Ara, does he walk around all night with a glass of whiskey and ice in his hand?"

"I think I'd have a few."

Burlane covered his eyes with his hands and his shoulders slumped. "You and Neely'd be a real pair. That stuff creeps up on you and before you know it, everybody thinks you're Buster Keaton. All of a sudden you're dizzy. An anchorman for CBS wants to interview you and all you can think of is you want to puke. After that it's sleepy time, and you wake up with a fucking headache that's tearing your brains out. No, no, Ara."

"So what would you do?" Schott asked.

"I'd toot a few lines of coke. The myth is that anything you can do well you can do better with coke. You can screw all night if you want to—just hump on and on—no problem. You don't feel sleepy. You have energy. You can go all night."

Schott smiled. He knew what Burlane was about to propose.

"The thing is Townes can't ask for it. He can't order it, not even from the people around him. But suppose a well-wisher, someone from his past, managed to get a little gift to him for his big night. So he opens the gift, seeing it's from Nathaniel Aldeburg, and what does he find?"

"Coke," Schott said. "Pure coke laced with R-Fourteen."

Burlane laughed. "Why, I think you might make

a good field man, Ara. Sure, and with a little note that says maybe, 'This is for your victory night. May it last forever. Congratulations. Nat.' Did they call him Nat?"

"We can find that out."

"If it's true, as the lab people tell us, that R-Fourteen can't be traced in an autopsy, there we have it. It's pure coke, certainly not enough to do him in ordinarily, but he's not used to the stuff."

"OD."

Burlane tugged at his belt. "FORMER BERKELEY RADICAL ELECTED PRESIDENT ODS ON COKE. People'd believe it. Coke and booze."

Neely looked fascinated by Burlane's idea. "The problem is getting it to him. They have people hired to intercept gifts and go through them, catalog them, and return them. Isn't that the way it works?"

Burlane shrugged. "We find a way around that. It can be done. I think you and Jackson should think about it."

"I agree," Schott said.

"Now, if Philby isn't working for the KGB, then he's working for someone else, am I right, Mr. Schott?" Neely said.

"That follows."

Neely felt the pressure closing in. He had been successful because he had never let emotion or passion get in the way of making the right decision. "So we need to find out who's following you?"

"I think so. Jimmy's got a little plan."

"Like I said before," said Burlane, "I think the

first thing we have to do—this afternoon—is to do a little running, have a little fun."

"To find out who's been following you?"

"It'd be nice."

"Meanwhile Jackson and I work on a way to get Nat's package to his old friend?"

"That's what I'd do."

"I agree," Neely said. Burlane was right even if he was a slob. Neely's career was in the hands of a man who flopped and scuffed when he walked. Neely read Burlane's dossier when he came back from Moscow, microfilm in hand, with his story of meeting Kim Philby at a meeting of professors and unionists. Jackson, with wisdom bestowed by Providence on survivors everywhere, had suggested Neely read Burlane's dossier. "Nothing could get you in more trouble than a red-hot in the field," he had said. In view of Burlane's many idiosyncrasies, Neely had asked Jackson why the Company allowed him to remain in the field.

"The reason," Jackson had said, pointing at Neely with his finger, "is that he gets things done."

Neely then understood Burlane's value. Neely and Jackson were much alike in how they thought and made decisions. Neely could tell they were simpatico when he first noticed the broadcloth of Jackson's shirt. Jackson had his shirts done in a laundry. Neely wore cotton broadcloth, not polyester; he had his shirts done in the laundry.

Neely liked doing business with Jackson. You can trust a man only if you are certain exactly how it is that he thinks. You never know how to do

business with a slob. Neely learned that in the
Army. A man neat on the outside is tidy on the inside. As far as Neely was concerned, this ob-
servation followed at IBM; he had no reason to believe it wouldn't work in the Central Intelligence
Agency.

A man with taste in shirts just doesn't slop
through life like an intoxicated duck.

Neely's thoughts were interrupted by Burlane.
"Ara and I are gonna have to borrow Jackson."

"What?" Jackson looked concerned.

"The first thing we'll have to do is send someone
out to a department store to buy some clothes.
We'll need matching jackets, with a checkered pattern maybe, fairly loud, one for Jackson and one
for me. Slacks, shoes, hat, everything has to be the
same."

William Jackson looked at Burlane uncertainly
and licked his lips. "I'm not a field man, Jim."

Burlane shrugged. "Neither was Ara last month,
now he's a vet. Right, Ara?"

Neely looked at his wristwatch and stood up.
"I've got a National Security Council meeting in
forty-five minutes. I think I should go. Somebody
might be asked one day how we seemed to be
doing over here."

"Business as usual," Jackson said.

Neely stood and cleared his throat. He leaned
awkwardly against his desk and made a tck, tck,
tck sound with his tongue. The duty had been
thrust upon him by chance and history. It was his.
He felt a rush of adrenalin. He hadn't felt this way
since he played touch football in his fraternity. He

had confidence. He was sure. He was ready. "Listen," he said, "history will never know what we do here. It will go with us to our graves."

Ara Schott stood and extended his arm level toward Neely and spread the fingers of his hand. It was a gesture an athlete might make, sealing a pact with his mates before the game. Burlane placed his hand upon Schott's, Jackson upon Burlane's, and Neely upon Jackson's. They felt at once inspired and uncertain, confident and afraid. They found themselves at the frontier of the logical extreme. The very reason for being in intelligence services, judiciously considered, impelled them to murder a man about to be elected President. It was the unspoken mandate given them by Congress and the President and even the public, although it would be denied.

Knowing what they did, they had to kill Townes. There was no alternative. If they succeeded, their act would go unacknowledged by history.

"We will not fail," Schott said.

"We'll do our damnedest," Burlane said.

"Yes," said Jackson.

"I'll go to the NSC meeting and fly the flag," said Neely. "You people bag your friend. Before we waste anybody we have to find an explanation to Ara's questions about the Yalta trip. By the time you get back I'll have come up with a way to get Townes his victory coke."

25

Burlane stressed the fedora when he gave his final instuctions to the gopher who was to do the shopping in a nearby mall. The gopher's name was Samuel McBride; it was his job to get things for Langley. The requests ranged from the hohum to the bizarre: a blue marble, a quart of donkey's blood, a vial of semen from a man infected with syphilis, a kind of safety pin manufactured in Poland; a screw with a certain kind of thread, the manufacturer's specifications for a Smith & Wesson .32 caliber pistol manufactured from 1934 to 1937 then discontinued, a book on witchcraft. McBride had no idea what was done with the fruits of his errands. The instructions were casually given, the requested article or snippet of information graciously received. The people at Langley appreciated his talents and McBride knew it. His superior called him a "creative" scavenger. They never asked him how he got things.

Burlane put his arm around McBride's shoulder. "Samuel, my man, I want you to go shopping. It's a simple job but it'll have to be quick. A local mall will do fine." He handed McBride a typewritten list. "Clean yourself on the way."

"SOP," said McBride.

"Now the fedora has to be distinctive. If a person is wearing it, you should be able to spot him at a distance by his silhouette."

McBride looked at the list. He knew immediately what was being planned. This wasn't the first time he'd been dispatched for matching outfits. Judging from the sizes, Burlane would be a player. "I'm on my way, Mr. Burlane. Give me maybe forty minutes or so. Getting clean takes a few minutes."

"On your way, my man," said Burlane. He turned and walked back to Schott's office to go over his plan with Schott and Jackson. Schott had proven his nerve. Jackson's ability to use his head in the field had not been tested. To Burlane's relief, Jackson listened carefully and asked questions. He was equally alert in the discussion of the fallback.

McBride returned thirty-five minutes later.

Jackson started to gather his items together to go put them on but was stopped by Burlane. "*You* don't put those things on here. Just me. Tell your secretary you're feeling sick to your stomach and are going to a drugstore to get some medicine, then home. Call your wife and tell her you're not feeling well."

"She's at school. She's a professor at American University."

"I'd forgotten, sorry. Even better. Get yourself clean now, then get into a public toilet somewhere and change clothes. And you'll get to College Park when?"

"Four-thirty exactly."

"And?"

"I'll go to the McDonald's, place an order for two Quarter Pounders with cheese, two small french fries, and two cups of coffee."

Burlane narrowed his eyes in thought. "When you've placed your order, go into the toilet there to the right of the counter. You'll take your brief-case with you."

"Oh, yes, the briefcase," Jackson said.

"There's one urinal in there and one stall with a door that'll lock. Claim the stall, lock the door, and wait."

"Maybe I should take the sports pages with me," Jackson grinned weakly.

"Okay now," Burlane said. "You're in the stall there waiting. I'll come in about ten minutes later. About four-forty, something like that. I'll place an order the same as you, then go to the toilet, same as you. If the throne's taken, you wait inside any-way. Just shift back and forth like you're about ready to dump a load right there. You want to finish it?"

"I go out front, get my order, and return to the car."

Burlane looked at Schott. "So all you have to do is wait, Ara. The two of you eat your food in the car. Bill, you have to remember to wear your hat in the McDonald's and in the car when you're eating."

It was Burlane's opinion—in which Schott and Jackson had concurred—that whoever was following them wanted to remain covert, but being in a foreign country didn't have the manpower to do it right. It was one man working alone, maybe two. Their pursuer or pursuers would have to take chances in a crowd. In the open they'd hang back; they'd have to.

Which is why the chosen McDonald's was on Baltimore Boulevard near the Beltway. It was surrounded by a used-car lot on one side and a parking lot on the other side. There were fast-food places on both sides of the street: Arby's, Kentucky Fried Chicken, Pizza Hut, Burger King. They were near the University of Maryland and their customers carried nylon backpacks filled with Victorian novels, chemistry texts, tomes on Socrates, and books on how to penetrate a zone defense in basketball.

The MacDonald's was in the clear. Their pursuers would have to pull over and wait.

So Jackson went first. He looked good in the tweed jacket chosen by McBride. The jacket had leather patches on the sleeves. The brown slacks were first rate. The fedora likewise looked good on him.

Jackson drove north on the Beltway by way of killing time before he got to the College Park McDonald's. He arrived at the appointed time, placed his order, paid for it, and disappeared into the toilet.

Burlane and Schott left fifteen minutes after

Jackson. Burlane drove. It was his task to spot the
hound if there was one. To do that he had to be
able to maneuver in traffic and have access to the
rearview mirrors. Schott rode shotgun.

It was in spotting the hound that the republic
entrusted its future to James Burlane's memory
and his eye for detail.

In matters of spotting a hound, Burlane was
without peers. He had good vision. He was a suspicious mother, especially if there was someone
lying covert out there who could step out of the
dark and cut his cock off, zip, shit! He was a suspicious mother and he had a memory that was
something else. Some people think a remembered
name is like a stored nut and have mental tricks to
match names to faces. Burlane could do that and
more. He was able to recall the details of faces. He
divided faces into thirds, as he had been taught.
He watched hairlines and foreheads. He could dis-
tinguish between all manner of noses, cheekbones,
jaws, and chins. Company sketch artists loved to
work from Burlane's instructions. If Burlane said
a man's eyebrows were wide, then by God they
were wide.

Burlane went south on the Beltway. The Pentagon and the Washington suburbs of Fairfax
County, Virginia, were on their left at the beginning.

Burlane drove at fifty miles per hour for three
miles, then sped to sixty-five. He drove in the fast
lane, then moved sharply to the right as an exit
lane approached. He braked suddenly, precipi-
tously. Then just as quickly he worked his way

into the fast lane again. There Burlane cruised, watching the rearview mirror as much as he did the traffic in front of him.

There are two ways to follow a car in open traffic. One is from behind, as in the movies. The other is from in front, using the rearview mirror. Burlane knew that one or two cars, laying covert, would have to do both. The trick was to remember cars and faces: cars behind, cars up ahead, faces passing, faces being passed.

"Do you have him?" Schott asked as Burlane slowed for the College Park exit. They were almost directly opposite the Company's headquarters in Langley, Virginia. This was Prince Georges County, Maryland, red-neck country.

The McDonald's where Jackson waited was on Baltimore Boulevard north and west of the University of Maryland, College Park, campus. Just past the main entrance to the Maryland campus the highway passed over a stream; beyond that on the left was the McDonald's chosen by Burlane.

Burlane considered Schott's question and checked his rearview mirror again. "He's back there. He's in a light-blue Honda." Burlane geared the Datsun into second.

"What else?"

"He's dark complexioned." Burlane checked his wristwatch. "Jackson's car there?"

"It's there." Jackson's car was parked across the highway.

Burlane parked the Datsun and got out. "Eyes forward now, Ara."

"Don't worry." Schott smiled.

Burlane went into the McDonald's and placed the same order as Jackson had a few minutes earlier. He paid and, without waiting for the girl to fill his order, turned, and strode into the men's rest room.

The rest room was empty except for Jackson, whose feet were visible below the partition to the toilet.

"Righto," said Burlane.

Jackson unlatched the toilet and handed Burlane an empty briefcase and a change of clothing.

Burlane stripped off his trousers with his back to the door that opened to the interior of McDonald's. "Stuff these in there, will you?" He handed Jackson his old trousers and motioned to the briefcase. "You and Ara take your time eating now. Don't be in a hurry. Don't look back. Do not." He stepped into his new trousers and began tucking in the shirt tail. "I'll be seeing you in an hour or so." He stepped aside to let Jackson leave.

"Good luck, Jim," he said.

"No big deal," said Burlane. He finished mashing his fedora and old clothes into the briefcase Jackson left with him. He waited five long minutes, then went out, briefcase in hand.

He left the McDonald's through the exit opposite the asphalt parking lot where Schott and Jackson sat in their car, suppressing an urge to look back over their shoulders. Burlane circled along the edge of the parking lot to the rear of the McDonald's, then through the used-car lot.

His mark was still parked in the blue Honda.

Burlane slid his briefcase under a parked pick-up with a cracked windshield and flat tire. That done, he took a deep breath and shambled over to the curb where the dark-complexioned man in the Honda sat staring intently down the boulevard.

Burlane always maintained in discussions of such kinds of duty that the best tactics is whatever is simple and direct. Too much finesse can get you in trouble, he argued. He followed his own counsel now, when everything there was to put on the line was undeniably there.

He strolled over to the driver's window of the blue Honda. He tapped lightly on the window. "Down," he said cheerfully, a smile on his face.

The man, who was half-Caucasian, turned in the seat, startled. He rolled down the window. "I. . ." He started to speak but stopped. He was facing the muzzle of a cocked .44 caliber automatic pistol.

"My name is James Burlane. I'm an agent of the Central Intelligence Agency. We're going for a small ride. If you twitch, I'll blow your balls off." He lowered the muzzle of the pistol. "You'll live, but it won't be fun."

The man's head jerked in the direction of the McDonald's.

"They're still eating Quarter Pounders with cheese."

"What are you talking about?"

"Cole Field House is behind the trees over there. They say the Terps'll take it all this year."

"What?"

"Scoot," Burlane said. He motioned to the far

side of the seat with his pistol.

The man moved, reluctantly.

Burlane opened the door and slid into the driver's seat. "I want you to slide your seat back and roll up into a ball on the floor there. Hands behind your back now."

"I don't know if there's room."

"If you don't want me to shoot you in the knee-cap for the hell of it, you'll fit."

The man did as he was told. He was a small man so there was room. He looked at Burlane with eyes that calculated odds. The eyes told Burlane he was intelligent and knew his business. "I just bought this suit," he said.

Burlane slipped a hand over his shoulder and retrieved an automatic pistol from a holster. "I'll spring for the cleaners. Do you have a name?"

"I can hardly breathe."

"Closer with the hands there." Burlane handcuffed the man's hands, running the handcuffs under the man's belt as he locked them shut. "I asked you if you have a name?"

"My name is George Stone. I sell industrial rubber supplies. I have ID in my wallet if you want to look at it. Are you some kind of cop or what?" He shifted in his tight space. "What I want to know is what's going on?"

"That's all I want to know too," Burlane said.

"I don't have anything more to say," George Stone said.

"We're going for a drive. You Moscow Center?"

Burlane couldn't see it, but George Stone smiled at that. He twisted on the floor.

The safe house they would use was in Loudoun County, near Sterling, Virginia, about twenty miles southwest of the District. Ordinarily, anyone driving from College Park, Maryland, to northern Virginia would have taken the Beltway north and stayed with it as it turned west then south again. Not Burlane. Burlane was now paranoid. What if whoever was running George Stone had laid him out there on purpose? He couldn't imagine why, but what if they had? If there were enough of them, they could run a rotation on him in traffic.

The only way to bend a rotation was with people of his own; Burlane did not have people.

Burlane decided to go straight into the District. In the District he could run cleansing routines that would screw the best rotation. He remembered reading where the FBI had fifty or sixty cars on the street when they followed Colonel Abel around Manhattan. Burlane had been in the field for fifteen years and had never killed a man. He would now if he had to; he knew that. Even if a cop stopped him, then that was tough for the cop. There were ends and means to consider: Less than one-tenth of the nuclear strike force of both the United States and the Soviet Union was capable of killing 90 percent of the other country.

Burlane checked the rearview mirror. "Who'd you say you were again?"

"Stone."

"George Stone?"

"Yes."

"You work for an industrial rubber supplier?"

"Langford's Limited."

"You're an intelligence officer, George Stone."

George Stone struggled on the floor. "What?"

"You want to tell me who you're working for?"

"I told you already."

Burlane sighed. "I tell you what, my man. I, personally, am going to see to it that you regret my having to go to a whole lot of extra effort to find out the truth. We don't have a lot of time to piss away."

"My name is George Stone."

"Sure, George. The deal is, with the situation being what it is and all, you can't count on your reputation for being pansies to help you out. Do you understand what I'm saying?"

"I think so," Stone said.

"Your cover isn't worth a pinch of shit, George. We're gonna drug you up and get the truth."

"My name is George Stone."

"After that I'm gonna have to waste you. This isn't the kind of thing where we can leave ends dangling."

"How long're you gonna keep me down here?"

"On the other hand if you'd care to help us out, we know how to scratch backs."

"My name is George Stone."

"Fuck," Burlane said. In Loudoun County, dammit, they would find out who George Stone really was and what the hell he was trying to pull. "Now I tell you what, George, we're going to have to swap cars. I got a friend who left one across the street we know damn well is not fitted with a tracer."

"A tracer?" Stone said.

"Otherwise I'd steal this car. Now what we're going to do is go across the street, and I'm going to get out, walk around the car, and let you out. You get out and you get in the other car and curl up on the floor just like now. No moves or I'll hurt you."

"What?"

"Anybody sees us they'll think I'm a cop, with you being in handcuffs and all."

It took James Burlane three hours of driving both to accept the fact that he was clean and to drive to Loudoun County, Virginia. It was just after 9:00 P.M. when he pulled up to the country home nestled in the trees. He saw there was smoke coming from the chimney. Schott or Jackson had built a fire.

"We're here," he said to Stone, who had not spoken since they left College Park.

"I probably won't be able to stand up."

"It's good for you, George. Teach you discipline." Burlane got out of the car and walked around to let Stone out. There was a bright moon, as there had been in Connecticut. There were lights on in both stories of the stone house. Burlane turned his back on a gust of cold wind and listened as leaves rattled to the ground from the trees that surrounded the farmhouse.

Stone was right; he could hardly stand up when Burlane pulled him out of the car. He looked around him.

"You won't see anything," Burlane said.

"My knees."

"There are trees here and leaves falling. A stone farmhouse, that's all."

George Stone said nothing. Then, "If you took off the cuffs, I could so some knee bends."

"You'll do okay," Burlane said. He gave Stone a nudge toward the front door, which opened now, revealing Schott.

"Jim?" Schott called.

"He calls himself George Stone."

"Anything else?" Schott leaned forward to get a better look at Stone, who approached the house with Burlane at one shoulder.

"He says he works for a company that deals in industrial rubber. No condoms, apparently."

"Everything okay?"

Burlane shook his head. "Do you think I'd be here if it wasn't?"

Schott stepped aside to let them enter. "You look a bit sore," he said to Stone.

"You'd be sore too if you'd spent three hours curled up on the floorboards of a car." Stone looked around the room, looked at Neely and Jackson, his face revealing nothing.

Burlane removed Stone's handcuffs. "You want to take a seat there."

Stone sat on the couch as Burlane had indicated.

26

The man who called himself George Stone was not a talker. He said nothing at all, in fact. He picked at a sore on his knuckle and stared impassively past the face of James Burlane, who stood before him now. Ordinarily, Ara Schott would handle the interrogation. That's if you stood by rank. But rank meant nothing here. They were all equals: Burlane, Schott, Jackson, and Neely.

Burlane was a field man. He was best able to imagine what it was like to be in Stone's shoes. There was an open if unspoken covenant among them that Burlane would do whatever was necessary to solve the puzzle that was Stone. Burlane regarded Stone as though the latter was a bloated toad, say, or the fetus of a seal.

"Now the deal is, Mr. Stone . . ." he said. "The deal is you were following us around last night, then again today."

Stone blinked. He was a handsome man with patient brown eyes. "I think there's been some mistake," he said.

"No, no." Burlane shook his head. "No mistake. I ran a pattern out there on the Beltway. It's not your fault I buttoned you."

"I don't understand." Stone looked perplexed.

"Sure, you do. You can't stay covert on a spooked rabbit if you're all by yourself. No way."

Stone blinked again and looked away from Burlane. "Would you please tell me what's going on here?" he asked Schott.

"He asks the questions," Schott said.

Burlane grinned. "These gentlemen don't have a whole lot of time or patience, George. You're not from Pennsylvania or Arizona, George, where you from?"

"I don't know what to say. My father was an Australian, my mother Chinese. I grew up in Macao."

"Which is how you got involved in industrial rubber, right?"

"Right." Stone looked partly relieved.

"Just how was that?"

"It was my grandfather's business. My mother was an only child."

"Frugal Chinese and all that." There wasn't time to do it without drugs.

George Stone smiled.

"You want to roll up your shirtsleeve, George?"

Stone turned stiff in the chair. "What? I don't understand."

Burlane shook his head. "Sure you do, George.

We're gonna hit you with a hypodermic needle and you're gonna tell us everything we want to know. You want to roll up the sleeve now?"

Stone rolled the sleeve of his shirt. "This has to be some kind of mistake."

"No mistake. You can either relax or I can tie you down. Your druthers. Lie down."

"It's all there in my ID." Stone lay back and closed his eyes. There was no sense in him arguing; everybody in the room knew that.

"Ara?" Burlane stepped aside.

Schott hesitated for a moment, then knelt before the couch. He found a good spot on Stone's forearm and without further word sunk home the needle. He emptied the hypodermic and removed the needle with a flick of his wrist. He stepped back for Burlane.

"Go ahead," Burlane said. "But give him a few minutes first."

"How do you feel, Mr. Stone?" Schott asked.

"Warm right now," Stone said.

"I wonder what they did before these marvelous drugs?" Burlane leaned close to George Stone, watching Stone's breathing.

"They had hoses, hot cigarettes, wired testicles, stuff like that." Schott looked at his wristwatch. "Mr. Stone?"

"Mmmmm," said Stone.

"What is your real name?"

"Gideon McTeague."

"Your father is a Scot?"

"He was Australian. He's dead."

"Your mother was Chinese?"

"My grandmother."

"Who do you work for, Gideon?"

"Mr. Hsiu."

"Could you spell that please?"

McTeague spelled it.

Schott looked at Neely then at Jackson. Burlane was grinning. "Hsiu Feng?" Hsiu Feng, according to Company estimates, was the chief intelligence officer of the Chinese legation to Washington.

"Yes."

"What were your orders, Mr. McTeague?"

McTeague's eyes remained closed. "I was to follow Ara Schott and James Burlane. I was to report everywhere they went, everything they did, everyone they talked to."

"Why was that?"

McTeague coughed softly. "Why was what?"

"Why were you told to follow Schott and Burlane?"

"I wasn't told."

"Why do you think?"

"I have no idea," McTeague said.

"How long have you worked with them?"

"Who?"

"Hsiu's people."

"Since 1973."

"Where were you trained?"

"In a school not far from Peking."

"How long were you in the school?"

"Ten months."

"How many were in your class?"

"Fifty in the beginning."

"What was the name of the man who lectured

you on Western intelligence services?"

"Kung Meo."

"How would you describe Kung Meo to me?"

"He had a scar on the right side of his face."

"Did he say where he was educated?"

"Yes."

"Where was that, Mr. McTeague?"

"Columbia University, I think it was."

"Did you know a man named Vincent Chan?"

"Yes."

"Who was he?"

"He taught us about the field. He'd been educated by the British."

"How are you supposed to communicate with Hsiu tonight?"

"I am to call him whenever I get the chance."

"You're working alone?"

"Yes."

"What do you do when you call?"

"I let it ring twice, hang up, then call back."

"I see. What else?"

"I say I'm George Stone if everything's okay."

"And if it isn't?"

"Just Stone is all."

"What if someone else called?"

"He'd assume I'd been had and you'd used drugs."

Schott looked at Neely. "I think we should talk. He can't lie to the drug."

Neely thought about that. "You want to take him downstairs and lock him up, Mr. Burlane?"

Burlane took Gideon McTeague to the lockup in the cellar of the house. When he returned he found his companions sitting around the antique kitchen table drinking coffee.

"More in the pot, Jim," Jackson said.

Burlane helped himself and joined his companions.

"Well?" asked Neely. He looked at Jackson.

"I think I'd ask Ara."

Schott smiled. "Jim?"

"I'd call Hsiu," Burlane said. "I have an idea he thinks we're thick-headed, stupid bastards right about now. Wouldn't you love to come down to a nice warm house like this, a good little wife?"

"Do you agree with Burlane?" Neely asked Schott.

"I do."

"Who calls?" Neely asked Burlane.

Burlane shrugged. "Why not Ara? He knows the answer, same as me."

Neely didn't know the answer. He was as yet too new to the business to be sufficiently paranoid. "Would you explain, Mr. Burlane?"

"I need a drink. This is a lovely old house, as I said." He stood up and opened the refrigerator, which was well stocked with beer and three-liter jugs of white table wine. Burlane retrieved an unopened half case of Heinekens. "The Company knows how to buy beer."

Neely was impatient. "You were about to tell me what the answer is. Do you know, Ara?" He looked at Schott.

"Maybe. But I'm willing to let James Bond here go first. Jim?" Schott looked at his wristwatch. It was eight o'clock.

Burlane was busy ripping cardboard. "You'd think they'd learn how to design a fucking box. Takes Houdini to retrieve a bottle of beer. You know the first signs. You couldn't shut up about them. There was Emil who knew my name, the kid who spoke perfect English, the boat off our starboard, the man on the golf course, the Soviet patrol boat that let us off, the rescue." Burlane popped a beer cap and tilted his chair back, teasing Schott a bit.

"And you think you have the answer to all that?" Schott teased back.

"Maybe," Burlane grinned. "Good beer."

"On the scale of the utterly bizarre and outrageous, one being low and a ten being high, where would you rate your conclusion?"

Burlane burst into laughter. "Dammit, Schott, I believe you're loosening up a bit. Not bad. Not bad at all. Well, let's see, first you have to consider all the pissing and moaning about Kim Philby. Think of the poor Brits, for Christ's sake, it was awful! Everybody had to suck a turd—MI Five, MI Six. And we trusted them. Beetle Smith had second thoughts about Philby, but nobody listened."

"Finish it, Jim," Schott said. He got himself a beer.

Burlane rested his chin on the palm of his hand, his elbow on the table. "So Philby's there in Beirut getting sloshed in hotel bars and pretending to be a journalist. He knew about Munich. The Old Boys' network couldn't hold out forever. He knew that."

"They were going to pin him."

"Sure they were," said Burlane. "They knew it. He knew it. Soviets knew it. Philby was in a jam. He'd worked up a thoroughgoing hatred of the Soviets by now, the pricks. He couldn't redouble, that would just be impossible."

"He had to go to Moscow."

Burlane nodded. "If he wanted to stay alive, certainly. If he's as spiteful and hateful as his legend, what could he do?"

Even Ara Schott had to grin at that one. "Yes, I would like to be the one who calls Hsiu Feng."

"Then go for it," Burlane said.

Schott started to take the receiver from the phone mounted on the wall, but hesitated and looked at Burlane.

"The one on the left tapes the call, the one on the right lets us listen in."

With a glance at an impassive Neely, Schott dialed the number Gideon McTeague had given him. He hung up. He dialed a second time. He punched both buttons on the wall.

"Yes," a voice answered.

"Mr. Hsiu?"

There was a pause. "Yes."

"My name is Ara Schott, Mr. Hsiu; we have your man Gideon McTeague prisoner in a safe house."

Hsiu Feng made a noise with his lips. "Prisoner?"

"Yes, we interrogated him with drugs."

"I see."

"We want to know why he was following us."

"If you don't know why, Mr. Schott, I'm sure I don't know exactly what to say." Hsiu's English was even and clear.

"A simple explanation would do."

"I am a little bit angry, Mr. Schott; can you sense that?"

"Yes." Schott grinned at Burlane.

"Well, then why are we talking? Why aren't you out there doing what you have to do?"

"What *we* have to do? I don't understand."

"You *do* understand!" Hsiu half shouted.

"We have no idea," said Schott.

"We spent the better part of two years setting everything up. Are you listening?"

"I'm listening, Mr. Hsiu."

"We held your hand across the Black Sea. Hasan is a captain in the Chinese Army. Our man hit the KGB when you were running across the golf course. Did you see that?"

"Emil?"

"In our pay, has been for years."

"The fishing boat on our starboard?"

"Ours. So was the patrol boat and the fishing boat that picked you up."

Schott was shaking his head. "Philby was back at the Tartar Palace in time for breakfast, I take it."

"He had a nice omelet."

"And his KGB tail?"

"He turned up missing. Nobody knows what happened to him. Philby said he didn't see him."

"How long?"

"For a while now," Hsiu said.

"Since Beirut?"

Hsiu didn't answer. Neither did he deny it. His silence was Schott's answer. Schott's face asked Burlane if he had a question.

"Indeed," said Burlane. He reached for the receiver. "This is James Burlane, Mr. Hsiu."

"The Turk gave you high marks, Mr. Burlane."

Burlane laughed. "And your nephew?"

"Yes, he also."

"Mr. Hsiu, has Philby mentioned the name of Milos Gereben in connection with Boris this past week?"

"Yes, he has."

"Do you have the details?" Burlane asked.

"No, we don't."

"He is KGB for certain?"

"KGB, apparently in place for some years now, Mr. Burlane. But as I said, Philby doesn't know his connection with Boris."

"Reports regularly does he?"

"Philby says straight to Konsomov."

Burlane leaned against the wall and stared at the ceiling. "Is there any possibility that Gereben has been running Boris?"

"No."

"You asked Philby that specifically?"

"Yes, I did. He said he wondered about that when he heard Gereben's name mentioned earlier this week. But he says he's made some checks and no, it's not possible. Gereben does not run Boris. He helped recruit him, along with Ostrov at Berkeley, but he hasn't been running him."

"Did you ask him if it was possible that Susan Townes might be running him?"

At the mention of Susan Townes's name, Ara Schott's chair scraped on the hardwood floor.

"No, I didn't Mr. Burlane."

"So you don't know what he thinks of the possibility?"

"I have no idea," Hsiu said.

"Question, Ara?"

"No question," Schott said.

"How long does it take for you to ask Philby a question and get an answer back?"

"I can't say exactly, Mr. Burlane. It might take days, maybe weeks. How long depends on circumstances."

"I want you to see if Philby can build a case against Susan and Boris's good friend Irv Cohn."

"We talked about Cohn."

"And?"

"Philby said it was possible but not probable. He didn't say why."

"Thank you, Mr. Hsiu. I'm giving the phone back to Ara Schott now."

"Could you remain at this telephone tonight in case we have to get in touch with you?" Schott asked.

"Mr. Schott, I want you to know that we've gone to all this trouble—including exposing our prize agent in Moscow Center—because we hate the Soviets as much as you do. The last thing in the world we need is a Soviet agent in the White House."

"You'll stay there then?"

"Certainly."

"You people must be getting anxious."

"Philby was onto him a little more than two years ago. We waited, hoping something might happen to his career."

"Thank you, Mr. Hsiu, we'll keep in touch."

"Please, anything at all I can do."

"Of course. Good-bye for now, Mr. Hsiu." Schott hung up and punched the replay button on the wall.

The four of them sat and listened to a tape recording of the conversation with Hsiu Feng. Nobody said anything for a moment.

Neely's beeper went off. He took the receiver off the wall and dialed Langley. "Yes?" he asked. He listened for a moment. "I'll call back in twenty, maybe thirty minutes," he said and hung up. He looked at Jackson, then Schott. "I have a call from Vasily Butov, the Soviet ambassador. He's given us a number to call. He says it's an emergency."

"I'll bet it is!" Burlane said. He popped another Heineken. "I like these green bottles, real class."

"What do we do?" Neely asked.

Burlane stood up and looked out at the clouds sliding past the moon. "If I were you, Mr. Neely, I'd enjoy the whole delicious circumstance."

"Please," Neely said.

"No, no, listen. Why do you suppose the Soviets are calling you?"

Neely said nothing.

"They're calling you to tell you something perfectly awful has gone wrong with their mole. They're afraid to go ahead and waste the guy for fear of getting caught and starting Big War Three. They have to tell you, there's no other way." Burlane hopped up on a counter and put his feet in the kitchen sink. "Derek Townes is KGB; he probably has been since 1964, like Philby said." He looked at Schott. "Our friend Philby has been working for the Chinese since he defected in 1963."

"The question is, what would he do if he worked for the Chinese and found out Townes was KGB?" Schott interrupted.

"He'd tell the Chinese, that's what he'd do. So the Chinese know this, and they're keeping an eye on the upcoming elections. Townes is James Burack's chosen. It was obvious more than a year ago this was going to be his only term. The Chinese can't just get on the telephone and make an allegation as outrageous as that! They can't try to tell us they got it from Kim Philby. Who'd believe them? Would you, Ara?"

"No," Schott said.

"Would you, Bill?"

Jackson shook his head. "Kim Philby? No way."

"Well," Burlane said. "The only thing they can do is have Philby tell you himself. They figure this has to be done right. They have to take their time. So Philby starts walking. A year later Townes starts by winning the Iowa caucus, then mashes everybody else in New Hampshire."

"So the Chinese decide they have to move."

Burlane stood up briefly and dug at the inside of his thigh. "They weigh everything carefully and decide the Americans should be given plenty of time. Given enough time, they think, we'll do what we have to do. So Philby slips me his note in March and plans the rendezvous for October."

"Why didn't they make the rendezvous earlier?" asked Schott. "In July, say."

Burlane considered that. "I had to ask myself

that too, Ara. Two answers strike me as logical. One is that he was telling the truth; October was all he could get because that's the only time the Soviets would give him. The other is that they thought Philby's story would be convincing in the extreme."

Schott finished the sentence. "They decided we shouldn't be given too much time to change our minds."

"Yes," Jackson said.

"I agree," Neely said.

"The Soviets didn't know they had to contend with another Trotsky until last weekend."

"You're saying they've just now found themselves in quicksand and they're grabbing for the closest hand available?" said Neely.

"That's it," Burlane smiled. "If somebody has to go under, better them than us. I say we play dumb and watch 'em squirm. After all, we don't have any reason to believe a bullshit story like that. Who do they think they are calling us on election eve with a lot of nonsense like that? They created him; they can damn well get rid of him themselves."

"He's right," Schott said to Neely.

"Sure, I'm right," Burlane said. "We just listen to their story, ask a couple of questions, and hang up. Don't take Butov seriously. He'll call back. It doesn't make any difference how much he pisses and moans, we shouldn't lend any credence to his story. Our pose ought to be that this is all just preposterous. Make him suck a big fart."

"And pray to God they waste Townes themselves," said Neely.

"Oh, they will," Burlane said. "And besides," he added cheerfully, "if they don't, we'll deal him out with a toot of coke." He looked at Neely. "You did figure out how to get the cocaine to Townes, didn't you?"

Neely looked embarrassed. "I'm afraid I can't think of anything that doesn't leave traces."

"Irv Cohn," Burlane said.

"Cohn?" Neely asked.

"Sure, Cohn. They've all been pals since Berkeley, haven't they? They had the same friends, probably knew the same girls. Our mark in Sweden, Ara, Aldeburg I think his name was. Did he hang around with both Townes and Cohn?"

"Yes," Schott said without hesitation.

"Then we have the stuff delivered to Cohn. Nobody's screening Cohn's mail. Cohn probably keeps anything he gets. There's this little celebration package from their old radical pal still keeping the faith up there in Stockholm. Do you think there's any way Townes does not get that coke? No way."

"So you get two dead men instead of one," Neely said.

"What else are you going to do?" Burlane opened himself another beer.

Neely's beeper went off. He telephoned Langley again. "Neely," he said.

"We have a call from the Soviet ambassador, sir. He says it's urgent that he talk to you at once. Very urgent, he said, sir."

"I know why Mr. Butov is calling. Everything is under control. Did he leave you a number?"

"Yes, sir, he did. He said it was extremely important that I get back to him at once."

"You didn't tell him where I was?"

"I have a number, sir."

Neely felt foolish for having asked such a question. "I want you to call him back and relay his call to me through a screen so it can't be traced. This is Situation Zebra Foxtrot, my ears only. You understand Zebra Foxtrot?"

"Yes, sir. I am to handle the remainder of these calls with someone with me to confirm your privacy."

"Who's in charge there tonight?"

"Margenta, sir."

"Have him pick someone."

"Yes, sir."

"Do not put Butov through to me until the conditions of Zebra have been met."

"Yes, sir."

Neely sighed and put his fingers on a dial mounted next to the buttons that recorded or broadcast calls. "What's the number for Zebra Foxtrot?" he asked Jackson.

"Alpha-Alpha-Hotel-Niner-One-Zero, this week," said Schott.

Neely dialed the code and sat down again. The call would not come through to the safe house unless conditions for Situation Zebra Foxtrot were met at the other end.

Four minutes later the wall phone rang again. It rang twice. Neely stared at the handle of the refrigerator and listened to the phone ring twice. He sniffed and turned his wedding band once. "I told them to have the refrigerator stocked. I don't think we should do business on an empty stomach. You three hungry?"

"I'm a cook," Burlane said.

The phone rang again. Schott looked at it. "The kid works fast," Neely said. He started to pick up the receiver but Burlane waved him off.

"Let him wait a couple of rings," he grinned. "They've got a microwave here and a freezer full of food. I see there's a pint of sour cream in the fridge."

The phone rang yet again.

"How about chicken tarragon on some nice noodles? There're some onions here."

Neely grinned. "I told them to stock the refrigerator with enough to last us a couple of days. There anything for a salad?"

"You betchum, Red Ryder. Cucumbers, green onions, fresh spinach if we want it, a couple of kinds of lettuce."

The phone rang. Neely picked it up. "Neely, here. A salad would be nice, Jim. There's some good white Burgundy to go with the chicken. You ever had white Burgundy? Who is this, please? Bet you didn't know there was such a thing!"

"Vasily Butov."

"There should be some white pepper up there if you'd like. Ambassador Butov?" Neely would have liked to have watched Burlane harassing Butov, but it was coming surprisingly easy and he was pleased with himself.

Burlane grinned and held his fist up in a victory salute he'd seen athletes give. "Go mo' fo!"

"I'm with some friends, Mr. Ambassador, so unless it's a terrible emergency . . ." Neely looked
offended.

"I have to speak with you on a most urgent
emergency," Butov said.

"Certainly, what is it, Mr. Butov?"

The four men in the kitchen looked at one
another. "Mr. Neely, this is most embarrassing to
me, I assure you, but it is my duty to inform you
that Derek Townes is an active agent of the Soviet
Union."

"What?" Neely started laughing.

"Who thinks," Butov continued, "that he's Leon
Trotsky."

"You're drunk, Mr. Butov. Please call me tomorrow." Neely hung up.

Burlane took Neely by the shoulders. "Well,
shit, boss, I didn't think you had it in you!"

Neely's beeper went off. "Yes," he said when he
answered the call. He punched both buttons.

"Mr. Butov's calling back, sir."

"You tell him very politely that I don't like
crank calls. If he calls back, put him off. Make him
wait an hour before you let him through. The President knows what is going on here. He is not to be
notified without my permission."

"Yes, sir."

Neely hung up. "Let's have your meal, Mr. Burlane."

"Your people're good shoppers," Burlane said.

"Imagine the fix he's in," Neely said.

Burlane started butchering a chicken. "Good
chickens. Poor fucker, there wasn't much he could

say without sounding like a stand-up comic."

"Can I help?" Schott asked. "I like recipes with sour cream. You don't just ease into a conversation like that."

"Look at it this way," said Burlane. "What if we had to call Ivan Konsomov and tell him the man about to be elected Premier was a psychopath who thought he was George Patton."

Schott gathered avocados, celery, and cucumbers from the vegetable tray. "The trick to a good salad is to dry the lettuce well and chill it before you put the dressing on. Green Goddess is my number, laced to the hilt with anchovies."

Neely and Jackson grinned. They were married men who were accustomed to having their food prepared for them. Neely checked the wall; it was 9:30 P.M. It would soon be Sunday. If the Soviets didn't blink, he'd have to send the cocaine to Irv Cohn and await the outcome. For whatever the difference in their ages, backgrounds, and opinions, it was clear to all four men in the kitchen of the Loudoun County safe house that they would never be the same after this awful night.

If they were lucky, they would have to bear a secret of secrets for the rest of their lives.

If they were unlucky . . .

"Hey, frozen asparagus!" Burlane yelled. "I'm gonna double the recipe on the chicken. The Company can spring for an extra bird here or there."

They had eaten their meal and loaded the dishwasher before the young man at Langley, following the instructions for Situation Zebra Foxtrot to the letter, allowed Vasily Butov through again. It was just after 11 P.M. The wind had kicked up outside. They drank coffee and listened to the branches rustle against the eaves of the farmhouse while the phone rang.

"This is Mr. Butov again, Mr. Neely. I ask you to accord me the respect of a representative of the Soviet Union. Our responsibilities are great. You must listen."

"Please, Mr. Butov, no more stories about Derek Townes being a mole or thinking he's Leon Trotsky. I'm afraid I'll have to ask you not to bother me with jokes."

"This is no joke, Mr. Neely. You must listen."

Neely cut him off. "No, *you* listen, Mr. Butov. We established direct lines of communication with you people to avoid a tragedy through lack of understanding. Better that we be absolutely straight about everything."

"Please, listen," Butov said.

"A man like you has no place being in the diplomatic service."

"Just give me a chance to explain what I have to say. This isn't easy over the phone. If I could just talk to a couple of your people."

"No," Neely said.

"You name the place, Mr. Neely."

Neely looked at Schott.

"Tell him sure," Burlane said. "Schott and I'll talk to him."

"You're right, of course, Mr. Butov. It won't hurt for us to hear what you have to say."

"Tonight," Butov said.

"Monday," Neely said. "I'm sure it can wait until Monday."

"No, tonight. You must hear what I have to say."

Neely motioned Burlane to the phone. "Mr. Butov, this is Mr. Burlane, who will arrange the details with you."

Burlane took the receiver. "Do you have something to take a note with?"

"I do," Butov said.

"You'll come alone now, is that understood?"

"It is."

"What will you be driving?"

"A gray Mercedes."

"I want you to smash out the right rear taillight. Drive north on Highway Seven toward Leesburg, Virginia. Pull over at the Inky Dink Truck Stop a few miles past McLean. Got that?"

"The Inky Dink Truck Stop," said Butov with a trace of disgust in his voice.

"You damn well make sure you're clean. If I have any reason to think you're not, then everything is off."

"When should I be there?"

"Any time between one-thirty and two in the morning."

"Agreed," Butov said.

27

James Burlane shook his head in disbelief when he saw Ambassador Vasily Butov step from the gray Mercedes dressed in a sharp blue suit. Butov was no more than five feet ten, Burlane estimated. He looked shorter than he did on television. He weighed maybe 240 pounds. His wattled face, which had been ravaged by acne when he was young, was devoid of emotion. He glanced up at the moon and straightened his shoulders. He had small, gray eyes that bulged slightly and glistened like wet marbles. He blinked once. He coughed and muffled the cough with his left hand. Butov had oily skin; Burlane could see his pores in the moonlight. If great calm and lack of emotion are the marks of poker players and gamesmen, Butov was the right man to acknowledge that his country had fucked up royally. He looked like a great, swarthy, cunning, imperturbable frog.

Burlane was excited. He was going to partici-
pate in what was unprecedented in more than
sixty years of relations between the Soviet Union
and the United States. Burlane regarded it as black
comedy. There was no heroism in Schott's having
to listen to Butov's sorry tale. And there certainly
was no honor in detailing how you had recruited a
man to betray his country, then squeezed him
until his brains popped. "Mr. Butov?" Burlane
asked.

"Mr. Burlane," Butov said.

Burlane had been paid a compliment. Butov
knew his name. "We'll have to use our car the rest
of the way."

"I understand. Will I be talking to Neely?"

"No, Ara Schott and myself."

Butov's lids lowered, hovered, then he blinked.
"It shouldn't make any difference, the story I have
to tell. Where will we be going?" He shook
Burlane's hand.

Burlane gestured up the highway. He looked at
Schott, who waited in their car parked next to the
outdoor telephone booth. "Not far from here."

"Oh," Butov said.

Burlane led Butov to their car and helped him
get in the backseat.

"You're not armed, I take it," Burlane said as he
left the parking lot.

"No," Butov said. "It was difficult to say what I
had to say over the telephone. I know it sounds un-
believable on the phone but it's true, every word
of it."

Schott turned and shook Butov's hand. "Mr.

Burlane and I will hear you out."

Nobody said anything more as Burlane turned off the main highway and followed several country roads through the Virginia countryside. He suddenly turned off the road and into an all-night diner. "This'll do. We can have some coffee."

Butov looked at the diner and smiled, as if wondering what history might say later. A red neon sign said simply, EAT. Underneath, in black letters on a white background, was SARAH'S. Sarah's looked something like a school bus painted white and with the wheels removed. It actually dated from the mid-1950s, when long, narrow diners were fashionable in the East and Midwest. In their day these diners—often featuring little more than a long, central eating counter—inevitably featured liver and onions with rolls, peas, mashed potatoes, and tossed green salad, and splendid breakfasts. The hamburgers served at lunch always featured slices of raw onion; the buns were grilled. Chicken-fried steak was a good bet, or fried shrimp.

They settled into a booth on which there was a napkin dispenser, salt and pepper in glass shakers with square patterns in the glass, a bottle of catsup, another of Worcestershire sauce, a third of A-1 sauce, and a heavy glass ashtray. The booths were hard-backed; the seats were empty except for a teenaged fry cook who wore a fluffy-topped paper chef's hat and one waitress, a tired-looking woman who looked stooped from the burden of forty years and an enormous beak of a nose.

They sat, Butov on one side, Schott and Burlane

on the other. Burlane was on the outside. "Coffee?" he asked.

Butov nodded.

"Three coffees, please," he called to the waitress.

The waitress acknowledged the order and took down three heavy ceramic mugs from a shelf.

"Now then, Mr. Butov," Ara Schott said.

"Derek Townes is an agent of the KGB."

The waitress arrived with the coffee and small plastic containers of artificial creamer. "Sure he is," Schott said. He helped the waitress with the coffee.

"He has been since 1964."

Schott sipped his coffee. "Good coffee."

Butov accepted a cup and waited until the waitress had left. "His code is Boris."

"And he thinks he's Trotsky." Schott shook his head.

"Please," Butov said. "You must hear me out, Mr. Schott."

Schott emptied some creamer in his coffee and stirred it with a stainless-steel spoon. "I like fiction. But you must remember that we're a democracy in this country. It may not be as efficient as your way, but it's up front and in the open."

"Please, Mr. Schott, no rhetoric." Butov took a sip of coffee and seemed surprised that it tasted good.

"You'll have to explain it all. On something like this we have to know everything."

"I'll do the best I can under the circumstances.

We first contacted him when he was in the Peace Corps in Nigeria."

"Through whom?" Schott asked.

"A man named Milos Gereben, a Hungarian refugee who's been ours since he was a teenager. He's now a practicing psychiatrist in Manhattan."

"How did that first contact come about?"

"Gereben was visiting his sister in Lagos. His brother-in-law was a chemical engineer with a British firm. Townes, as you know, did a tour of duty in Nigeria in the Peace Corps."

"That was after he finished his bachelor's degree?"

"Yes."

"Gereben is Townes's control?"

Butov waited as though he didn't want to answer. "Yes," he said.

Schott swallowed. He took a sip of coffee. He started to ask Butov another question but was interrupted by Burlane.

"He ran him from where?"

"From his residence in Connecticut. He has a home on the Long Island Sound."

"You're saying he maintained contact since he recruited him in Nigeria?"

Butov looked out of the window at the end of the booth. "Well, there was Ostrov."

"Ostrov?" Schott asked.

"Gereben convinced him to return to school to study under Nicholas Ostrov, a professor of economics at Berkeley."

"Ostrov is yours?"

"He's ours," Butov said.

"But Ostrov didn't run him?" Burlane interrupted again.

Butov looked at Burlane. "No, Gereben did."

"Is Irv Cohn yours?" Burlane asked.

Butov looked puzzled. "You're talking about Townes's assistant. No."

Schott said, "You're telling us the KGB sponsored Derek Townes's political career from the beginning and that you ran him through a shrink named Gereben?"

"We saw to it that he received whatever necessary money he needed. Beyond that he did it pretty much by himself."

"So what went wrong?" Schott turned his palms up. He watched Butov's face closely. "What's this stuff about Trotsky?"

Butov caught the attention of the waitress and held up his mug for more coffee. "We don't know for sure. Gereben suspects, and we agree, that the pressure was too much for him. Something happened."

"What?"

"We don't know for sure, as I said. He had problems—memory loss, times when he seemed to lose control."

"So what exactly happened?"

"He thinks he's Leon Trotsky," Butov said.

Schott looked at Burlane.

"He does. Believe me he does. He knew what was happening to him. As the election grew closer it got worse. So he finally went to Gereben, who hypnotized him."

"His control," Burlane said.

"Yes. Gereben hypnotized him and there he was, a schizophrenic, thinking he was Leon Trotsky. He wrote a biography of Trotsky when he was in college."

"Do you have any way of proving this?" asked Schott.

Butov reached into his jacket pocket and removed a cassette tape. "Gereben recorded the conversation. This is a copy of the tape he made."

"Do you really expect us to believe a story like this?"

Butov blinked once. He wet his lips with his tongue. "You play the tape, Mr. Schott. Decide for yourself. Run voice prints if you like. I want to ask you what motive Townes could possibly have to record a tape like this? And how would we possibly come by it if Gereben were not our man? How? I ask you."

"With Ivan Konsomov, anything's possible," Schott said.

Butov started to get angry. "What I'm telling you is true, Mr. Schott. Do you really believe I'd bring you here to tell you an insane story like this if it weren't true? Do you really believe that? Believe me when I tell you I have some amount of pride."

"Derek Townes is on this tape saying he's Leon Trotsky?"

"Yes."

Schott half smiled. "Why don't you just leave him in place?"

Butov looked amazed. "Do you have any idea of the hatred Leon Trotsky felt for Joseph Stalin in his last days?"

"Stalin's gone long ago. He was repudiated by Khrushchev more than twenty years ago."

"Trotsky's back and he still hates," Butov said.

"You mean Townes." Burlane smirked.

"Townes, Trotsky, what difference does it make? He could punch the ICBM button. He could see us in rubble so the noble workers could pick up the pieces." Butov glanced at the waitress and lowered his voice. "If you remember, the real Trotsky predicted the First World War would bring down the Czar and he was right."

"So what do you expect us to do, even if we believed you?"

Butov leaned across the booth and lowered his voice even more. "Stop him for the sake of us all."

"We just don't go around shooting people." Schott felt Burlane's knee nudge his own and knew that Burlane must be stifling laughter.

"Not even if your President believes he's Leon Trotsky?" Butov looked amazed.

"What do you think, Jim?" Schott asked Burlane.

"I don't believe that shit for a second." Burlane looked offended.

"But the tape . . ." Butov began.

"Horseshit," Burlane said.

"You must stop him."

Schott did his best to look offended. "You must be on drugs, Mr. Butov. We're not some banana republic police state. We represent a democratically elected government. We just don't go around shooting people."

"Play the tape, gentlemen." Butov's face turned hard.

"If you think he's Trotsky, why don't you get rid of him? If what you say is true, he's your responsibility. You created him."

Butov's face flushed. "Are you telling a foreign government to assassinate a candidate for President of the United States? Am I hearing you correctly?" He looked in the direction of the waitress again.

Schott looked at the waitress also. He took a sip of coffee that was now tepid in the ceramic cup. "No, Mr. Butov, I'm just telling you we're not going to clean up after your mistake if you made one."

Butov held up his hands. "Look at it this way. Derek Townes is guarded by the Secret Service. What if we tried to get him and got caught, what then?"

Schott shrugged. "There'd be a bit of a fuss. We'd get a bigger budget at Langley. So would the Pentagon. We can't take a man out on such a preposterous allegation as this."

"Check it out."

"Check it out? How? Be reasonable."

"Play the tape, please!"

Schott picked up the tape. "I don't know what's on this, but I assure you it's not enough."

"So what will you do?"

"We'll play the tape and talk it over."

"The election is Tuesday, Mr. Schott. What is this now, Sunday morning? You don't have time to talk it over."

Schott turned to Burlane. "Are you curious, Jim, why these people waited until now to tell us this if it's true?"

"I'd like to know that," said Burlane.

Butov rested his forehead in his hands and stared at the table. "We didn't tell you before now because we didn't know until a week ago."

Schott had finished his coffee. "Shall we be taking Mr. Butov back to his Mercedes?"

"I don't know why not." Burlane got up.

"Please," Butov said.

"I'm sorry, but this just makes no sense," Schott said.

"I agree," said Burlane. "Do you really expect us to drive out here in the middle of the night to listen to this kind of shit? You better tell Comrade Konsomov to lay off the marijuana."

Butov got up reluctantly. "You will tell us, then, what your final decision is? Play the tape and you'll change your mind."

"I think you'll have a long wait, Mr. Butov."

"You have my number. Call anytime." Butov followed the Americans out of the diner.

Nobody said anything as Burlane drove back to the Inky Dink Truck Stop.

"Listen to the tape," Butov said in parting.

"We'll listen to it, but don't lose sleep waiting for a call," said Schott.

When Butov had gone and they were on their way back to the safe house, it was Burlane who spoke next. "He told one lie."

"Oh?" Schott said.

"He said Gereben was Townes's control. Philby said he checked out that specifically and the answer is no. I believe Philby."

"Then who's running him?"

"Susan Townes, I'd say," Burlane said.

Schott felt his mouth turn dry. "Susan Townes?"

"Sure. She's been with him since the beginning. She can come and go as she pleases. With her the Soviets are assured of communication with him anytime they want, no questions asked. The deal is, why lie about her? With so much on the line, why would Butov lie about her?"

"I don't know," Schott said.

"He doesn't want her burned."

"I can't imagine why."

"There's a reason why, you can bet on that. Konsomov doesn't go out of his way to protect someone like that without a reason." Burlane braked the car.

They were back at the Loudoun County safe house.

Jackson and Neely were waiting for them when they opened the front door.

"Well?" asked Neely.

"He gave us a copy of the tape," said Schott. He held it out in the palm of his hand.

"I see." Neely took the tape.

"I don't see how he could possibly believe we'd go for a story like that even with a tape. It's now Sunday morning; we couldn't possibly act before Tuesday." Schott sat down.

"He didn't expect us to believe it," said Burlane. "He just wanted to tell us in advance and give us a copy of the tape."

"I'm not sure I understand," Neely said.

"To tell us what's happened and give us warning in case their man gets caught. They want to explain now, beforehand, not after the fact. Get caught and everything's in chaos. This way we're warned. If something goes wrong, they can come to us for help." Burlane opened the refrigerator and got himself a beer.

"Having decided at the eleventh hour to waste their prize mole, they had to warn the Americans, humiliate themselves as insurance. Poor Butov was selected to debase himself and would probably be hit later so that his Comrades could purge themselves of the awful memory."

"That could be," Schott said.

"I say we go to bed," said Burlane. "Maybe it'll be on the tube in the morning."

Neely's beeper went off at a quarter after eight. He told Langley he'd be in shortly and got dressed. He woke up the others and they watched the details on television.

Presidential candidate Derek Townes had been murdered in his East Norwalk vacation home.

Reports were that the assassin had escaped in the predawn darkness.

The four Company men sat in the Loudoun County safe house, unshaven, tired, drinking James Burlane's coffee, as a network anchorman relayed the opinion of a local coroner that Senator Townes had been struck down with an ice pick.

"Mr. Larcarna said the senator would have died within minutes," the anchorman said.

Twenty minutes later the Company patched through a call from Susan Townes for Ara Schott. She was crying.

"I need someone, Ara," she said.

"I'm terribly sorry, Susan." Schott didn't know what to say next. He was aware of Burlane listening to the conversation from across the room.

"Please, Ara."

"Hold on, Susan." Ara Schott felt overwhelmed. The whole awful thing was almost too much for him to handle. Now this. Sweet Jesus!

Schott looked at Burlane and knew Burlane was right: There were two separate reasons why Butov insisted on talking to them in the middle of the night. The first was to warn them the KGB was about to correct its mistake and to give them a copy of Gereben's tape as proof. The second was a diversion. Kim Philby was right about Gereben. Gereben did not run Townes.

Comrade Butov had lied. The Soviets were scheming pricks to the very end.

Schott lowered the receiver. "That night I interviewed her . . . I slept with her, Jim. She's a Soviet agent, I think." Schott swallowed. "She was lovely."

"They always are the first time," said Burlane.

Ara Schott was a desk man, a virgin in the manner of theorists, and ideologues. "God, what do I do, Jim?"

Burlane tugged at the crotch of his trousers. "You go see her. If she says she wants romance, give it to her. Konsomov doesn't know anything about Philby and the Chinese. He couldn't possibly think we have any reason to suspect her."

"I can see that," Schott said. He looked at the back of the hand that muffled the receiver.

"We leave her in place," Burlane said. "There'll come a time when we can use her."

"You know, Jim, this is a bullshit way to live your life."

"I've considered that. A guy with a nose like I've got, and dandruff, what am I going to do, sell shoes?"

Schott put the receiver back to his ear. "Yes?" he said.

"You have to come, Ara," Susan said. "You told me to call and I'm calling. You can't say no. I've got a life to live. I'm free now. I'm not married any longer." She started to cry again.

"Susan, listen, because of Derek's assassination, I'm in a room filled with people. Can you give me a number so I can call back in ten minutes?"

"Oh, thank you, Ara." She gave him a number.

Schott settled on top of the stool by the kitchen wall. He didn't want to tell Burlane that he couldn't get his mind off Susan, that he sat around daydreaming about her. It was hard enough telling Burlane he'd slept with her. "Well, what do I do?"

"She got to you, eh?"

"Yes," Schott admitted.

"That can't make any difference, you know. You work for the Company. You have a job to do. You have to do it."

"Christ, Jim, I just don't know if I *can* do it."

"It's different out here, I know. I've been doing this shit for years now. You nine-to-fivers at Langley, you think you're fighting the war. Well, friend, this is what it's like for us soldiers. Welcome to the goddam club.''

"Is it really worth it, Jim? What could we gain, really?"

"We just cannot pass up an opportunity like this!" Burlane looked hard at Schott. Burlane hated the Soviet Union, not for ideological reasons, but because the murderous, lying fuckers who ran the place bullied everybody. When there was a chance for a coup this sweet, Burlane's pulse raced. He was a competitor. "We just cannot let this pass. We just cannot."

Schott had never seen Burlane look so intense. Burlane's eyes were hard, demanding that Schott do what was required of him as a professional. "I guess I have to call her then," Schott said softly.

"You're damned right you do, pal."

"I suppose she killed him too. The reports are she's the only one who saw the assassin. A woman about to become First Lady, what reason would she have to murder her husband?"

"She probably did." Burlane put his arm around Schott's shoulders. "She's an interesting looking woman, Ara. It doesn't have to be such bad duty. It's all in how you look at it. You need to settle down. Do you good."

"How can I do this?"

"There's no 'how' to it, Ara. You just do it. Remember, she was running a mole about to be elected President of the United States. When Townes went nuts, they even tried to have us waste him. Susan's still in place. She knows you like her. Maybe she likes you too. In any event, the Soviets do what they have to do. Derek's body is still warm and here she is, the bereaved widow, looking for a sympathetic shoulder and maybe a dinner later on when she feels better. Philby had no choice. Derek Townes had no choice. She has no choice.''

"Am I any different from them?"

Burlane looked out the window and sighed. "I honest to God don't know how to answer a question like that. There just seems to be no end of bullshit in this business. It never stops." Burlane turned suddenly and looked amused. "One thing though, I do like the ice pick touch. You have to hand it to Konsomov. By God, if you have to murder Leon Trotsky a second time, there's only one way to do it—an ice pick. No other way."

"Konsomov's sense of humor."

"He's more fun than the East Germans, you have to give him that. Look at it this way: If you and Susan really click, you can get together and decide between you which side to screw."

Schott picked up the receiver and began dialing. "Yeah, well sure, Jim. Anything for a friend."

"I agree the whole thing s-s-sucks," Burlane said, mimicking Kim Philby. "We should give the Chinese a little gift, you know—chocolates, a juke-box, an old Ford, something. And when this is over, I'm going to take a hot shower, get some sleep, and find myself a lady with a real nice butt." Burlane looked wishful. "We could start with a good meal, go to a movie maybe, and top the evening off with a joint and a little fooling around."

Schott listened to the phone ring and stiffened slightly when Susan Townes answered, "Hello?"

Burlane said, "Listen, Ara, do you think you could ask her if she has any girlfriends who'd like to date an interesting man. Tell her I know how to show a woman a good time. With all the women running around these days, you'd think it'd be possible to meet a fun lady once in a while."